Virtual Vengeance

A journey from man to machine

To Shari, VIRTUALLY Yours

Thomas J J Starr

ISBN: 1492236756
ISBN 13: 9781492236757
Library of Congress Control Number: 2013915870
CreateSpace Independent Publishing Platform
North Charleston, South Carolina

Author's Note

The world's first computer-based teaching machines were developed and widely used at the University of Illinois in Urbana-Champaign, Illinois, during the early 1960s. Technologically, the PLATO learning system was far ahead of its time. PLATO terminals employed a touch panel and a plasma display screen with bit-mapped graphics. The display screen also featured overlaid images from a microfiche projector. Twenty-five years before the World Wide Web became widespread, PLATO terminals scattered about the campus were networked together into an online community with e-mail, multiplayer games, instant messaging, and chat rooms. PLATO was created by Professor Don Bitzer and others at CERL, the Computer-based Education Research Laboratory at the University of Illinois. The PLATO system offered instructional material on one hundred subjects. Funding for PLATO came from the military and the National Science Foundation. The PLATO system did not use a mind scanner like the one described in this novel.

This is a work of fiction. The characters, names, places, and institutions are the product of the author's imagination or are used fictitiously. Any resemblance to actual persons, businesses, and events is coincidental.

There really is a Coordinated Science Lab at the University of Illinois, but this work of fiction does not accurately portray the CSL that exists today or in the past.

"Computer science is no more about computers than astronomy is about telescopes."—E. W. Dijkstra

"Our scientific power has outrun our spiritual power. We have guided missiles and misguided men."—Martin Luther King Jr.

PROLOGUE

The undergraduate classes in computer science at the Lomonosov Moscow State University were easy for Yuri Petrov—too easy. He was one of the brightest people in his class, and everyone knew it, but this did not make him popular. On the contrary, it isolated him. Like most twenty-year-old men, he was bored with ordinary life and wanted excitement. Females were first on his mind, but his efforts in that arena were futile, so he focused on discovering just how far his intellectual abilities could take him.

Yuri's best friend Dmitri spent much of his time with smitten girls who fawned over him. He was tall and blond and wore the latest fashion, dress shirts with a colorful flower print and tight-fitting white slacks. Yuri, on the other hand, spent his time with books and computers. "Bulldog" was the nickname Dmitri had given Yuri due to his short, stout frame, broad face, and coarse black-brown mop of hair. Yuri had a jaunty disposition but wore plain black t-shirts and black trousers regardless of the occasion.

Dmitri understood Yuri better than anyone else, including Yuri himself, which made sense considering that they had been best friends since primary school. Dmitri knew that a girlfriend was what Yuri really needed. Billing Yuri as "the smartest man in Russia," Dmitri had persuaded a number of girls to go on dates with Yuri. Yet despite extensive charm coaching and a new outfit from Dmitri, none of the girls hung around for more than a date or two.

Dmitri was well aware of Yuri's computer prowess and was eager to put it to the test by hacking into computers around the world to steal credit card numbers. Yuri did the hacking and Dmitri dealt with the sordid people who were willing to pay for the numbers.

<hr/>

As on many nights before, the two friends were huddled over the highly modified computer in Yuri's bedroom at his parents' third-floor apartment. Cigarette smoke and empty Coke cans filled the cramped room. Yuri's father was a professor and head of the chemistry department at the Lomonosov Moscow State University, so they lived in the comparative luxury of a four-room apartment. The otherwise drab rooms featured his parents' prize possessions, fine Persian carpets.

"*Da!* I've found the hole," rejoiced Yuri, leaning back and pumping his fist in victory.

"I enjoy watching a master at work," Dmitri encouraged. "Your method of finding security holes in Isoft's operating system is brilliant. Every time they issue a security patch, you analyze it to find the hole before most people install the new patch!" This was not the first time Yuri had successfully found the vulnerable point to the patches made by Isoft's mediocre computer programmers. In fact, it was the fifth time this year.

"Now," said Yuri, lighting a cigarette with his left hand while rapidly zigzagging the computer's mouse with his right hand, "we use the hole to install a secret back door in thousands of people's computers before they patch the hole."

"And then," said Dmitri with glee in his voice and a glimmer in his eye, "we use the back door at our leisure to take credit card numbers."

Dmitri masterminded the criminal operations and his plan was simple. The gang that bought the credit card numbers bribed the local police to ignore their activities. Dmitri did it for the excitement, the money, and the girls who liked the money. Yuri did it for the sport of outwitting the most sophisticated computer systems in the world, specifically those of the corporate empires in America. Since Yuri had no interest in the money from their exploits, Dmitri kept all of the money, but he provided Yuri with an endless supply of cigarettes and Coke.

"You are smarter than the American computers," said Dmitri, clapping Yuri on the back.

"One day," Yuri boasted, "I shall make a computer that's really smart, as smart as a human." He mused about how aspects of the human brain could be applied to the design of computers.

Yuri was pulled back to reality by his mother shouting angrily in the other room, "Go away! You stupid politsai, there are no criminals here."

"Where's your son?" a policeman's voice demanded.

Confused, Yuri looked to Dmitri, who was more accustomed to dealing with the police. The wide-eyed alarm on Dmitri's face flooded Yuri with fear. They had to escape; the police were dangerous thugs.

"Stop!" cried his mother as the policemen barged into the apartment.

They had never expected the authorities to bother them, but Yuri had insisted that they be prepared. Dmitri tossed an escape rope out the third-story bedroom window and leaped out, holding the rope with both hands.

"Go away! No one here is doing anything wrong. Leave us alone!" shouted his mother as she tried to stop the intruders.

Yuri jammed a sizzling emergency flare into a prepared hole in the side of his computer. As Yuri grabbed the escape rope, he glanced back at the smoking computer and smiled as he saw a brilliant flash of white shine from every opening in the case. The packet of white phosphorus attached to the hard drive had ignited. He scrambled awkwardly out of the window as three policemen with AK-47 assault rifles burst into his bedroom. It was a long three stories down, and the rope tore into Yuri's fleshy hands as he struggled down the side of the building. He finally made it to the ground and was about to run when he heard a shout from the window above: "Politsia. Halt!"

Yuri flinched at the sound of a gunshot just a few meters away. He looked around to see where the shot came from and saw an officer standing near the building entrance with an automatic pistol aimed at Dmitri. His friend had dropped to the ground, clutching his belly and groaning in agony. The officer swiveled, and the smoking pistol pointed at Yuri's head. Yuri heard a sound from above and looked up to see two AK-47s pointed directly at him. These were state police, infamously more brutal than the local Moscow cops. He was scared stiff, unable to decide what to do, his heart pounding.

The state policeman with the pistol strode up to Yuri and said with vodka-scented breath, "Come with me," in a tone suggesting that Yuri would not like what the officer had in mind. What would the policeman do with Yuri? Yuri wondered if the officer could be bribed into letting them go or if he should just cooperate and hope they would let him live. He looked for an answer in the policeman's face, but all he saw was a heartless brute.

The police made no attempt to help Yuri's friend, so Yuri slowly bent down beside Dmitri, looking at the policeman to be sure this was acceptable. Shocked by the flowing blood, Yuri pressed his hand over the gaping hole in Dmitri's belly to try to stop the bleeding. Dmitri cried in pain, so Yuri eased his pressure on the wound. The flow of blood increased, staining the dusty dirt black. Yuri gently pressed harder. The blood was warm, but Yuri shivered with fear. Dmitri's eyes were wide with terror.

"Tell me how you stole the credit card numbers from American Express," the policeman said callously, looking down at them.

"We have nothing to say," Yuri said in defiance.

"I am sure your computer will tell us everything we need to know," the policeman said, his eyes smiling.

"You won't get anything from that melted heap." Blood gushed out between Yuri's fingers with a rhythmic pulse. Yuri pressed his other hand on top of the first one, trying to stop the bleeding, but to no avail.

"Ah, yes. It seems your friend needs a doctor." The officer pulled a two-way radio from his belt. "If you were more helpful, I might call for an ambulance." The policeman laughed cold-heartedly. Both of Yuri's hands were now covered with warm blood.

"Why are you after us? I only stole the numbers of some rich Americans that nobody cares about," Dmitri begged, coughing up blood.

Yuri knew that the police never arrested hackers who stole from Americans. Everybody hated the rich, all-powerful, perfectly educated Americans who would not share their miraculous teaching machines with the old world.

The policeman gestured with his radio. "You were not careful to check *every* number. In addition to the American accounts, you stole two numbers belonging to Turks. You can have the Americans, but not the old-world people."

Dmitri's face was turning pale as he lied. "It was all my fault. I confess. I hacked into the victim's computers and stole their account numbers. Yuri is innocent." Dmitri glared at Yuri, silently demanding that Yuri keep quiet.

"That will do," sneered the officer as he called for an ambulance. The policeman seemed to be satisfied with one culprit. Maybe Yuri's father could bribe the police to let Yuri go.

"Don't let the corrupt commissars push you around," Dmitri whispered to Yuri, squeezing Yuri's blood-covered hand weakly.

"I promise," vowed Yuri with tears welling up in his eyes.

The ambulance arrived three minutes too late.

×

1

Twenty years later, the University of Illinois quad bustled with students as Professor Yuri Petrov pedaled his ancient Schwinn bicycle to class. He had replaced the low-slung racing handle-bars with high-rise "choppers" befitting a rather plump forty-year-old professor. The quad was a postcard scene with the warm sun sparkling from the dew on the grass, leaves fluttering in the light breeze, and young, lean students playing Frisbee, oblivious to the troubles that plagued other parts of the world. Yuri chuckled at his old-fashioned notion of a postcard; no one sent postcards anymore. As Yuri absorbed the surrounding vitality, he felt younger. Riding a bike on the quad was prohibited, but Yuri had never respected authority—not the corrupt Russian police and not the meddlesome micromanagers at the University of Illinois.

Two years ago, the opportunity for access to the most advanced technology in the world and ample research funding had motivated Yuri to move to America. Life in America was like a pleasant dream compared to the nightmare of Russia. He hated being told what to do by the petty Czars who ran every niche of life in Russia. America had its small-minded bureaucrats too, but they only told you what *not* to do, so Yuri was free to do anything else.

As Yuri approached the red brick digital computer lab building at the University of Illinois, he pressed a button on a remote control in his pocket. A radio receiver secretly installed by Yuri signaled the handicapped entrance to open just in time for Yuri to ride his bike into the building, through the main hallway, and pedal directly into the lecture hall where his students were waiting. It was an auditorium-style lecture hall from a bygone era, with big chalkboards and two hundred antique wooden seats with foldout lapboards, but only twenty students were in the class. All of the students sat in the first row, at Yuri's insistence. He wanted them as close as possible to see what they were thinking by looking into their eyes and watching their expressions. He wished he could reach inside their heads like the teaching machines.

Very few teachers remained in the United States, and Yuri was beginning to regret being one of them. The smart graduate students in his computer heuristics programming class became bored easily, so sometimes he thought he would have to resort to singing and dancing to keep their attention. That would teach them—watching an overweight Russian immigrant with a deep, gravelly voice sing and dance. All of the teachers from grade school through undergraduate college were long gone. Education was so much better once students stopped going to school. Only a few graduate-level classes remained.

Midway into his lecture, a young, plain-faced woman with mouse-brown hair raised her hand. "Professor, are heuristic inference algorithms used in teaching machines?" Yuri knew this was not a spontaneous question; it was coerced. He had to force the students to interact. To stimulate his graduate school students, he had rediscovered a teaching trick often used by seventh-grade teachers in the old days. On the first day of class, he told his students that one-fourth of their grade would be based on the number of good questions they asked each week. "That is a good question." He recognized Julie Mountcastle, who had been a student in the artificial intelligence class he had taught the previous semester. She was a bright student who scored well on exams, but he doubted she would shake the world. He hoped one day to find a student who could challenge him intellectually.

Yuri made a tick mark by her name on a clipboard. "You, Miss Mountcastle, and every other student here were taught by machines since you were four years old. So maybe you should know a little more about teaching machines."

Yuri loved to lecture, and it would be some time before he answered her question. "The breakthrough that made teaching machines possible happened right here at the University of Illinois, twenty-five years ago, when the resolution of magneto-encephalographic brain scanning attained the ability to detect the state of each synapse in the brain. While brain scans helped to diagnose many neural disorders in the brain and other parts of the body, the real breakthrough was the real-time analysis by a supercomputer to detect the creation of new synaptic links between the neurons in the brain. The new links signaled that something had been learned and that the knowledge had been stored in long-term memory."

To retain the students' attention, Yuri walked and gestured as he lectured. "The supercomputer used to analyze the brain scans was the first application of the neural network computer architecture we will study in this class."

A hand went up from a young man on the left side. "So how did detecting the formation of neural links lead to the teaching machine?"

It was another good coerced question. Another tick mark went on the clipboard. There was hope for the class, even though he had to treat them like children. "The education department at the university conducted research with volunteer students attached to a brain scanner. The students would listen to live instructors using different teaching methods, and the education researchers used the brain scanner's immediate indications of learning to observe what worked and what didn't. They found that some methods worked better than others, but mostly they found that the best method of instruction differed for each student. Impressive results could be achieved by customizing the method of instruction for each student. Professors have always loved the instant feedback they receive when they see their pupils suddenly understand, when the light goes on. In these experiments, that was literally the case because a big green light would flash on when a new piece of information clicked into long-term memory. Since it was not practical for professors to customize their delivery for every student, the neural-scanning feedback was applied to computer-based instruction."

"Since teaching machines have made human teachers obsolete, why are you teaching us?" It was Julie Mountcastle again.

Yuri made another checkmark and chuckled to himself; he loved students with spunk. He reached into his pocket, retrieving a piece of candy wrapped in plastic, which he reserved for the best questions. He tossed the candy to Julie as if he were rewarding a dog for performing a trick. "I am here to teach you the difference between man and machine. Standing before you is a living contradiction. I am an expert in the technology used in teaching machines, and yet I believe that students should be taught by humans and not machines. Unfortunately, since Congress passed the Education Modernization Act, very few teachers remain. Some, like me, teach classes so specialized and advanced that it is not worth creating the teaching programs, and some teachers remain for dance and athletics."

Yuri noticed the students shifting uncomfortably in their seats. He looked at the clock and saw he had lectured past the end time again. "That's all for today."

As Yuri bicycled back to his office in the Coordinated Science Laboratory, he noticed a road crew repainting the centerline on the roadway. The newly painted line consisted of the written phrase "Dexus cars—driven to succeed," repeated over and over to form a line. They were painting over the faded old line advertising Global Motors cars.

Yuri cursed to himself in Russian, *"Takuiu kartinu obosrali. They have covered this nice scene with their crud."* Yuri's swearing satisfied a subconscious desire to maintain his extraordinary proficiency with more than two thousand Russian swear words. Few countries had fostered a dialect of cursing as rich as Russia had. For those gifted in the art, Russian cursing provided a creative and sophisticated form of expression. Yuri never swore in English, just as a person holding an acetylene cutting torch would never use a hacksaw to cut a thick steel plate.

———

Kent Fechner, President of Strategic Accounts at Sellco, Inc., knew the phone call was from Alfred Grossberg. No one else would call him using Mod II triple DES encryption. Mod II was available only to people with the highest level of top-secret security clearance. Alfred had always been paranoid, even when he and Kent Fechner were drinking buddies in law school. Despite the high-tech security, their conversations were always cryptic.

"Hello," said Kent.

"I have a new message for Mercury. When can you deliver it?" asked Alfred.

"Monday."

"How's Mercury doing?" Alfred sounded worried.

"A hundred and fifty million last week with a score of eighty-eight percent," boasted Kent.

"You're amazing."

"So what's the new message?"

"Slaughter is the right choice."

"Is this necessary?" Kent did not want to waste any of Project Mercury's precious silver bullets.

"The Senate canvas shows we will lose otherwise."

"OK. You owe me, big time."

"I know. By the way, you'll be amused to hear my secretary became a big Pepsi drinker after completing a one-hour first-aid refresher course. She never drank soda before that."

"There's millions like her."

The next day Kent Fechner departed for a vacation in Africa. His recreational reading for the trip was essays criticizing religious beliefs, written by Friedrich Nietzsche, Voltaire, and Chuang Tzu. Seeking the most authoritative versions, he read each essay in its original German, French, or Chinese.

—•—

Julie Mountcastle stepped into Yuri's office and was astonished by an explosion of organic designs and shimmering colors. The walls and the floor were covered with oriental carpets, each with a unique abstract design. Yuri seemed amused by Julie's bewilderment.

"You like my collection, Julie?" asked Yuri, proudly straightening his dwarfish posture.

"Yeah. There's such diversity in the designs. Are they from different countries?"

Yuri pointed about his office. "Turkey, Iran, India, China, and over here I have the Stans: Turkmenistan, Kazakhstan, and Afghanistan." Yuri picked up a smaller rug from the floor and held it facing Julie. "Watch the colors." Yuri tossed the rug around and caught it upside down with the same side facing Julie. He held it for a second, tossed it again, and caught it right side up. He repeated this twice more.

"The colors change completely." The change in appearance amazed Julie.

"The reflected light changes because of the orientation of the fibers. No oil painting can do that." Yuri replaced the rug and then dropped heavily into his worn office chair. "Now, what can I do for you?" he asked pleasantly, engaging her with a curious sparkle in his eyes. Anyone talking with Yuri quickly realized that they had one hundred percent of his attention, and he expected the same in return.

"I came to ask you about the circuit modules you showed us yesterday. You said each module contained hundreds of millions of picoprocessors. How can enough processors to model the brain fit into a module the size of a large book?" inquired Julie. She sat down, knowing Yuri's answers were never simple. Computer science was not the only reason she had come to visit. She wanted to get to know Yuri better. Everyone else on campus seemed boring and common by comparison.

Julie saw he was delighted by her interest. "There is no need for teaching machines to model the entire brain," he responded, gazing into her eyes. "To detect learning, only one percent of the brain is tracked at any time."

"I remember you saying in class that the surface area of a silicon wafer is about the same as that of the neocortex in the human brain," Julie noted.

"Yes, but I think it is just a coincidence. The other interesting comparison is heat dissipation. The circuit module consumes thirty watts of power, just a little more than the human brain."

Julie was trying to think about what he was saying, but she actually was paying more attention to his elaborate gestures, his foreign pronunciation, and the passion reflected in his lecture. During his lectures last semester she had grown to admire the honest conviction she saw in Yuri. She wished she too could find the professional inspiration he exhibited.

Despite his dwarfish appearance and foreign perspective, she found him intriguing. Everyone she knew had neatly styled hair, but Yuri had an unruly mop of coarse hair that should have been cut two months ago. His hair was varicolored: mostly black, some brown and silver. Yuri was a fascinating, unique person and she loved to listen to his lively lectures.

Yuri was now drawing a graph rapidly on the whiteboard. "Heat dissipation is proportional to switching speed. The clock speed of the picoprocessors is turned down to one-thousandth of the speed of normal computers. This is because human neurons take five milliseconds per operation, one million times slower than the common computer. By operating so slowly, the circuit temperature remains within safe limits."

Listening to Yuri's lecture was like trying to drink from a fire hose. "Professor, you're so excited about computers. Why do you find them so fascinating?"

Yuri mulled this over; maybe he had detected her limited interest in computers. "Consider the history of technology. The steam engine amplified man's muscles to achieve the impossible, such as digging the Panama Canal. The telephone and radio amplified man's ability to communicate with anyone anywhere instantly. Computers amplify man's mind to a new realm of possibilities. The Internet has connected computers to form a worldwide community of shared intelligence. We have evolved from individual intelligence to a communal intelligence. Isn't that fascinating?"

Julie was uninspired. "Sure, but what makes it so interesting for you?"

"Computers make life better by making complex things simple." Julie still did not understand. "When you drive a car, you take for granted that all you need to do is press on the gas pedal. What if you had to minimize fuel consumption and exhaust emissions by continuous manual adjustments to the fuel flow, air-intake manifold, and valve timing in response to the air temperature, engine temperature, altitude, throttle position, and speed? What if you also had to constantly manage the power delivered to the hybrid electric motor and the charging of the batteries?" Julie had no answer, so Yuri continued. "Computers are our willing slaves who toil endlessly on the most boring tasks." Then Yuri asked, "What inspires you?"

"Well, I have bachelor's degrees in accounting, organic chemistry, computer science, and French."

"And in which of these fields would you like to make a career?"

"I rated well in all the courses, but I don't think I'd like to spend my life in any of these fields. I plan to try classes in some other fields to see what they're like."

"You shouldn't be a perpetual student trying courses at random. You need to look inside yourself to find what makes you passionate."

Julie had known her life was adrift, but she was aroused when she heard someone else tell her to correct it. Yuri had been the first person with the honesty to confront her. She said she would think about it and asked if they could talk about it further sometime.

Julie was about to leave when Hamilton von Helmholtz, the head of the Coordinated Science Laboratory, stepped into Yuri's office. As an afterthought, Julie turned to Yuri and invited him to dinner at her apartment on Friday.

Yuri was partway into declining when Helmholtz interrupted brusquely. "Don't be a bore, Yuri. You shouldn't miss the experience of a lifetime. Miss Mountcastle is famous on campus for her fabulous cooking." Looking at Julie, he said, "Yuri is in for the best meal in town, isn't he?"

"I was planning on something nice," Julie replied, slightly embarrassed.

"OK, but please don't make too much work of it," Yuri relented.

"Great. I'll see you at six, Friday night. Apartment 314 at 616 East Green Street." Julie left with a spring in her step.

———

"You're a lucky dog," confided Hamilton, picking a strand of hair from his traditional dark gray business suit. The silk tie, perfectly knotted and tied under Hamilton's square chin, was a new one that Yuri had not seen before. This tie was monogrammed with Hamilton von Helmholtz's initials, "HvH." Yuri committed the tie to memory as tie number forty-six. Secretly, Yuri played a game to see which was bigger, Yuri's memory or Hamilton's tie collection. Thus far, Yuri was winning, but he was getting worried. Hamilton pretended to be a scientist, but a real scientist would never waste his time and money on such vanity. Yuri owned only one tie, which would likely be worn next when he was in a coffin.

Noticing Yuri's attention to his tie, Hamilton checked to see if it was straight and then resumed talking. "My wife's idea of cooking is putting a frozen meal in the microwave." Hamilton changed context with no indication. "I haven't received your fifty words. It's overdue."

"My work summary hasn't changed. Use what I provided last time," replied Yuri, noting that American bureaucracy was nearly as bad as Russian.

Hamilton von Helmholtz required every person on his staff to file a fifty-word statement summarizing their current work every six months. He memorized the name, title, and fifty-word statements for every person in his department. This, plus some general information about the department, was useful for one of Hamilton's favorite activities: serving as a tour guide of the Coordinated Science Laboratory. These tours always started in the main lobby with him standing besides his extra-large framed portrait, a welcoming smile on his handsome Germanic face. Hamilton was proud of his knowledge and the many innovations produced by his department. However, he never invited questions during his tours because he did not understand the details of what his people did. The collection of fifty-word statements was all he needed to know. The exception was Yuri; he kept a close eye on Yuri.

Hamilton's management philosophy was a practice in the conservation of energy. He made no effort that did not advance his career or help to expand his empire. He had no time for meaningless discussion of strategic direction or making scientific contributions himself. Hamilton's time was spent hiring the best talent, insulating his people from campus politics, and tirelessly raising funds. He rarely micromanaged their work, since he had little interest in their specific projects. He had advanced to the position of department head through skillful politics and by publishing papers about computer programming languages early in his career that benefited from the excellent work of his graduate students.

2

There was no satisfying the shareholders of Pharmor, a US-based pharmaceuticals company. They had become accustomed to the sustained growth in Xarim sales for the past several years, and now sales had leveled off. Xarim's colossal sales volume, second only to aspirin, was not enough. The shareholders wanted more growth. Isaac Hodgkin was vice president of sales at Pharmor, and it was his job to find a way to reignite the growth in sales. The past several years had been easy for Hodgkin; it had been like riding a jet fighter with its afterburner set to maximum. He had looked good no matter what he did because each year sales records were broken. Now the figurative jet fighter had reached its maximum altitude.

This was Hodgkin's chance to become part of the greatest legacy in pharmaceuticals. The story of Xarim's growth began with its acceptance as the most effective and safest drug to reduce the risk of stroke and heart disease. Years of clinical and long-term studies had proved it to be remarkably safe. The second and most dramatic phase of sales growth occurred when it was discovered that Xarim produced a slight reduction in excess body fat. Hopes of a third phase of growth had been sparked by laboratory experiments suggesting that Xarim might improve brain function. While the studies demonstrated improved blood flow to the brain, several studies of human subjects failed to show conclusive improvement in brain function. A different approach was needed to increase sales. Xarim had been advertised for many years, but now it was time to bring in the superstar of advertising.

Sellco's distinction from the other big advertising firms located in Manhattan was highlighted by its idyllic location in the prettiest part of the New Jersey countryside, near Chatham. Isaac Hodgkin craned his neck as the Sellco limousine drove though the extensive natural landscaping, which would put most golf courses to shame. He had passed an impressive stone archway and gatehouse as the limousine entered the Sellco property. The curving drive wandered deep into the forested grounds and eventually broke into the open with a manicured lawn surrounding what appeared to be a huge tiered garden. Isaac was still searching for the Sellco headquarters building. Broad stairways, stone terraces, and waterfalls could be seen in the embanked gardens. Green-tinted window slits peered out between layers of verdant vegetation. Isaac realized that the tiered garden was the Sellco headquarters building only a moment before the limousine stopped at the main entrance. The building's architect had clearly been influenced by Frank Lloyd Wright and the legend of the hanging gardens of Babylon. No parking lot was visible; it must have been buried under the building with the loading docks.

It was obvious that the limousine driver had signaled the vehicle's impending arrival when a sharply dressed executive assistant greeted Isaac as he stepped out of the limousine. They strolled through the entrance containing a legend describing the geographic origins of the fifteen types of marble decorating the lobby. A glass-walled elevator took them to an executive meeting room dominated by a long, oiled teak table. Green-tinted windows on one side of the meeting room provided a vibrant view over the luxurious landscaping and forest beyond. Windows on the other side looked out through a broad, clear sheet of water falling onto a stone terrace. The mesmerizing view through the thin sheet of water was fascinating. A butler requested Isaac's choice of beverage and delivered a cappuccino as Isaac sat at the vast meeting table.

A thirty-year-old man arrived wearing a finely tailored suit, artfully styled hair, and a sincere smile. He delivered a firm handshake. "I'm Miles Huxley, vice president of strategic accounts. Please call me Miles. I trust that your trip went well." Isaac noticed that Miles ordered a cappuccino also. Pleasant greetings were exchanged, and Miles asked a few questions about Isaac's professional background. The conversation moved smoothly into Isaac's personal interests, and Miles casually mentioned his skiing trip to Tahoe the previous week. Miles sounded like a competent skier, and Isaac always enjoyed talking about his favorite pastime. Miles asked about Isaac's favorite ski runs at Tahoe. When Isaac mentioned the wonderful new ski lodge that had opened last year, Miles jotted the name of the lodge down on a pad of paper and asked insightful questions about the lodge. Isaac was relieved that Miles seemed to be a nice guy, not a tacky salesman.

——◆——

Miles had read the client analysis of Isaac Hodgkin three weeks ago; it mentioned Isaac's avid interest in downhill skiing. Isaac took at least two major ski trips per year. Before last week, Miles had been skiing only once in his life. During the past week, Miles had taken two days of ski lessons near Tahoe and had talked for hours about skiing with people at the ski lodge.

He enjoyed becoming an instant expert on a new topic. The sole purpose of the two days in Tahoe was to prepare him for the four minutes of important skiing small talk today.

Miles made a hand gesture to the butler; motors lowered translucent shades over all of the windows. The brilliant views from the windows on both sides of the meeting room would have been a major distraction during the meeting.

"Xarim is an excellent product in need of correspondingly excellent promotion," said Miles, starting his carefully prepared presentation. "Sellco will create a comprehensive plan that will assure that Xarim reaches its full potential. No other advertising firm can provide what Sellco will deliver."

"And why's that?" interrupted Isaac.

"Let me explain exactly how Sellco is different." Miles tapped a touchscreen built into the table, and an image appeared on a projection screen built into the wall facing Isaac. "Sellco is distinguished by our people, our channels, and our targeting." A second slide appeared. "Sellco's staff is formed by the most intelligent minds on the planet. Ask anyone who has applied for a job at Sellco; they'll tell you that only the most qualified candidates are invited to be interviewed. They'll also tell you that the week-long series of tests, interviews, and practical exercises was the most intense experience of their life. We press every applicant to the intellectual breaking point. Only one applicant in a hundred is invited for an interview, and we hire only one in six of those who are interviewed. Another ten percent wash out during their first probationary year." Miles glowed with pride. "Working at Sellco is exhilarating. It is a supercharged atmosphere where one is surrounded by the greatest intellects in the industry. No other advertising firm has this caliber of intelligence."

Sellco's reputation as a brain trust was widely known, as were the high fees they commanded. Miles glanced at the executive assistant who was sitting across the table, looking intently at a video screen embedded into the conference table. The table was arranged so Isaac could not see that the executive assistant was looking at two live video images of Isaac taken from hidden auto-tracking video cameras. One image was a tight, close-up frontal view of Isaac's face; a second image showed a full-body infrared-enhanced view in profile. Additionally, the screen showed his pulse rate, continuously taken from the instrumented chair.

The executive assistant was called a "mind reader" at Sellco. He was especially adept in reading facial expressions, body language, and vocal inflections. Sellco always had a mind reader present at major client meetings, since they recognized that most of their staff had relatively poor abilities to read these subtle indications. Miles saw a message from the executive assistant appear on his private video screen: "Move on; getting bored."

Miles presented his next slide. "Sellco has created many unique advertising channels. Let me show you two examples that you see every day, but may not have known that they were provided exclusively by Sellco." Miles turned on the power to a computer sitting at the conference table; the screen immediately lit up with an advertisement for Meganet Internet service. "The advertisement shown on every computing device during the boot-up cycle is provided through an exclusive agreement with Sellco." Miles tapped his touchscreen and familiar music played softly in the background. The music was a series of short songs whose lyrics promoted specific products. "I'm sure you recognize this as 'elevator music.' In fact, it is played in nearly every elevator and public restroom in the country under exclusive contract to Sellco. Extensive psychological testing has proved the effectiveness of audio advertising in elevators and restrooms. People are more receptive and less distracted there."

Miles turned off the music and advanced to his next slide. "This brings us to targeting. We communicate with the individual, not the general population. Whereas other advertisers show the same advertisements to wide demographics, we recognize the unique interests of each individual. The restroom audio advertising provided in the men's room is different than in the women's room, and the audio advertising in a five-star restaurant restroom is different from a two-star restaurant." A new slide was projected, showing a comparison of a World War II bomber scattering many bombs across a city versus a modern jet fighter dropping a single smart bomb on a target. "Other advertisers broadcast the same advertisement to every TV in a city. Sellco TV advertisements are selectively inserted for each household. We have a purchase probability profile for every household in the country. The TV advertisements you see are different than your next-door neighbor's. If you don't have a cat, you will not be shown advertisements for cat food. You will be shown an advertisement for arthritis medicine only if someone in the household is over a certain age. Not only do we select what ads are shown, we know what ads are watched. We get feedback from every TV, telling us what channel is being watched, how long it has been since the person pressed a button on the remote control, and if an infrared sensor in the TV detects the presence of a person in the room. We know if our ads have reached their target."

The executive assistant noticed that Isaac needed a restroom break even before Isaac was conscious that he needed to go to the restroom. "Take a bathroom break" appeared on the screen facing Miles.

Later, returning from the bathroom, Isaac said in an amused tone, "I noticed the eerie silence in the bathroom. It's been a long time since I was in a public bathroom without hearing music and ads."

This was one of the many perks of working at Sellco. Miles tried to downplay it. "We try to minimize distractions in our offices."

"And I noticed a pad of notepaper and some pencils are stationed in every toilet stall."

"You'd be surprised how often good ideas occur there. We wouldn't want to lose any of them." Miles chuckled.

Then he launched directly into the next part of his presentation. "So what results does Sellco advertising provide for a mature product like Xarim? PepsiCo signed on with us a couple of years ago. In the past eighteen months, Pepsi has gone from a forty-one percent market share to fifty-three percent. It's the same product as before. This is the power of superlative advertising."

"What happened to the Pepsi sales volume during this period?"

Miles extemporized, "Yes, I see your point. Market share is nice, but sales volume is what most interests you, and it would also be interesting to see how the Pepsi sales volume compared with the general consumer spending trend for the eighteen-month period." Miles took a long sip from his cappuccino and glanced at his video screen, where the executive assistant had just sent a message after quickly referencing the backup materials for the meeting. Miles continued, "During the eighteen-month period, Pepsi sales volume increased nearly twenty percent while total consumer spending increased one percent. Pepsi's net income increased three billion dollars. They paid less than half this amount for advertising."

Miles returned to his prepared material with a slide showing an Olympic-style awards presentation with bronze, silver, gold, and platinum levels. "Sellco offers several levels of service. PepsiCo is one of our Platinum Program clients." Miles could see that Isaac had heard of Sellco's Platinum Program and assumed that he had heard how expensive it was. "The Platinum Program is the pinnacle of advertising. The best of Sellco's staff is assigned to the Platinum Program. Platinum advertising gets top priority placement in the most effective channels; we fine-tune the selective targeting most accurately. Simply put, the Platinum Program provides the ultimate results."

A message from the executive assistant appeared on the video screen facing Miles, "Need more; try the Olympics sponsor." Miles projected an image of the US Olympic downhill ski team with Pharmor's logo superimposed on their uniforms. "To provide you with one example of the opportunities that are available only to platinum clients, we could make Pharmor the official corporate sponsor of the US Olympic ski team." Miles went on to explain that the Pharmor logo would be on the team uniforms and crossover placements elsewhere. As a sponsor, Isaac and his wife could spend an expenses-paid week with the ski team as the team trained near Tahoe. He could ski with team members during training, get tips on his technique, and give the team advice on competition strategy. The US ski team would treat their sponsor like royalty.

Miles glanced at the message from the executive assistant: "Receptive—go for the kill." Miles continued, "No compromise is allowed for our service to platinum clients. The Platinum Program provides an excellent value for the very few who can afford it. The prime resources needed to support platinum clients permit the support of only three platinum accounts at a time. There is now one opening in the Platinum Program that could be secured if a contract is completed within ten days. I'm sure that Pharmor sees the value in getting the very best results. Does this interest you?"

Isaac nodded in agreement. "Sold!" the executive assistant messaged.

"To save time, let's go through the major parameters for the contract terms and conditions. This way, my staff can prepare a first-draft contract that best serves your needs. Of course, what we say now is open for change later during the detailed review of the contract. No commitments are needed today. Is that OK with you?"

Isaac agreed, showing no awareness that this method of conditional consent gently placed Miles in control and stripped Isaac of his defenses. They quickly worked out the details, including the two-billion-dollar annual fee and performance guarantees.

Isaac would never learn that Sellco's Platinum Program was even more effective than Miles had described. None of Sellco's clients were ever told the real reason for the Platinum Program's phenomenal performance: Project Mercury. Miles was one of only ten persons in Sellco who knew of Project Mercury, and he could not mention Mercury's existence to anyone else. The most that Miles could do was point to the astounding past results of the Platinum Program and suggest that the results came from the sophisticated application of the best advertising channels.

3

Susan Hebb, a professor of sensory neurophysiology, entered "the Persian carpet store," as Yuri's office was affectionately known at the Coordinated Science Laboratory. Yuri straightened his posture as he always did when he saw Susan. Try as he might, he could not match her towering height. Yuri always reminded her of a bulldog, stocky and friendly. He had a wide, rough face with premature wrinkles. Despite being a few years older than her, he had a more youthful idealism and inquisitiveness.

Susan ignored most men, but Yuri's emphatic, enthusiastic personality had been impossible to ignore when they had first met two years ago. At first he had seemed pushy and rough, but she soon learned he was just a cute puppy dog who wanted attention. He quickly became her closest professional colleague and a surprisingly good friend. Although her statuesque figure attracted the lustful attention of men, she was well practiced in deflecting unwelcome advances. While Yuri had never said anything to suggest that he wished to be more than a good friend, she wondered if maybe he was afraid of telling her his true feelings since he had seen her rebuff other men.

"Happy fortieth birthday," she said, handing an envelope to Yuri and hoping that her choice was suitable for Yuri's worldly taste.

Yuri had a mischievous twinkle in his eyes. "Don't you know? The proper number base for counting birthdays is base sixteen, not base ten. I am really twenty-eight years old today."

Susan got the joke and winked with her good eye. She wore a black eyepatch on one eye, the result of a nasty bout with cancer when she was twenty years old. While an eyepatch could appear dashing on some men, she thought it was less attractive on a woman. She had been devastated when her fiancé dumped her immediately after the surgery to remove her cancerous eye. She was thirty-four years old now and had convinced herself that she had no need or interest in men. Susan had devoted herself to her work.

"You computer nerds always think in powers of two and powers of sixteen, don't you?" She pointed at the clock on Yuri's wall that ran counterclockwise and had to be read backward. "I'm surprised that your warped clock doesn't have binary numbers on its face."

Yuri chuckled as he sliced the envelope open with a Swiss Army knife. It contained a birthday card that had been generated by a program at a music sales website and printed by Susan. The card told Yuri that Susan had purchased music by an artist named "Fourplay," and he could download the music using the code provided on the card. Yuri looked up, "Thank you. Who's Fourplay?"

"It's a turn-of-the-century group of four jazz musicians. I think you'll enjoy it." Shortly after his arrival at the Coordinated Science Lab two years ago, Yuri had started their tradition of giving each other gifts of music for birthdays and Christmas. It had become a competition to see who could find the most wonderful, obscure pieces of music.

Yuri typed the website's URL into his computer's browser and then entered the code from the card. The smooth jazz played from his computer. Most men were hard to read, but it was easy to see that Yuri was pleased. His head bobbed in time with the music.

"*Oj!*" exclaimed Yuri in Russian. "I am a bee surrounded by pretty flowers, so lucky to have a friend with such good taste in music." She always enjoyed it when Yuri fed her need for recognition.

With a dramatic flourish, she placed a paper bag on Yuri's desk. As she opened the top of the bag, a dense fog wafted from the open bag and drifted across Yuri's desk. "And here's something for us to enjoy with the music."

As more fog spilled forth from the bag, she extracted two ice cream cones: chocolate chip for herself, and for Yuri, his favorite, French vanilla. She had loaded the bag with frozen carbon dioxide from the bio lab before visiting an ice cream shop in town.

As they ate the ice cream, Yuri inquired about the function of the hippocampus region of the human brain. The Coordinated Science Laboratory often provided the opportunity for cross-pollination between scientists from different disciplines. Susan explained how the hippocampus played a vital role as the brain's filing clerk. Yuri seemed to be fascinated by the human brain's power coming from its ability to retrieve associated sequences of information from a hierarchal storage of memories. She explained that on most occasions the brain did not compute answers; it retrieved the answers from its huge, well-structured memory.

Yuri had asked her about the human brain on several previous occasions. He was such a curious person, in both senses: he persistently asked odd questions, and he behaved and thought in unusual ways. Susan had learned to respect and even enjoy

Yuri, whereas she had noticed that most Americans showed distaste for Yuri's strange, old-fashioned mannerisms.

"What is this fascination you have with the human brain?" she asked.

"The brain is the ultimate computer. Our most powerful computers are cheap toys by comparison. I think we can learn to make better computers by understanding the human brain."

"That sounds interesting, but today I need to ask for your help with an experiment in my lab," she said. They finished the ice cream cones and walked to Susan's human perception and sensory systems lab. "I have been funded to develop a system that automatically measures the effectiveness of advertising material by observing the motion of a test subject's eyes."

Yuri smiled as he imagined what he and Susan must look like walking down the hallway. Her tall and slender physique contrasted Yuri's stout frame. She had all of the deliciously feminine curves that Yuri thought a woman should have, not the boyish rail of a figure that the high priests of fashion worshiped. His unruly black-brown hair and rugged complexion had nothing in common with Susan's refined appearance. The light band of freckles that splashed across Susan's nose complemented her fiery red hair, which was pulled back in a clip with a French braid finish. He had not worked up the courage to tell Susan of his ardent desires. American women were so unapproachable.

Like all of CSL, Susan's lab was lavishly equipped with leading-edge instruments. Susan showed Yuri a helmet containing two miniature video cameras pointed at the subject's eyes and a third video camera pointed where the subject was looking. "This system is already in general use, but its measurements require lengthy analysis by skilled psychologists. We are trying to develop a computer-based analysis of the subject's eye motion to provide an immediate score of the effectiveness of trial advertisements shown to the subject. I was hoping that you could suggest the right type of computer algorithm to perform the data analysis."

Yuri grunted. "There is too much advertising already. There must be better work to do."

"Come on, Yuri," pleaded Susan playfully. "Put on the helmet. I think you'll find it's fun." Yuri could not refuse Susan's charm.

A knob at the back of the helmet adjusted it for a snug fit. Susan told Yuri to look at a projection screen with a numbered target in each corner and a fifth target in the center. "First we must calibrate the system. Look at each target and call out the number."

Yuri moved his eyes. "One, two, three, four, five."

Six lines of text appeared on the screen. "Now read it silently." She waited until he was done and then said, "Press this green button and look at the playback screen. You'll see exactly where your eyes were fixating as you read the text."

On the playback screen, Yuri saw the view of what he had been looking at just before he pressed the button. The bright red crosshairs were dancing in small jumps along the first line of text. Then the crosshairs quickly jumped to the second line of text, and they continued this jerky motion through the remaining text. Wherever the crosshairs went, they left a series of small red dots that slowly faded away.

"The red crosshairs show the points of fixation of your eyes as you read the text," she said. "We call the red dots 'breadcrumbs,' and they show a short-term history of the points of fixation. Press this white button and the system will replay the scene."

Yuri pressed the white button and was fascinated by the record of his eye movements. He had expected the eyes to move in a smooth continuous path, but instead he saw the crosshairs perform a series of jumps. "My eyes were jerking about wildly; why didn't I notice that while I was reading?"

"The eye's fixation point jumps every three hundred to five hundred milliseconds; these are called saccades. This is how your eyes normally scan any image. Your visual cortex combines the images from both eyes and smooths the jumps between fixation points to produce a perceived stable visual model of the world." Susan pointed to the "breadcrumbs" on the screen. "Notice that your eyes were jumping one to three words at a time."

The motion of the red crosshairs entranced Yuri. "Do you mean that I do not read each letter of every word?"

"No. Skilled readers perceive up to three words at once. Now look at this." Susan placed a new image on the projection screen showing an advertisement for the Trek 7800 bicycle. The gleaming bicycle was shown with a muscular man on one side of the bike and a fit-looking woman on the other side wearing cycling gear. Text extolled the laser-mitered joints of its tapered aluminum frame and its Shimano derailleur. Yuri took in the advertisement and noted some of the mechanical details of the bicycle.

He pressed the green button and was astounded to see the pattern of fixation points shown by the red crosshairs. His eyes had first zeroed in on the woman's face and then had proceeded to explore every bit of her anatomy in detail. There were breadcrumbs all over her body. Next the crosshairs jumped to a very brief scan of the man, then back to the woman, then a little longer on the bicycle, back to certain key parts of the woman's anatomy, and lastly to the text. With Susan looking over his shoulder, Yuri felt exposed and betrayed by his eyes. This system revealed private thoughts in his mind that he did not know himself. Oddly, Susan seemed oblivious to his embarrassment.

"Oh, I am sorry for my wandering eyes. I didn't know what I was doing," he apologized.

Susan laughed heartily. "That's normal. Men always first inspect any female in an image. Don't feel embarrassed; it's OK. Here, try it again. This time, try to not look at the woman." She showed another bicycle advertisement for a more traditional style of bicycle with a different man and woman. Susan was having fun; Yuri was not.

He pressed the green button and the playback showed the red crosshairs starting at the bicycle. "Yes," he thought, "I can control my eyes." But then the crosshairs darted to the woman's face, back to the bike, to the woman's chest for an instant, to the bike, to the woman's hips for an instant, to the bike, and then to her legs. Yuri was really peeved now.

Susan laughed again. "Don't fight it, Yuri. Males can't help but check out any woman in the image. Advertisers have known this for ages." Susan took a step toward the door to the hallway. "I'll be right back. I'm going to get a Pepsi; do you want one?"

"I'll take a Coke, please." Yuri still had the helmet on as Susan walked to the door. He suddenly realized what he was doing and pressed the green button. The playback screen showed Susan walking to the door with red breadcrumbs tracing the curves of Susan's shapely figure. "*Vot eto stanok.* What good hardware for making love," he muttered to himself as he contemplated the eye-tracking system and Susan's figure.

Susan strode back with two cans of soda, her hips swaying deliciously. Yuri decided to follow Susan's advice and did not fight his eyes. He took the helmet off and thanked Susan for the Coke. He provided some advice to Susan about how to automate the analysis of the data collected by the eye tracker and then said, "It would be interesting to experiment with the benefits of integrating this eye tracker into a teaching machine. Today's teaching machines can tell if students are paying attention and if they have learned something, but they do not know exactly where a student is looking. Sometimes the teaching machines can be misled if a student learns something other than the intended lesson. By integrating eye tracking, the system could better assure that the right item was learned."

"That's brilliant! Why didn't I think of that?" Yuri had never seen Susan so excited. "This could be a breakthrough for teaching machines. Yuri, would you mind if I performed a set of experiments to test your theory? I will be sure to give you credit for the theory."

"You deserve credit too. We can work on this together." Yuri looked forward to working with Susan. He knew that she craved having her name associated with an important professional accomplishment and was happy to help her gain recognition.

4

———

The next day Yuri began work on how to integrate the eye-tracking cameras into a teaching machine. His first step was to investigate the video display circuits. He sat alone in his laboratory talking to a digital signal analyzer connected to the guts of a teaching machine. "Zoom out display...stop. Scroll down... stop, select rising edge." The voice recognition system had been trained on his voice, so it had no trouble with his thick Russian accent.

A close-up view of the printed circuit board appeared in the goggles Yuri was wearing. In the foreground, he saw the computer-generated drawing of the printed circuit board, and in the background, the real circuit board. By positioning his head correctly, he could align the two images.

Dirty-hands work was unusual for a computer scientist. Any other engineer would rely on computer simulations of the circuit, or if they got desperate, maybe a debug-mode data dump. While Yuri generally trusted people, he never trusted computers to behave correctly. Too many times, he had seen the statement "computers never make mistakes" proven wrong. Relying on a misbehaving computer to diagnose itself made no sense.

The circuit board had tens of thousands of connection points, but the voice-controlled goggles made it easy to find the right place to connect the signal analyzer probes. His hands were full, and Yuri wished he had a third hand to handle the microprobes. Each microprobe was numbered and color-coded with two bands of color. The set of sixty-five microprobes made a pretty palette of bright colors from the entire visible spectrum. The goggles had magnifying lenses at the lower portion of the visual field for fine work. The close-up of the circuit board looked like a grand metropolis with multilane copper superhighways flowing among buildings of various shapes and sizes. There were capacitor skyscrapers, transistor water towers, integrated-circuit warehouses, and resistor housing developments.

Steady hands were required to attach the microprobes without knocking others loose. He double-checked the connections and then turned to check the status of the second computer, which he had programmed to emulate the signals from the brain scanner to the teaching machine. Rather than having a human subject connected to the teaching machine, Yuri had a second computer take its place. The teaching machine was busily teaching a lesson on clothing fashion design to the dummy student.

The digital signal analyzer showed the stream of information flowing to the teaching machine's display converter. The data appeared normal, and Yuri proceeded to look for the information he needed to determine the coordinates for displayed objects. Just as he had almost isolated the coordinates, the data jittered for an instant and then returned to normal.

Most technicians would have ignored the data jitter as a loose microprobe and proceeded once the data had resynched. Yuri, however, knew his microprobes were firmly connected, so he pressed the MANUAL MEMORY CAPTURE button the instant he saw the data jitter. His quick reflexes had caught the data jitter while it was in short-term memory, and he used the REVERSE TIME function to search back in the digital signal analyzer's memory to the event. Sure enough, this was not a loose microprobe; the clock signal was solid, but every data bit had been affected. He stored the event in a file he named GLITCH-1 and then examined the data jitter one sample at a time. It was only a few milliseconds in duration, and he did not recognize the data patterns. The data in the GLITCH-1 file did not match any of the standard information formats used in the teaching machines.

Yuri was curious. This was a standard production teaching machine running standard software. There was no reason for it to have a glitch like this. He was concerned that a data jitter could subtly impair the effectiveness of the teaching machine. The source of GLITCH-1 needed to be found.

Yuri reconnected every microprobe, making extra sure it was connected solidly to the right point. Next, he rearranged the grounding connection for the digital signal analyzer to make sure it was rock solid. Then he double-checked the clock synchronization settings. He would not be fooled by sloppy instrumentation technique. Yuri programmed the digital signal analyzer to AUTO MEMORY CAPTURE the instant a pattern matching GLITCH-1 appeared.

He waited several minutes watching the data patterns, but everything was normal. His attention began to drift when he saw the data jitter on the display screen. He looked for the AUTO MEMORY CAPTURE confirmation, but there was none. The data jitter had not exactly matched GLITCH-1. Yuri cursed as he jabbed the MANUAL MEMORY CAPTURE button. He was too late; the event had fallen out of the memory buffer. Whatever it was, it had occurred again, but differently.

Yuri sat with his finger near the MANUAL MEMORY CAPTURE button and his eyes riveted to the digital signal analyzer screen, waiting patiently. He dared not to glance at his watch to see how much time passed, but he knew it was a long time. It was tedious and he began to talk out loud. "Come out and play, my friend; I want to take your picture."

As if on command, the displayed data jittered. Yuri jabbed the MANUAL MEMORY CAPTURE button. "Caught you!" he exclaimed. He scrolled back in the analyzer's memory and stored the event in a file named GLITCH-2. This event had the same duration as GLITCH-1, but the data were different. He checked his watch; it had been exactly thirty minutes between this and the previous event. Yuri's intuition was buzzing. There was something interesting behind these mysterious glitches.

He checked GLITCH-2 against the standard information formats, but there was no match. He tried a decryption program, but the code-breaking algorithms could not sink their teeth into files this small. Yuri cursed to himself, "*Zaebla menia eta bliadskaia golovolomka*. This bewitched puzzle has screwed me up."

The data jitters occurred every thirty minutes like clockwork, so it became easier for him to catch them. Eventually, he caught a third unique sequence, which he stored in a file named GLITCH-3. Then he found that the subsequent events exactly matched the three GLITCH files in a repeating pattern of GLITCH-1, GLITCH-2, GLITCH-3 spaced thirty minutes apart. No new versions of glitches appeared. This was time-consuming work, and he needed to think about what to do next.

———

Yuri did his best thinking when he smoked, but smoking was not permitted in the building. When he had first arrived at the university, Yuri had tried smoking outside CSL's entrance. He grew weary of the stares from everyone who entered or exited the building. Most of them had never seen a person smoking except in old movies. He could not have attracted more attention if he had been juggling flaming torches. Smoking in America had become so rare that stores no longer sold cigarettes; they had to be ordered at a boutique website. Eventually he had found a place where he could smoke without becoming a spectacle or getting rained upon—a chemistry lab in the south wing of the building. Yuri had developed a good rapport with Clarence, the good-hearted organic chemist who ran the lab. Unlike most bald white men's, Clarence's shiny black head made him look handsome. The shine on Clarence's head matched his sunny personality. Whenever Yuri came to the lab, Clarence greeted him with a welcoming "hello."

Yuri sat next to a fume hood in the rear corner of the chemistry lab and lit a cigarette. The fume hood efficiently sucked every bit of smoke out of the building.

Clarence greeted Yuri with a glass beaker containing a pale yellow liquid. "Yuri, drink some of this and tell me what it tastes like to you."

Being a trusting soul, Yuri suppressed the suspicion that it looked like urine. "It tastes like water. What is it?"

"It is a tasteless food additive. When it is metabolized, it produces identifiable molecules in the exhaled breath. A gas analyzer built into future TVs could then detect if a person has consumed a tagged product. The TV will then report the result via the Internet to the sponsor of this research, Sellco." Clarence handed Yuri a plastic tube. "Blow into this." Yuri blew into the tube, and Clarence seemed to be pleased with the results.

Yuri returned to smoking his cigarette under the fume hood as he pondered the data glitches. Smoking had the strange property of simultaneously calming his feelings and stimulating his thinking. Yuri gazed at the gallery of glassy shapes in the chemistry laboratory. The Erlenmeyer flasks, Liebig condensation tubes, beakers, pipettes, and graduated cylinders were perfectly organized. Reflecting on the glitches, Yuri said, "What are you, my curious little gremlin?"

Clarence turned from his mass spectrometer. "What's that?"

"Nothing; I was just talking to myself." Clarence went back to his work. If Clarence could tolerate Yuri's smoking, then talking to oneself was nothing. Everyone at the Coordinated Science Laboratory was a bit crazy in his or her own individual way, but Yuri suspected he was considered the oddest of the bunch.

A kitchen timer beeped and Clarence removed two loaves of bread from an oven in the lab. He placed the loaves next to two other loaves that had been sliced. A numbered tag sat next to each loaf. The aroma of the freshly baked bread made Yuri salivate just like a dog in the conditioned-reflex experiments conducted by Ivan Pavlov. Yuri reached toward the sliced bread. "May I have a piece? It smells delicious."

"No. Sorry, Yuri, the bread is an experiment. I haven't finished the tests to confirm it is safe to eat."

"But it smells so good."

"It has an additive to make the freshly baked aroma last much longer. I'm developing it as a favor for my sister, who recently opened a fancy French restaurant in Milwaukee. Imagine what it'd be like if her restaurant always had this wonderful aroma."

They chatted about his sister's restaurant until Yuri noticed that Clarence seemed to have completed his work at the mass spectrometer. "Clarence, could you help me for a while? I need your brain."

"OK, but I want it back when you're done," replied Clarence, ever the joker.

They went to Yuri's lab and hooked Clarence up to the teaching machine's brain scanner in place of the mock student that Yuri had previously connected to the teaching machine. Perhaps the glitches were somehow caused by the computer-simulated student that Yuri had been using.

"Just act like a student and take this lesson on clothing fashion design," said Yuri. "I will be observing the operation of the teaching machine."

"OK, but I must warn you that by teaching fashion to a chemist you may produce a fascist. Ha, ha." Yuri did his best to humor Clarence.

It was not long before the digital signal analyzer triggered upon detecting GLITCH-2. Just as Yuri thought, the glitches were not an artifact of his mock student. Yuri wondered if the glitches were linked to the instructional program.

"Clarence, I need to change to a different instructional program. What subject would you like to take?"

"Portrait photography." Yuri pulled up the subject menu on the teaching machine.

"Which lesson?"

"Lighting techniques for photographing naked female subjects," said Clarence, grinning mischievously. Yuri selected the lesson without a word; he needed to keep his volunteer happy. Thirty minutes after the last event, GLITCH-3 appeared. Yuri found the series of nude photographs on the teaching machine's screen quite distracting, but he kept his eyes on the teaching machine's display screen when the digital signal analyzer beeped to indicate it had been triggered. No artifact was visible on the screen during the beep, only an interesting study in the shadows created by different lighting angles.

Yuri thanked Clarence and said he had completed his observations.

"I hope you found your observations stimulating. Mine were," quipped Clarence as he left.

Yuri pondered what he had learned. The glitches occurred when different instructional programs were played, and the thirty-minute interval remained invariant. Later, with his mock student connected to the teaching machine, he tried several other instructional programs. The same pattern of glitches resulted with every program, and no artifact was visible on the teaching machine's display. The glitches did not belong there. What were they? Yuri performed an autocorrelation analysis on the GLITCH files. There was a strong autocorrelation; this indicated there was some sort of information in the GLITCH files. These were not random patterns. There was information hiding in there. Yuri muttered to himself, "You are a shy demon. Show your colors."

———

"Good grief! Not more Spam." Susan Hebb gave a dejected sigh as she looked at the computer screen.

"It's been more frequent this month. This time I am ready for it," proclaimed Julie Mountcastle, pulling a bunch of fresh chives from her bag.

For nearly a year, Susan and Julie had served as volunteer cooks at a kitchen that served homeless and needy persons. Julie loved to cook, and Susan enjoyed learning from Julie. Chatting with Julie was much better than talking to men. It seemed to Susan that most men could only talk about three subjects: sports, gadgets, and sports-gadgets. Each Tuesday they would check the computer at the Salvation Army kitchen to see what was to be prepared that night. For the fifth time that month, the menu was fried Spam and instant mashed potatoes.

Julie pulled a jar of Dijon mustard and some other cooking supplies from her bag. "We're not serving a slab of Spam and a mound of potatoes again. Get those muffin pans down from that shelf." Susan was intrigued as to what Julie was going to create.

They used a large food processor to mix Spam, eggs, oatmeal, and milk. The two friends talked as they filled each cup in the muffin pans two-thirds full with the Spam mixture.

"You work a lot with Professor Petrov. What d'ya think of him?" said Julie, intent on her cooking.

"He's brilliant. Working with him is like trying to keep up with a race car when you're riding a bicycle."

"Yeah. But what do you think of him? I mean, don't you think he's interesting?"

"Sure, he's one of a kind and works harder than anyone I know. Yuri's like a machine." Susan wondered what Julie was driving at.

"Machine!" disputed Julie. "He's nothing like a machine. Yuri really cares about what he's doing and is not afraid to show his feelings. He's more human than most people." Julie's emotional response surprised Susan.

Julie mixed brown sugar with mustard and vinegar and then showed Susan how to spoon the glaze mixture into each cup in the muffin pans.

"I just meant that I admire how dedicated he is to his work," explained Susan, "and Yuri's very nice about helping others too. But, you know, it's ironic how much he works on the technology used in teaching machines, given that he doesn't like to use teaching machines himself."

"Maybe it's something you have to get used to as a child."

"Or maybe he's just an old-fashioned Russian."

"Well," said Julie defensively, "I think he has a lot to teach all of us, and not just about computer science."

This remark caused Susan to reconsider her thoughts about Yuri. "Yes, I think you're right."

After the Spam mixture had baked in the oven, Julie showed Susan how to use a pastry bag with a large star nozzle to place a pretty swirl of mashed potatoes on top of each Spam cupcake. Julie placed a sprinkle of chopped fresh chives on the top and stood back for a look. "A little creativity makes a big difference."

Susan had never imagined Spam could look so good.

5

—

Alfred Grossberg felt Doug Lefler's eyes zero in on him like the targeting system of a fighter airplane. Alfred was the only big fish in the sea of junior staffers at the Washington, DC sales seminar for the US Customs and Border Patrol Agency. Doug Lefler was the vice president of sales for Security Scanning Systems, and Alfred sensed desperation in Lefler's presentation. Triple-S needed to hook a big one soon, or Lefler would be out of a job.

Lefler made eye contact and switched on his charisma like a light bulb. "Mr. Grossberg, would you care to be our volunteer for the demonstration of the IS-250?"

Alfred Grossberg was not impressed by Lefler's style and had no wish to be on stage, but there was no way of saying "no" without appearing to be a jerk. He acted pleased to be selected.

The nervous salesman followed his memorized script. "The IS-250 is so simple to use that the only instructions you need are on this sign." The sign had no words. Its pictures showed a pair of eyeglasses with a red, slashed circle through the glasses and a person standing on painted footprints looking at a blue light while holding the eyeglasses in his hand. "Go ahead," Lefler said with a showman's smile as he waved his hand at the IS-250. As

Alfred stepped into the portal and made a right turn, he heard a servomotor and saw a module with four optical lenses quickly move to his eye level. A blue light followed by two brief flashes of white light was emitted from the center lens, and in less than a second the light in the center flashed green.

"Thank you, Mr. Grossberg," Lefler said with feigned confidence. "You're done and the IS-250 correctly identified you. You can all see how quick that was. In trials with untrained public volunteers, we consistently get a throughput of one person per four seconds with an accuracy exceeding ninety-nine point nine nine percent. We'll guarantee those numbers in a contract. No other product comes close, ladies and gentlemen. The alternatives don't compare. Facial recognition is worse than ninety-nine percent, assuming your subjects don't play games with makeup or move their jaw. Fingerprint scanners are a little better, but they require hourly cleaning. Voice prints can be faked, and background noise is a big problem unless you put the subject in a soundproof booth."

Lefler projected a simplified diagram of the IS-250. "You may have noticed that the IS-250 resembles the magnetic detector portals that are commonplace in all airports and government buildings. The public has accommodated to the magnetic detector portals, and people are comfortable walking through them. As Mr. Grossberg approached the IS-250, the ultrasonic sensor detected his exact height. By the time he was centered on the footprints, the optical module had moved to exactly match the height of his eyes. The portal and footprints unobtrusively constrain the person so that their eyes are positioned within two centimeters of a reference point. This is aided by the blue light, which provides a fixation point. The beauty of the IS-250 is that the subject touches nothing. This makes the subject feel at ease. There is no worry of picking up germs, no worry of exactly where to place your head. Since nothing is touched, there is nothing to clean. It took the world's best optical engineers to design an imaging system with the required resolution to take its picture at a distance of ten to twenty centimeters from the subject's eyes."

"What were the two flashes of light for?" asked one of the small fish.

Lefler presented his "What a brilliant question!" face and replied, "The flashes illuminate both the iris and the retina of both eyes for the image capture. The IS-250 is the only system to capture a high-resolution image of both the iris and the retina. No one has successfully fooled an iris scanner with overlay contact lenses." He made a dramatic pause. "Except in spy movies, of course." Lefler chuckled at his own joke; no one else seemed amused. "The IS-250 takes no chances by scanning both the iris and the retina." He projected a typical snapshot of a family with a dog where everyone, including the dog, had bright red dots at the center of their eyes. "I am sure that you have all experienced the dreaded red-eye effect in your family pictures taken with a flash camera. Well, the IS-250 puts this effect to good use by emitting a low-power flash to illuminate both the iris and the retina. The red dot you see in the eyes in this family photo is the light reflecting off the retina at the back of each eye. There are two flashes of light to ensure that it gets a good image if the subject blinks at the wrong time. Furthermore, the IS-250 will not be fooled by a replica contact lens because the system looks for the eye's dynamic reaction to the flashes of light. The flashes are low-power to avoid temporary blindness. Mr. Grossberg, did you notice any visual discomfort or afterimages?"

Alfred shook his head.

"Of course, you didn't; the IS-250 is designed to provide a totally pleasant experience. Even the color of the paint was chosen to be pleasing."

Lefler pointed to a pair of small radio antennas at the top of the IS-250. "These antennas scan and record any RFID chips on the person as they pass through the IS-250. You may not know that radio frequency identification—RFID—chips the size of a flea are imbedded in virtually every item sold in stores: clothes, shoes, medications, packaged food, and cosmetics. These RFID chips have replaced the old UPC bar codes for tracking store inventory. Where the old UPC bar codes indicated that the item was a brown, size nine, men's Nike Prosport-II shoe, the RFID is a unique serial number for every item. Two identical bottles of aspirin have different RFID codes. The ensemble of RFID codes found on the person scanned by the IS-250 is stored together with the other information collected by the IS-250."

The new technology was better than Alfred had imagined. It would fix the hole created by the privacy nuts who had forced the stores to disassociate credit card purchase records from RFID scans at the checkout station. The IS-250 would associate the RFID chips that clung to everyone like fleas with the person's identity. This would effectively turn all of the existing RFID scanners at stores, gas stations pumps, tollbooths, and libraries into secondary population-tracking stations.

Doug Lefler fidgeted with the projector controller in his hand as he moved to a slide showing the IS-250 connected to a national network of computers. "The IS-250 transmits a compressed copy of the scan via a secure VPN connection to a national database of eye scans. In less than a second, a positive identification match is made, and confirmation is returned to the IS-250. The green light Mr. Grossberg saw indicated a positive match. In the very rare case of a red light, no match was found and a rescan is taken. If the system identifies the subject as being on a list of persons wanted by the law, then a hidden signal is provided to the security staff at the site. But that's not all," he said, sounding like a television pitchman.

"Law enforcement officers love the IS-250 because while it is capturing the eye scan, it also takes a full-face photograph of the subject. The facial photo and the height measurement play a role in the identification algorithm, and they are uploaded to a central law enforcement database together with the date, time, location, and subject's identity. Imagine having up-to-date facial photos of every person who walks through a screening station. The era of ten-year-old mug shots is history."

Alfred noted that Lefler did not mention that privacy and civil rights groups had organized fervent opposition to systems like the IS-250 because they would permit the government to track everyone's movements. This had stopped all but a trickle of sales for the IS-250.

Lefler had run over time and people were starting to leave. "Thanks for coming, and please be sure to pick up a brochure and my business card as you leave." Lefler's assistant by the door made sure that no one got away without a brochure.

The room emptied quickly, but Lefler shone with hope when he saw Alfred Grossberg approach. "How quickly can you install ten thousand units across the country?" asked Alfred.

"Ten thousand?" said Lefler with barely controlled delight. "We estimate that twelve hundred units would be enough to service all points of entry to the country."

"I'm thinking of that plus every aircraft departure screening point and government building in the country. The threats to the security of our country are both internal and external."

"I agree completely, sir," Lefler said eagerly. "I was just thinking of the points of entry as the first phase." Lefler looked like he was about to jump for joy. "We have two factories on contingency contracts, and we could have twelve hundred units installed at all points of entry within six months of a signed contract. I can get back to you in three days with a firm schedule for all ten thousand units." Lefler paused to raise a delicate issue.

"I can send you a public policy study we have prepared to help address the privacy concerns. If the administration will back the use of this system, we will be happy to help efforts to overcome the opposition."

"Mr. Lefler, if this nation can't trust its law enforcement agencies, then who can it trust? The president's 'Strong America' program needs this to defend our homeland against a growing flood of people who would destroy what the privacy freaks take for granted. Our country is under attack every day by foreigners who envy our high standard of living. Yes, I think the administration will back this system, and we may just have what it takes to convince everyone else that this is right. We have some work to do first. Send me your public policy paper and I'll get back to you when we're ready to get serious."

Alfred had already wasted too much time with this twit. Doug Lefler hardly had the chance to say "Thank you, Mr. Grossberg" before Alfred walked out with the brochure in his hand thinking, "Slaughter is the key to Supreme Court approval."

———

The retina of the eye has a blind spot at the point where the optic nerve attaches to the retina. The blind spot is not perceived because the mind fills in the space with an estimate of what it thinks should be there. Similarly, Susan had a partial blindness to the subtleties of human facial expressions and body language. Her mind made up for what she did not see in the faces of others, but sometimes it was confusing.

Hamilton von Helmholtz was strutting about Susan's office blathering on about how great the Chicago White Sox were and how he had bet a bundle in the departmental betting pool. She could not tell if he was just trying to treat her like one of the guys or if these repeated lectures on professional sports were an attempt to develop something more intimate.

"This new pitcher, Garrison," Hamilton said with authority, "was slow in the first couple of games, but in the last game he was really in the zone. Take it from me: the White Sox are your best bet."

Susan had almost finished writing her proposal for the new research project on integrating eye tracking into teaching machines when Hamilton had interrupted her with this banal talk of sports. She was doubly bored by his chatter because she had no interest in him or baseball and even less interest in gambling. Susan checked her personal calendar on her cell phone in an effort to signal her extreme disinterest, but she could not bring herself to tell her boss to leave. She just waited for him to burn out.

Hamilton was just starting to wind down when Takashi Fujikawa stepped into Susan's office. Takashi was a senior engineer for the campus computing infrastructure department; his job was to keep all of the computers at the University of Illinois running smoothly. The title "senior engineer" did not seem fitting to Susan, since Takashi was only twenty-nine years old and behaved like he was nineteen. Takashi had come to America as a young child, but since he was machine-taught, he acted and thought like any other American.

Takashi must have heard Hamilton's praise for the White Sox. "You're wrong; Garrison's changeup pitch still isn't working. The Cubs' outfield is way better than the White Sox', and the Cubs' new closing pitcher is awesome."

To Susan's dismay, Hamilton was fired up again. "So are you putting your money where you mouth is, Takashi?"

"Oh, yeah, and I'm going to enjoy taking your money. You didn't hear that Samuels has been suspended for the remainder of the season, did you? They found out he's taken DNA modification treatments."

"I'm not worried about Samuels; the White Sox have more pitching depth than any other team in the league."

Just when she had hoped that Hamilton would go away, Takashi had shown up. Now the two men were going at it full volume with Susan as a bewildered bystander. She could not figure out what they were arguing about, since both of the teams seemed to be from Chicago. Did Chicago have two baseball teams?

The two men ignored Susan and continued their baseball banter, standing a meter from Susan as she returned to typing on the computer in her office. She had given up on the incomprehensible conversation and did her best to ignore the male dominance contest. Hamilton would never admit he was wrong. Takashi was thoroughly American; there was no trace of the traditional Japanese avoidance of causing dishonor to others. Susan was relieved when Hamilton signaled for Takashi to leave with him.

———

"Send me the access code I need to monitor Petrov's computers," Hamilton ordered Takashi when they were alone.

"OK. Is there anything special I need to do?"

"No, I just want to keep an eye on Petrov. He's an odd one, y'know."

6

—

Yuri arrived bearing a sensational phalaenopis orchid in a matching purple and white ceramic pot. There are few universal truths in this world, but Yuri believed that one could never go wrong by giving flowers to a woman. Yuri was right. Julie was delighted by the orchid and placed it on the dinner table, set to one side so that they would have a clear view of each other. Yuri noticed that she had done her best with a subtle application of makeup and stylish clothes, but there was no hiding her plain face and short stocky legs. She was the antithesis of Susan's statuesque curves. Julie wore her hair like it was her best feature, which it was. Her shoulder-length, mousey-brown hair had bold blonde highlights. Yuri was dressed in his usual abnormal style: black tie, black shirt, black belt, black pants, black socks, and black shoes.

After she had thanked him for the orchid and lit a pair of candles, Julie poured a little *crème de cassis* in each champagne glass and then filled the remainder with chilled champagne. "This drink is called Kir Royal," she said, handing Yuri a glass. Lively bubbles danced toward the surface of the rose-tinted drink. An aroma of peach mixed with other fruity fragrances caressed Yuri's senses.

The volume on Julie's television had been turned down, but Yuri found that the frenetic images on its screen distracted his enjoyment of the Kir Royal, so he asked Julie to turn the television off.

"You want the TV off?" asked Julie, puzzled.

"I wish to give my full attention to my host and the meal."

"I always have the TV on. Everyone knows the importance of advertising to being a well-educated consumer."

"Do you believe everything that you are taught?"

"That is what teaching machines are programmed to do." She did not seem to understand what he was saying, but turned the television off to please him.

Yuri proposed a toast: "To you discovering your true passion." The Kir Royal was delightful.

Julie placed two small plates on the table. "This is an *amuse-bouche*, a beginning amusement." On each plate was a large firm mushroom cap filled with finely diced lobster and mushrooms in a bubbling hot cognac butter cream sauce with a parsley garnish. "Use the small spoon," she said with an impish smile. Small was an understatement. The incredibly tiny spoon's volume could be measured in microliters. Clearly, the spoon's function was to ensure that the course would be enjoyed slowly. Yuri felt slightly foolish using a spoon that would be suited to serving mice, but made a contented sound as he took a second small bite. "Have you thought more about your interest in computer science?"

"I certainly appreciate the importance of computer science. There must be computerized controllers hidden inside almost every electronic device in my apartment, but I really don't share your fascination with computers. I don't think I'd like to make a career of programming computers."

"You are a fine student and are doing well in my class, and you are welcome to continue, but frankly, you're wasting your time. I think you should drop this class and find something that inspires you. Please don't get me wrong; I enjoy having you in my class. I want to do anything I can to help you reach your potential, but I am sure you can find something more fulfilling."

Yuri held his breath as he waited for her reaction to his blunt statement. She nodded acceptance. Yuri felt that might have been the first time someone had the courage to tell her to find herself.

"You're right; I really don't know myself." She paused to think and then brightened. "But for now, we have a meal to enjoy."

How could Yuri discover the real Julie? They finished the *amuse-bouche,* and Julie soon returned with chilled serving plates holding slices of foie gras with *coulis de framboise de Bourgogne* and fig chutney on the side. The bright red raspberry sauce was drawn in a serpentine line around the edge of the plate with a dot of sauce at the inside of each curve. The course was served with a warm baguette wrapped in a linen towel. It was nothing like the usual uninspired but consistently satisfactory American food.

The slice of foie gras was small, but each bite was packed with a mouthful of savory, robust flavor. The bread was hard and crisp outside, soft and warm inside. Its aroma left no doubt that the bread was freshly baked. Without a word, Julie had established a lingering pace for the meal. Every bite was to be slowly explored and enjoyed. Yuri surrendered to hedonism. *"Skazochnaia havka—kak s neba upalo.* This is the food from the old-time fables, like it fell straight from the clouds," Yuri thought to himself.

"What did you want to be when you were a young child?" asked Yuri.

"I wanted to be a gymnast. I spent most of my childhood taking gymnastics classes and performing in competitions. I was pretty good up to a point. Then I realized I had stopped improving, and everyone else was passing by me. By age fifteen my body had changed, and I no longer had the build to be a competitive gymnast. After that I lost interest in gymnastics."

"That is one of the few classes still taught by human teachers. Even though you lost interest in gymnastics, I am sure that the extensive interactions with teachers and other students at an early age benefited you." Julie had better interpersonal skills than most other people. This confirmed Yuri's theory that the poor socialization exhibited by most people was the result of a childhood spent with teaching machines instead of interacting with humans.

"So what did you want to be as a child?" asked Julie, toying with her hair.

"I wanted to be an astronaut and explore the unknown. My parents named me in honor of Yuri Gagarin, the first man in space."

"I have a hard time imagining you as an astronaut," said Julie, giggling.

"When I got older, I realized that I would never get through astronaut training with my poor hand-eye coordination and my trouble with motion sickness."

"Both of us have been cheated by our bodies."

"Perhaps it was for the best after all."

"Why did you leave Russia and come here?"

"There is very little money for research in Russia; you don't know how good you have it in America. Here, there is no limit to what I can do. What forced me to action was the loss of my family. My parents and my wife were killed in a battle between the police and a gang of Chechen terrorists who seized the university where my parents and wife taught." Yuri tensed as he recalled the horrific day that the murderous police had unleashed a fusillade against the building where hundreds of hostages were held. In desperation, the Chechens had shot many of their hostages. Yuri had rushed to the massacre site and found his dead parents clinging to each other. What made his blood boil was the reckless police accidentally shooting his wife.

He sighed and took a sip of water. "My wife and I had just celebrated our first anniversary the week before she was murdered. I had no other family, so there was nothing for me in Russia."

Julie had an anguished frown. "That must've been such a shock for you."

"Such tragedies were common in Russia. The police were as dangerous as the criminals. I miss my wife and parents, but I am glad that I came here. The American police are better, but as we said in Russia, don't trust the police any further than you can throw a ruble."

"Do you feel at home here?"

"No, not when human-taught people are treated like subhuman deviants. You are one of the few people who treat me with respect."

"I hope that I can make up for the rudeness of others."

Julie went to the kitchen and soon returned with the entrée: two plates of *rôti de gros turbot au four* with *éventail de pomme a la coriander fraîche* and an aromatic cream of clam sauce in two tones artistically swirled on the warmed serving plate. On the side of the plate was a baked apple cut into a fan of fine slices accompanied by sautéed green beans. Julie displayed remarkable skill at preparing and serving a complex series of courses while maintaining a leisurely atmosphere and focusing her attention on her guest.

"Confess—you are hiding a master chef in the kitchen," Yuri said in mock accusation.

"No, only the two of us are here." Julie winked.

With each bite Yuri heard the crunch of the crust, which was followed by a rush of rich flavors from the moist fish. Whereas the sense of hearing loves harmony and vision loves symmetric forms, Julie's creations presented tastes that were a beautiful mélange of complementary flavors. Julie was masterfully conducting an exotic symphony for all of the senses.

He closed his eyes and took a deep sniff of Burgundy wine, and when he opened his eyes, Yuri saw Julie drinking in every nuance of expression on his face. Julie was feeding off his pleasure. Her soulful eyes were more expressive than Susan's demure style.

The conversation with Julie was pleasant, but it lacked the intellectual stimulation of talking with Susan. He wished Susan were sitting across the table from him, glowing in the warm candlelight. While Susan was pleasing to his eyes, her powerful intellect was the true attraction. A conversation with Susan was like that evening's meal, full of unexpected delights, complexities, and craftsmanship.

His reminiscing about Susan ended when Julie returned carrying two hot plates holding a rack of lamb with a velvety Dijon mustard breadcrumb sauce accompanied by *gratine dauphinois* and garnished with carrots and cucumbers prepared to look like zinnias. The vegetable garnish was sliced in fine detail according to the ancient Japanese art of *mukimono*. The first bite confirmed that the entrée was another culinary masterpiece.

"Only the kings of France dined so well. This meal is too good for me. It must have cost a small fortune."

"Don't worry about the cost. My dad is a full partner at a law firm in Chicago. He's loaded and showers me with money."

"My parents were wealthy too. I inherited a good sum of money from them. It has allowed me to do what I enjoy, not what pays the most money. You must have spent the whole day preparing this meal."

"I enjoyed every bit of it. Nothing gives me more joy than giving pleasure to others." That confirmed what he had suspected about Julie's interests.

Yuri raised his glass of Bordeaux wine. "You have succeeded splendidly." He was in a glowing mood, and that seemed to please Julie.

Yuri had lost track of the number of courses Julie had served when she returned from the kitchen bearing two warm ramekins with *soufflé de Grand Marnier*. At the table, she poured a thick, warm *crème anglais* sauce over the top.

"Have you ever taken a lesson from a teaching machine?" Julie asked.

"I have tried it a few times, but only completed a couple of lessons. I learn what I need from books."

"Books! Only you and the university's museum of antiques have books. Who needs dusty old books when everything is online?"

"I do; it is the way I was taught, and I still enjoy the feel of a real book in my hands."

"Don't you enjoy the teaching machines?"

"Not really."

"You're very old-school." Julie winked playfully. "You should try teaching machines more. Everyone enjoys the lessons. It feels good while the lessons are playing. Haven't you heard about the 'learning high' that students experience while on the teaching machines?"

"The lessons are programmed to present the material in the way that the student finds most pleasurable; it enhances learning. However, I do wonder if the addictive nature of teaching machines distracts people from applying what they have learned." Realizing that he was starting to preach, Yuri changed tack. "Speaking of pleasure, this meal is delicious. Do you always eat so well?"

"Not every day. Only when I am entertaining someone special."

"You certainly make me feel special."

The soufflé was gone much too quickly despite their efforts to devour it slowly. Julie poured an aged cognac into a pair of stemmed glasses. They retreated to a comfortable sofa in the living room to enjoy the cognac as jazz sax music played in the background.

They talked about the meal, and then Julie went to the kitchen for the last time. She returned carrying a tray with cups of steaming coffee, cream, sugar, and a pair of chocolate truffles. Julie sat on the sofa near Yuri. The gastronomic symphony ended with a lingering fortissimo chord. As the chocolate truffle slowly melted on his tongue, a cosmic evolution of taste proceeded from roasted bittersweet to rich sparkles of fruit.

Yuri thought about the meal and Julie's obvious enjoyment in pleasing his palate. "You should be a chef at a fine restaurant."

"I've looked everywhere," Julie sighed, "but the best I have found is serving as a volunteer cook at the Salvation Army. I've given up looking."

"Susan Hebb mentioned that to me. Then I remembered that Clarence at CSL has a sister who recently opened a French restaurant in Milwaukee." Yuri unfolded a piece of paper from his pocket and smiled. "I have a gift for you."

The paper showed an e-mail to Clarence from his sister. Julie read,

Dear Clarence,

Thanks for telling me all about Julie. I have been searching for a young, creative chef for my restaurant, and Julie sounds perfect. I would love to give her a try and see if she lives up to your tall tales of the meals she serves. It is amazing she can prepare such fine meals by herself in an apartment kitchen. Tell her that she is welcome to come here for a "tryout."

Love, Jan

Julie's eyes widened and her jaw dropped as she read the paper. "Yuri, this is great!" she squealed like a teenage girl. "Oh, thank you."

Yuri was unprepared for Julie's swift attack. His arm automatically wrapped around her as she kissed him. It was no little "thanks for caring" kiss. The kiss was full-force, on the lips, with her fingers running along his scalp and her warm body wriggling up close. This was a "let's go all the way" kiss.

The conflict within Yuri's brain was intense. The limbic region of his brain wanted to know if Julie was as good in bed as she was in the kitchen. However, his anterior neocortex knew that she was not his type, and it was wrong to consume Julie as if she were another plate of food to be left in the kitchen sink when done. As her teacher, his ethics would not allow it. Besides, she was too young for him.

As these confusing thoughts circulated in his head, Yuri finally realized that she had been interested in *him* and not computer science for the past two semesters. This was a revelation for him. He was astonished that a young woman would be romantically interested in an overweight smoker with prematurely graying hair and foreign behaviors. He wondered: if this were Susan, would his reaction be very different? He must find a way to retreat without hurting Julie.

—•—

Julie felt Yuri's body tense and knew something was wrong. She looked at his face and without a word knew she had taken his concern for her as a more intimate interest. She had fallen for Yuri's unconventional, authentic character. He was an intriguing maverick with a good heart. Julie had fooled herself; the signals she had detected were naïve honesty on Yuri's part. Yuri was a special person and a fine friend, but it was foolishness to try for anything beyond that. She must find a way to retreat without making Yuri feel awkward.

Julie acted first. She drew back with a lingering touch of her fingers. "I guess I got a bit carried away by your gift." She tried to focus on the delightful invitation in her hand and to forget about her desire for Yuri. "You found the right path for me."

Yuri seemed relieved. "Do you really think so?"

"I'm sure. This is exactly what I've been looking for, and eventually I'll become the executive chef at my own restaurant."

Yuri thanked her for the extraordinary meal and suggested it was time for him to leave.

7

Susan sighed. This could well be the last faculty club luncheon she would ever attend. The bland food was certainly no attraction, and this month's speaker was a new low. Dr. Eccles, a frail eighty-five-year-old retired professor of sociology, was droning on about the lack of creativity in the younger generation. It was almost self-parody.

"In my day," he lectured in a thin voice, "students learned from real teachers. Some of the teachers were far from perfect, and we had to struggle to learn. That struggle taught us how to think. Each teacher presented a different point of view, and that taught us to be innovative."

A slide appeared on the large screen. "Note the average age of the winners of *Think Magazine's* top one hundred innovators of the year for the past fifty years." The statistics showed a clear trend of the innovators getting older in recent years. "In my day, the young folks were the creative ones. Our society is slowly losing its creative powers."

Susan gave a dismissive sniff at the simplistic analysis. She was reminded of the famous quote attributed to the British Prime Minster Benjamin Disraeli, "There are three kinds of lies:

lies, damn lies, and statistics." This, Susan thought, was the same generation-gap speech given by old fogies to the young whippersnappers for eons. Still, one thing about the speech personally disturbed her. She knew that she was very highly ranked in her specialty, yet when she compared her work to the discoveries made by the past great names of neuroscience, nothing she had done was even close to their breakthroughs. She longed to prove herself by making a major discovery.

She dismissed the lecture. He was out of touch. There was a lot of good research being done at the Coordinated Science Laboratory by her and other scientists from fourteen fields.

She looked over at the head of CSL; Hamilton von Helmholtz was not eating the generic food or listening to the geriatric speaker. Hamilton was in the back of the room talking in a low voice with the head of the psychology department. She felt sorry for the psych head; Hamilton was using one of his power-projection tactics. The head of the psychology department was backed up against the wall, and Hamilton was standing with only ten centimeters between their noses. Susan could not hear what they were talking about, but Hamilton clearly had the upper hand.

Later, she saw Hamilton mingle with the heads of the music and math departments. She knew Hamilton; he was here to find opportunities for his personal advancement, gather gossip, and call in favors. Also, it seemed that he enjoyed displaying Susan, like one who shows off a fine piece of a coin collection.

As they walked back together to the Coordinated Science Laboratory, she asked Hamilton, "Why don't you ever invite Yuri to the faculty luncheons?"

Hamilton grunted. "I prefer to keep the odd ones in their cages. CSL has a professional image to maintain. God knows what he might say to others." He smiled. "Still, he has done more than his share of creative work."

The more she thought about it, the more she felt like a middling technician in comparison to the brilliant work done by Yuri.

"Have you completed the olfactory memory project yet?" Hamilton demanded.

"Almost—the folks in the psychology department have nearly finished writing the paper."

"Make sure your name with the Coordinated Science Lab is the first author listed on the paper."

"The psych department won't stand for that. The entire theory and experimental design was their work, and they wrote most of the paper. They deserve it."

"I will call Jackson over in the psych department and tell him that he can forget about my support for the approval of the new wing on his building if we're not listed first on this paper. Don't worry; I'll fix it."

Susan noticed that a new banner was trailing from the drone aircraft circling far above them. The long banner read, "Tell a friend: Xarim makes you fit and trim." The primary function of the unmanned aircraft perpetually circling above the city was to carry an array of radio antennas used for metropolitan area telecommunications services, but the advertising revenue from the banner must be a big plus.

"Do you have any new ideas for research?" Hamilton asked Susan.

"Yes; Yuri and I were working on the Sellco eye-tracking project yesterday, and he came up with the idea of integrating an eye tracker into teaching machines."

"Great; write up a project proposal and I'll talk to the folks at National Business Machines about funding the work. So are you working with Yuri on this?"

"Yes."

"Keep Yuri on the sidelines. I don't want him taking a prominent role in this."

"Why's that?"

"Yuri does fine work, but he is such an odd coot. I just don't trust him with our clients."

Susan quietly fumed. She had also distrusted Yuri initially, but as she got to know him better, his strangeness had become an endearing quality. Now she was quite fond of him and had developed distaste for the anti-old-school prejudice shown by most people. Yuri's foreign background made people's prejudice even worse.

———

Yuri noticed that Julie had not attended his class that morning, but she did arrive at his office later that day. She excitedly told Yuri that she was on the way to her new job at the French restaurant in Milwaukee.

"This job and some instruction on a teaching machine will teach me everything I will need to know to open my own restaurant before long," Julie said, full of hope.

Yuri was pleased. "Good for you. So, have you found a new home?"

"I'll move into my parents' summer home in Port Washington. It's a nice drive to the restaurant, and my parents won't be there."

"When are you going?"

"Tomorrow. I just stopped to say goodbye and to thank you. I can't thank you enough for your help. I hope you don't mind if I keep in touch."

"Please do. I am sure you will enjoy success. The key to success is to do what you enjoy."

"Thanks again." She kissed Yuri on the cheek. This time it was a "thanks for caring" kiss.

8

⎯⎯

As far as Josh was concerned, he had the best job in the world. It was a steady job that paid him to rip around the Potrillo Mountains of New Mexico on a dirt bike protecting the greatest nation on earth. Also, he had learned amazing tracking skills from his partner, George, who was part Native American. Of course, old-fashioned tracking skills were rarely needed nowadays.

Both he and George had a radio-linked display built into their helmets that showed real-time, high-altitude, surveillance-drone imagery so detailed that during their idle hours they had fun zooming in on the nude sunbathers at a resort near El Paso. In addition to displaying images from the drone, each helmet contained a two-way radio, a dimmable visor, and a miniature air conditioner. The helmets also had a water sip tube running to a backpack that contained a water bladder and a tiny fuel-cell power supply. Thanks to its lightweight materials, the daytime version of the bullet-resistant helmet weighed less than two kilograms.

They had two hundred kilometers of US border to patrol; none of it had any sign of civilization other than the fence. A sign was posted every one hundred meters with a warning in twelve languages: "DANGER—DO NOT ENTER—DEADLY HIGH VOLTAGE AND RADIATION." The signs were attached to a three-meter-tall chain-link fence topped with coiled razor wire. After the chain-link fence was a one-meter-deep ditch. Next was a pair of two-meter-high wire-screen fences spaced two meters apart with wire screen over the top to form an enclosed wave-guide channel flooded with deadly microwave radio energy. Anyone entering the wire-screen channel would be literally cooked.

Four strands of wire with five hundred volts of electricity were mounted above to discourage anyone from climbing over the wire-screen channel. The high-voltage wires performed the secondary function of carrying power to the microwave transmitters located every kilometer. Lastly, there was another three-meter-tall chain-link fence topped with coiled razor wire and more signs.

A four-meter concrete wall would have been more effective, but Congress did not want to construct a reminder of the Berlin Wall or the Great Wall of China. The fence had begun as four strands of barbed wire for the entire length of the border. As intrusions were detected, a series of changes were made year after year to make the fence taller and meaner. It was called stepwise improvement, but one political wag called it a step-foolish folly.

When Josh had first started with the US Border Patrol, he had wondered why live patrols were still needed; surely no one would try to cross the fence. Later, he learned that he earned his salary every week. Mostly they were kept busy trying to keep suicidal idiots away from the fence. Dirt bikes were much less expensive to operate than helicopters, and Josh was glad of it; he preferred to be on the ground. The US Border Patrol made sparing use of their fuel-hungry helicopters.

Josh and George had stopped at the top of a favorite hill that offered a bit of shade under a lean-to and a fine view of the fence. They took a break to sip hot coffee from a thermos. It was a fine, clear day that would get good and hot by the afternoon. They kept an eye on the fence, occasionally using their binoculars since those offered a more natural perspective than the drone video.

"Look, that golden eagle has his eyes on something," George said, pointing at the handsome creature.

Josh looked through his binoculars at the golden eagle sitting on the top strand of high-voltage wire. The high voltage was of no concern to the golden eagle since it was not grounded. Suddenly the eagle spread its large, dark brown wings, swooped down, and snapped up a small lizard. The eagle perched on a rock as it ate its breakfast. Josh loved this part of his job. He saw nature as it was meant to be, not an artificial replica in a zoo.

"I wish I had eyes like that golden eagle. Its distance vision is three times better than a human's, and its visible spectrum extends to ultraviolet," Josh marveled.

The radio headsets in both of their helmets came alive. "Base to sector five: we have two vehicles approaching at coordinate two-fifteen. You'd better hurry."

Josh pressed his transmit button. "Two vehicles at two-fifteen. Roger. How long till they reach the fence?"

The radio responded. "Estimate fifteen minutes. Vectors have been sent to your helmets."

They both looked at the heads-up display built into their helmets. It showed the drone image of two large SUVs moving as fast as they could through the rough terrain, about twenty kilometers per hour.

"Crud, look at the front SUV" said George. "There's a cutting plow mounted on the front. It will get through the fence before we can get there."

Josh zoomed in to see the angled steel plates mounted across the front of the SUV with a sharpened steel blade sticking straight out at the center. He had seen this before and knew what was about to happen. "We can head them off at Ranger Pass if we hurry." It was the Wild West all over again.

Josh and George mounted their dirt bikes and raced cross-country. A two-kilometer detour was required to skirt around a vast field of house-sized, silvery sunflowers whose mirrored petals formed parabolic dishes that concentrated sunlight onto cylinders suspended at the focus of each parabola. The heated hydrogen gas in each cylinder drove a piston engine connected to an electric generator. The thousands of generators produced enough power for a city of a million people.

They were both expert bikers and enjoyed racing each other, making good time except where they had to dismount their dirt bikes and half-carry them through a steep gulch. Josh looked at the drone view in his heads-up helmet display; the SUV had stopped at the fence. The illegal aliens had used bolt cutters to cut through the first fence. Ten people were carrying sandbags to fill in the ditch between the fences. The intruders were making quick work of it. In a few minutes, the SUVs would be ready to ram through the remaining fences. Josh half hoped that they would make it through the fence and not get stuck in the middle like the truck Josh had found two weeks ago full of dead people cooked alive by the microwaves. Wherever this happened, the fence repair crews always posted a big steel cross at the site, partly to warn others and partly to place another obstacle in the path.

Josh and George pressed their dirt bikes for every bit of speed on the level ground as they slalomed through the scattered prickly pear cactus. There was a long way yet. Over the radio headset they heard from the base, "Base to sector five: both SUVs made it through the fence. The SUVs have veered northwest. Keep up your current course and you should arrive in time to intercept at Ranger Pass."

Through labored breathing and the screaming motorbike engine, Josh shouted, "Roger, base; intercept at Ranger Pass." The two bikers were climbing now, with rooster tails of dirt flying from the tires.

The two officers reached Ranger Pass in time to find a good position for the ambush and catch their breath so that heavy breathing would not interfere with their accuracy. They saw the two SUVs approaching quickly. The SUV with the angled plow was in front.

"Base to sector five: be advised that there is an El Paso news chopper approaching from the east," the radio reported.

"Roger; I see the news chopper," Josh answered. The news helicopter was closing quickly. They had seen news helicopters a few times before. With a TV news camera on them, everything would be done by the book.

"You take the one in front," George suggested.

The two officers both had M16A6 automatic rifles with upgraded telescopic sights and loaded with 5.56mm Mk262 Mod 2 rounds to improve the accuracy. The use of lethal force was prohibited, but they were also under orders to not let any illegal aliens slip through. They were trained to fire in single-shot mode for accuracy; there would be no auto-mode, wild spray of bullets. The people in the SUVs had seen them, and the SUVs were dodging left and right to evade the anticipated rifle fire.

Josh and George had been taught exactly the same lessons by the teaching machines. Like synchronized ballet dancers, they went through the steps: drop to prone position, extend and seat the bipod on the front of the rifle, check the ammunition magazine, dial in the range on the scope, check that the selector is set to SEMI for single-shot, acquire target, take a breath in and hold it, aim, squeeze, POW, aim, squeeze, POW, aim, squeeze, POW.

The second SUV blew a front tire and flipped onto its side. This action would make the El Paso evening newscast.

George and Josh targeted the remaining SUV. Aim, squeeze, POW, aim, squeeze, POW. Some of the bullets made it through the steel plow covering the entire front of the SUV, but the bullets were deflected from their targets: the tires and the engine. The SUV would be past them soon.

"Use your artillery," shouted George.

Only Josh's weapon had a grenade launcher attached to it. Unlike the army, who used fragmentation grenades, the US Border Patrol was only issued flash-bang grenades. The flash-bang grenades made a large explosion without shrapnel and would harmlessly stun anyone near the explosion. Josh aimed just in front of the SUV to maximize the stunning effect on the driver. With a loud boom, the grenade launcher lobbed the flash-bang grenade a little closer to the SUV than Josh had intended. The grenade exploded when the SUV's gas tank was five centimeters above it. The SUV burst into a ball of fire and rolled forward engulfed in flames. This event would make the nationwide evening newscast.

"Nice shooting, hot shot," chided George.

"Damn." Josh would have a lot of explaining to do; he pressed his radio transmit button. "Base, this is sector five. One vehicle has exploded; the other vehicle has crashed. Estimated five or six dead. We need a medevac chopper and an incident inspection team."

This was not the first time that Josh or George had killed an illegal alien, so they knew the grilling they would receive. Together, the officers mounted their dirt bikes and went to help the people in the SUV that had flipped onto its side.

9

———

Yuri was in his lab attaching signal analyzer probes to circuit modules deep inside the teaching machine. He had already tried and ruled out the obvious sources of the noise glitches in the teaching machine. Now he was testing to see if the signal was coming from the powerful magnetic fields used by the magnetoencephalographic brain scanner circuits. He searched for both time-domain and frequency-domain correlations, but again nothing matched. Instead of the goggles, he was wearing headphones to listen to the signals. Since the ears naturally performed a Fourier transformation of the audible frequencies, the ears could detect patterns the eyes could not. The glitches were so hard to isolate that it almost seemed as if they had been intentionally hidden.

One side of Yuri's lab was dominated by a large supercomputer whose dull gray panels hid densely packed stacks of processors and silicon memories. A steady roar came from the many large fans that constantly struggled to keep the supercomputer from melting due to the heat it produced. A long workbench on the other side of the lab was covered with stacks of test equipment, personal computers, and tools. Two teaching machines sat on rolling carts next to the workbench.

Near the workbench, the lab's window looked out at the CSL loading dock with its large trash dumpster and tall liquid nitrogen storage tank. Yuri had replaced the ugly view by fitting a large high-definition video panel exactly into the window frame. The video panel was fed a live view from a webcam that faced out from the front entrance of the Coordinated Science Lab, thus the scene showed the grassy engineering quadrangle with a large water fountain and trees. The perspective of the live video image was adjusted to match the angle of view for the person closest to the faux window. This was accomplished by infrared sensors near the window. The resulting scene was a perfect illusion. Yuri's lab had the best view in the building, and the fitted high-definition panel fooled most visitors into believing that it really was a window facing the engineering quadrangle. Depending on Yuri's mood, he sometimes changed the view to a live webcam on the beach at Hanauma Bay in Hawaii or a webcam in Yosemite national park.

———

Susan ignored the now-familiar trick window as she strode into his lab. She saw he was wearing headphones, so she waved at him. Yuri did not notice her. She walked up behind him and decided to conduct an experiment of her own. Holding her hand a half-meter from him, she slowly moved her hand from behind him to his front. Yuri did not notice the hand until it was almost in front of him; then he startled and wheeled around as he took the headphones off.

"Up to your psychological games again?" he asked.

"Your peripheral vision sucks."

"Is that a psycho-technical term?" he teased.

"I should run a retinal scan on you. The poor peripheral vision could be a sign of retinal degeneration caused by your smoking. On the other hand, it could be just a temporary effect from the stress caused by the hard work you're doing." Susan had recently become interested in studying the effects of stress. "One symptom of stress is losing track of time." She pointed at her watch to make the point that he was late for their chess game.

"Oh, sorry," he said innocently.

Being late was a part of Yuri that would never change, and she always forgave him.

———

The chessboard was in Susan's lab, and Yuri welcomed the distraction from the brain busting effort to track down the source of the glitch in the teaching machine.

Yuri loved to play chess, and Susan was the only worthy opponent he had found on campus. Susan's frequent victories at the chessboard brought out the competitor in Yuri. Susan's technique was masterful but conventional, and Yuri knew that eventually he would find a way to beat her. He blamed his long losing streak on her ability to distract him. Yuri's concentration faltered as the result of his attraction toward her and due to her habit of holding a conversation while they played.

Yuri had several theories to explain Susan's loquacity during their games. Theory number one was that she was unaware that it disturbed him. Yuri had dismissed this theory after repeatedly asking her not to talk during the games. It seemed that Susan tried to play quietly, but her effort failed. Theory number two was that talking was a tactic to disrupt his thinking, so he would lose the game. While he liked this theory, he knew that Susan would not stoop to such behavior. Theory number three was that this was all a devious psychological experiment; Susan did not enjoy playing chess, and she was really studying the effects of verbal stimulus on reasoning. Now this was something that Susan might really do. She seemed to enjoy studying him like a laboratory animal. Theory number four was the most credible: Susan could not stop talking. Anyway, Susan was distracting even when she was quiet. Yuri stole glances at her when he thought she would not notice.

Yuri loaded a special program he had written earlier that day into a teaching machine near the chessboard and put on the teaching machine's scanner helmet.

"What are you doing?" asked Susan. "Have you devised a program to help you play chess better?"

"No; this program will record my brain activity while we play chess. I am studying how the brain works. Playing chess and talking with you should be a good test."

The recorded data would test a theory he had for how the brain developed understanding from raw information.

Susan opened the chess game as usual with a book move. Yuri adjusted the helmet for comfort. "I had a sumptuous meal at Julie Mountcastle's a few days ago. You would have found it a fascinating study of the simultaneous stimulation of all five senses."

Susan kept her eyes on the board. "There are seven human senses, not five."

"Seven senses? That is nonsense." Susan's sense of humor seemed to have missed his joke, so he restated, "Non*sense*. A joke, no?"

Susan seemed to get the joke this time, but then went on seriously. "In addition to sight, sound, touch, smell, and taste, there is the vestibular system in the inner ear that provides the sense of balance and the proprioceptive system that senses the position of joints in the body. One could argue that humans have eight senses by including the ability to sense the amount of humidity in the air." Susan changed the topic. "I attended a lecture at yesterday's faculty club luncheon where the speaker claimed that the younger generation lacks creativity. Do you think that's true?"

Diplomacy was called for here because he suspected Susan's generic question was really stimulated by her personal self-doubts. "There surely are still some who are creative. Yet I do think that many of those who have been machine-taught from a young age have lost the benefits of seeing diverse viewpoints and styles presented by many different human teachers. Having all their lessons spoon-fed to them has deprived them from learning how to deal with the situation of exploring beyond the bounds of current knowledge. Still, here at the Coordinated Science Laboratory, we see a lot of good original work."

"Do you think I need to improve my creativity?"

Yuri swept his hands to gesture universal inclusion. "Every person in the lab, myself included, could benefit from more creativity."

"How can this be accomplished?"

He often coached his students to be more original. It was good to see Susan's wish to improve, though Yuri felt she was more creative than most machine-taught Americans.

"The first step of creativity is curiosity. We must ask 'what if?' We must force our minds to go where no one has gone before. Abandon the conventional paths. Look at problems backward, upside down, or from the viewpoint of an alien race. Give serious consideration to silly and impractical approaches. Often it is necessary to think in the background for days or weeks to give the brain a chance to search for distant associated patterns. However, the most important part is to not be afraid to pursue unconventional ideas."

"The need for diversity in the teaching machine programs has long been known. Every student has the choice of different versions of instruction: practical knowledge or theory-based, analytical or synthetic. Also, starting at the tenth year, students can choose among many specialized topics for intensive instruction." He understood why she was defensive. Susan had been machine-taught from an early age and continued to take lessons from the teaching machines.

"I am sure this helps, but it is not the same as having a variety of different instructors who can serve as role models and provide inspiration. Also, today's students have lost the interaction with other students. In a real class, the students learn concepts from each other along with social skills."

Susan took a gulp from her can of Pepsi. "So do you think that teaching machines are inherently bad for the students?"

Susan was especially talkative today, but Yuri had given up asking her to not talk during their games. He moved a pawn to help open up his queen and bishop. Then he tapped on the screen of the teaching machine to focus its scanning on the anterior portion of his cerebral cortex. "Teaching machines are marvelous teaching tools, but they are overused to an extreme. The machines have become the entire educational system instead of being a tool used by human teachers to enhance the classroom."

"Once teaching machines were proven superior to the best human instructors," she explained, "the government funded the introduction of teaching machines in all schools based on the savings from eliminating most of the teachers. The teaching machines cost less than human teachers and achieved better results. The government couldn't pay for both. Besides, human teachers still exist. All children attend physical education classes taught by human instructors. The PE classes emphasize team sports to help develop social skills."

"How many hours a week were you in physical education class as a child?" he asked.

"Five."

"This is like giving a flower five drops of water per week. Students need human instructors to train the mind, not just the body."

Susan's move took one of Yuri's pawns out of the game. It almost seemed like retaliation. "Your move."

Yuri muttered, "*Kozel!* Mindless male goat!" Yuri had paid the price for becoming more interested in their conversation than the chess game. The conflict on the chessboard propagated into their conversation with Yuri's continued provocation. "There are other dangers. Nearly all children and most adults use teaching machines every week. The resulting potential to influence so many people presents a great risk for the instructional material presenting only one point of view or promoting special interests."

Susan parried. "The teaching machines are designed to not run an instructional program unless it has been certified by the federal department of education. In addition to a technical review by the department of education, every instructional program must pass a review by independent reviewers at three different universities. As a graduate student, I served as a program reviewer, and I know several people who still perform the reviews. The reviewers take their responsibility seriously and are well trained to find any bias or improper political influence. In addition to the official certification process, there are independent watch dogs such as FOE, the Foundation for Oversight of Education."

Susan drove her queen deep into Yuri's side of the board, presenting no immediate threat other than pinning one rook. Yuri searched to see if there was more to this move or if it was just a tactic to disrupt his envelopment strategy. He tried to read her intentions by seeing where she was looking, but as usual, she had a poker face. Yuri did not worry about maintaining a poker face himself because he had learned that Susan failed to notice subtle clues in facial expression or body language. Like many others, she almost seemed to have a mild form of autism. Susan's semiblindness to reading the body language of others had nothing to do with her missing eye; he was sure it was entirely due to her lack of socialization as a child. Susan's weakness was particularly striking since she knew so much about human perception. Yuri wondered if she had chosen her field of study to compensate for her weakness. Conversely, Julie's nonverbal communication skills were excellent. No doubt this was the result of her many years of human instruction in gymnastics as a child.

Susan seemed to be enjoying her success on the chessboard and in their verbal sparring. "You're particularly paranoid today. You must see demons in every corner of government."

"There is too much trust in our government. The American people showed how tame they were when they approved the ratification of that unnecessary amendment to the Constitution last year. Now President Sherrington is appointing loyal cronies to head every department of the government." Yuri was referring to the surprisingly easy ratification of a constitutional amendment that changed the Senate vote required to approve presidential appointments of cabinet positions and ambassadors. The required two-thirds Senate majority vote had been changed to a simple majority vote. This had been prompted by a destructive battle between the Senate and the previous White House administration that had delayed the approval of two cabinet positions and the ambassador to China for eighteen months. Despite vehement protests by a small minority, the constitutional amendment had been ratified. Astonished political analysts were still trying to figure out why this violation of conventional political wisdom had occurred.

Yuri continued, "I am still amazed that the American people would approve a change to the Constitution to address a one-time problem. Now the Sherrington administration is trying to get a friend of the president appointed to fill the vacancy in the Supreme Court. The nominee, Robert Slaughter, has mediocre judicial qualifications. His main strength is his loyalty to President Sherrington."

"I saw an article," countered Susan, "that said Robert Slaughter had a lot of experience for someone of his age. It's about time that someone younger than sixty years old was appointed to the Supreme Court. Everyone knows that Slaughter is the right choice."

Yuri saw that Susan was becoming agitated. It would be better to move to the safer ground of their common interest in the interrelationship of computers and the human nervous system. Susan was interested in how computer technology could help overcome the human frailties. Yuri, on the other hand, sought ways to overcome the shortcomings of computers. Yuri changed the context of the conversation. "I saw an article in the *Journal on Artificial Intelligence* that compared the most advanced computer-based intelligence to the mind of a mouse. Why do you think computer scientists have failed to do better?"

"Computer scientists seem to be fixated on processing power. The raw computing speed and memory capacity of today's computers exceed the abilities of the human brain. More powerful hardware is not the path to true intelligence. Intelligence depends on understanding what to do with information from the senses and the memory."

The theory agreed with Yuri's intuition. "So the key is in developing algorithms that extract the pertinent essence from an ocean of raw data. This is so easy for humans. How does the brain do this?" He had a theory that was being tested right then by the teaching machine scanning his brain, but he wanted to hear Susan's thoughts on the matter.

"The neocortex stores sequences of patterns as abstractions in a hierarchal structured memory. Memories are not single items, but sequences of related items. Part of our intelligence comes from storing memories in a way that facilitates the next step: the subsequent matching of patterns and connecting of related items. This includes finding relationships between seemingly unrelated items in the memory as well as finding relationships between what the senses present and our memories. The brain is constantly comparing what the senses find with a model of the world that resides in our minds."

Susan paused to take a sip of Pepsi, but it was empty. Yuri had noticed that Susan quickly gulped down her soda, while he usually nursed a can for an hour. "I think that another aspect of intelligence is in our senses. Again, the key is getting the right information and not raw computing power. Consider the common housefly; its aerial acrobatics put the flight control systems on our most advanced aircraft to shame. Yet the fly's brain has less processing power than a scientific calculator. The fly's aerial abilities are due to specialized vision in its compound eyes and a precise sense of inertia."

Yuri took a sip from his can of Coke. "The artificial intelligence researchers have tried programming algorithms for pattern matching and associative links. This works only within tightly constrained fields such as the game of chess. Programming works if the programmer can fully describe what must be done under every condition, but programming an all-purpose intelligence is beyond us."

"The human brain learns automatically," said Susan. "It is not programmed. Some types of neurological therapy try to program the brain; the results are dismal. I doubt artificial intelligence is possible."

"Trying to attain true intelligence will be difficult without fully understanding how the brain processes information. Since we don't fully understand how the brain works, maybe we should just find a way to blindly copy it."

Susan traded a pawn for one of Yuri's knights. It was becoming a game of attrition that he could not afford. Yuri noticed that the nails on her long, supple fingers were always perfectly manicured. When she moved pieces on the board, it was never a hesitant sliding move. She swiftly picked up the piece and resolutely snapped it down as if to say, "Take that!"

"I started taking that new Xarim drug for cardiovascular health a couple of years ago," commented Susan, "and I noticed that it helped me lose six pounds with no effort. You should try Xarim. You could afford to lose a few pounds, and it would reduce your blood pressure too."

"I do not like taking drugs when I am not sick."

"You don't like taking drugs! What d'ya think those damn cigarettes you smoke are? Nicotine is a powerful drug," Susan exclaimed, wide-eyed.

Yuri recoiled. "Wow, you have really got your dandruff up."

Susan's puzzlement gave way to an explosion of laughter. "Oh, that's a good one, Yuri. I think you meant to say that I had my dander up...but seriously, you should stop smoking."

"I like smoking. I do my best thinking when I smoke." Yuri took a sip from his can of Coke.

"You're one of a kind, Yuri. Everyone takes Xarim, but you don't. You're the only person I know who smokes. Hell, most people drink Pepsi, but you drink Coke."

"I like Coke. In Russia we thought that Coke was the American thing to drink."

Yuri moved his queen in a feint. In a few moves, Susan had sprung an elaborate trap for his queen. His queen went down, taking a pawn with it and presenting Susan with the choice of losing either a rook or a knight in the next move. He hoped the squeeze play would be adequate to mask his next moves. Susan took the conventional choice and saved her rook. In two moves, Yuri had checkmate.

Susan gritted her teeth. "You intentionally sacrificed your queen, didn't you?"

"It was a big risk, but it was the only way to win." He had discovered a weakness that he might be able to exploit again. Susan had been taught to play chess by a teaching machine. While she played better than most, her style was similar to that of other machine-taught players. Yuri thought to himself, "This proves what a good old-school education can do."

———

A couple of days later Yuri found a postcard in his mail tray. Paper mail was a rarity, and he had not received a postcard since he had immigrated to America. The postcard was from Julie, and it showed the harbor at Port Washington, Wisconsin. She must have sent a postcard instead of an e-mail as a poke at Yuri's old-fashioned ways. The postcard read:

Dear Yuri,

My job is great! I am learning a lot. The people here really appreciate my talent, and I am showing them some new ideas. My parents' summer home has a nice view of Lake Michigan. The address is 256 Lake View Road, Port Washington, Wisconsin, 53074. It is less than a mile from downtown Port Washington. Come up and visit any time; there is a spare bedroom here, and I will feed you until you burst. Thanks again for the great advice.

Bye for now, Julie

———

As he entered Yuri's office, Takashi Fujikawa saw Yuri using a magnet to attach the postcard to a cabinet.

"A postcard. How quaint," teased Takashi. He and Yuri shared the bond of being among the handful of immigrants at the University of Illinois. Also, Yuri was one of the few people who could hack computers as well as Takashi.

Yuri opened the jar of colorful jelly beans on his desk, which Takashi always nibbled on during his frequent visits to Yuri's office. Takashi took a generous handful.

"The postcard is from one of my past grad students. It's nice when they remember to stay in contact."

"I stopped by to warn you that tomorrow I am running a network-wide search-and-destroy for nonstandard software. You should hide your homebrew programs on your super-computer. Your private archive will be safe." Very few people received this warning, but Takashi was careful to not provoke someone who could outmaneuver him in cyberspace.

"Thanks for the warning. I'll do it now before I forget." Yuri spun around in his desk chair and entered the password for his private archive.

Takashi stood behind Yuri nibbling jelly beans and silently chuckling to himself as he watched Yuri's typing. For such a brilliant person, Yuri could be remarkably naive at times. He should not type his password with someone watching every keystroke.

"Also, I want to thank you for saving my hide last week. I was at my wits' end trying to find a cure for that stealthy virus in the campus network," said Takashi gratefully.

"It takes a hacker to stop a hacker." Yuri had earned Takashi's trust and admiration. Takashi gave Yuri special treatment, such as allowing Yuri to tunnel through the software firewall in the campus network's gateway router. Yuri had convinced Takashi that the custom-designed suite of defensive software on Yuri's supercomputer provided better protection than the campus firewall, and Takashi trusted Yuri to watch out for himself in the wilds of the Internet.

"I've got an extra ticket for tonight's baseball game. Do you want to join me?" invited Takashi, taking another handful of jelly beans.

"A young stud like you can't find a better date?"

"I struck out. Besides, I'd like to hear what you've been up to lately with the teaching machines."

"Thanks anyway; I have work to do."

"You're a workaholic, Yuri," winked Takashi, leaving to find Susan. He did not want Yuri to think he was prying into his work, so he would ask Susan what she knew about Yuri's research.

10

—

This was Maria Felix's first visit to the White House. The hive of activity buzzed around her as she waited for her meeting with Mr. Grossberg. When she had been appointed as director of the US Customs and Border Patrol Agency immediately after the Sherrington administration had taken office, it had been made clear that changes must be made quickly to stop the flow of illegal immigrants and potentially dangerous visitors. Maria thought she knew why she had been called to meet with Mr. Grossberg, the president's most trusted friend and chief of staff.

As she sat down in Mr. Grossberg's office, he said sternly, "I expect that your department has been busy dealing with the Mexican border car demolition."

Just as she had expected, the White House was going to pile more criticism on top of the heat she had already received from the press. "Yes, we have a thorough investigation of the New Mexico border incident underway. Thus far, it seems to have been a freak accident. The officers followed the correct procedures, but I'll personally talk with them."

"I know that your officers are superbly trained, and they deserve our gratitude for their difficult and dangerous work.

I hope you'll not be too hard on them. I'm sure they feel bad enough already about the incident."

The meeting was not going the way Maria had expected. "I understand, Mr. Grossberg, but they will be reminded of the rules that prohibit lethal force except for self-defense."

"Certainly remind them of the rules, but I hope there'll be no punishment or reprimand. They were doing their duty. Besides, an incident like this goes a long way toward discouraging the crazy people who want to violate our borders."

Maria was astonished. It almost seemed that Mr. Grossberg was pleased by the outcome of the incident. She did not know what to say.

Grossberg continued, "Your people are faced with the impossible task of holding back a tide of humanity desperate for a shortcut to the good life here in America. Last year we doubled the budget for the Customs and Border Patrol Agency, and I must say that I am impressed by how effectively you have used the funds. Yet dangerous foreigners are still leaking through our borders. I have concluded that your agency needs more than money; you need better tools to do the job right."

"We could use more helicopters and fuel."

"That is really a matter of funding, and I will see that you get more help there too. What I was talking about are new tools to improve not only customs inspection, but commercial aviation security as well. Maria, have you heard of the IS-250 from Security Scanning Systems Incorporated?"

"Yes, sir. It is a virtually foolproof identification system using advanced eye-scan technology. We'd love to have it, but we can't get past the privacy and civil rights issues."

"Leave the privacy nuts to me. I think we know how to win that battle. I've already talked to Baxter at Homeland Security, and I want your department and his to develop a plan to deploy the IS-250 at every point of entry to the United States, every domestic and international aircraft and rail departure check-point, and every government building checkpoint. Work up a combined budget request to cover this plan. Oh, and include those helicopters you need too."

A dismissive wave of Mr. Grossberg's hand indicated that the meeting was over.

11

———

Where others would have given up long ago, Yuri continued to investigate the mysterious glitches in the teaching machine. He tested several teaching machines, and they all exhibited exactly the same curious behavior. What intrigued him the most was that the strong autocorrelation in the glitches suggested there was information in the patterns, yet every other analysis found no recognizable information. "I know you are hiding something, my little demon," he muttered to himself. Yuri was a bulldog; the bigger the challenge, the more determined he was to overcome it.

Since the teaching machine could not be made to freeze the display of one video frame at a time, Yuri connected a specialized video monitor to the machine. Then he stepped through the GLITCH-1 file manually, one frame at a time. Each still frame showed a meaningless pattern of colored dots. The pattern in each frame showed some organization, yet he could not make sense of it. On a whim, he programmed the digital signal analyzer to display all five video frames that constituted GLITCH-1 in sequence and then to repeat the sequence again and again. He pressed the EXECUTE MACRO button on the digital signal analyzer. In shock, Yuri dropped his can of Coke on the floor when the auxiliary video monitor clearly showed, "Drink Pepsi; it makes you sexy."

"Vot ty, bliad', chto mne podstroil! You whore, now I can see what you are!" he exclaimed. Yuri repeated the process for the GLITCH-2 file and saw the message, "Xarim makes you fit and trim." The GLITCH-3 file yielded, "Dexus cars—driven to succeed." He closely watched the teaching machine display when he played the GLITCH-1 file once at normal speed. There was a brief, barely noticeable flicker. The hidden message became visible only when he had jury-rigged the system to repeatedly play the GLITCH-1 file. Yuri had learned enough about the human visual process from Susan to know that the colored patterns of dots on each successive video frame were creating an optical illusion by taking advantage of the differing image persistence of the two types of light-sensing cells in the retina. The "rod" cells retained an image longer than the "cone" cells.

These were subliminal messages. They were not noticeable to the conscious mind, but perceptible to the unconscious mind. Like everything we see, these messages were automatically filed into the memory of the person viewing the screen. The person would not know he had seen the message, but it would become part of his memories without the application of conscious judgment regarding the validity of the information. This was a back door into the mind. Every thirty minutes people were seeing hidden advertisements that would be far more effective than conventional advertising. Yuri was furious. These subliminal advertisements exploited innocent students, and federal laws prohibited subliminal advertising. Who was behind this foul abuse of good technology?

He had been working for a long time and his bladder demanded attention. The likely source of the subliminal advertising occurred to Yuri while he was listening to the familiar music that came from the loudspeakers in the bathroom. A song about Harley Davidson motorcycles played, followed by an insipid song with the lyrics, "You make choices every day. With Sellco advertising you make informed choices." Yuri noted that this month the coupons printed on the toilet paper were for Pepsi.

Yuri returned to his office and checked the Sellco website for the list of their major clients. Pepsi, Dexus, and Pharmor were listed as exclusive clients of Sellco. It was nearly midnight and he was tired. Yuri decided to get some sleep and deal with his discovery when he was fresh the next day.

———

The next morning Yuri decided that he would first see what he could learn from looking into the software in the teaching machine. He discovered that, in addition to projecting the subliminal messages, the program detected if a message had been stored in the subject's memory. Sellco could immediately track the effectiveness of its subliminal advertising. The program that generated the subliminal messages would have been impossible to find by conventional search methods. However, now that Yuri had found the subliminal messages by hardware inspection, he could work backward using the digital signal analyzer to find where the program was located.

The program was fiendishly hidden in the bowels of the teaching machine's operating system. Being in the operating system subverted the intense certification process for the instructional programs. Since software updates to the operating system were broadcast via the Internet to every teaching machine weekly, the subliminal messages could be updated as well. The updates were carefully secured, so this almost certainly meant that someone inside Isoft Corporation, the maker of the operating system, was helping to distribute the subliminal messages. The messages were stored in encrypted form, so that if someone performed a global search of the software for "Pepsi makes you sexy," it would never be found. Whoever had done this had earned Yuri's respect for their technical cunning and his abhorrence for their whorish perversion of technology. Scientists had developed these machines to improve mankind, not to brainwash people.

After thinking over the situation while smoking a cigarette in the chemistry lab, Yuri decided to talk to the responsible person at Sellco. Contact information from their website gave him a starting point. Sellco's large bureaucracy did not intimidate Yuri; he had been raised in a country where bureaucracy had been elevated to an art form. He knew that a frontal assault would be rebuffed, so he adopted the ploy of claiming he was a professor at the University of Illinois who had discovered an interesting idea for how to insert a video advertisement before the start of each instructional session on teaching machines. Once he found the responsible persons, he would know where to search for more proof that Sellco was the source of the subliminal advertising.

He picked up the phone, noticing that the Cavalry Insurance jingle had been replaced by, "Tell a friend, 'Xarim makes you fit and trim.'" The traditional telephone dial tone had long ago been replaced by targeted advertising jingles that were selected to match the purchase potential profile of the calling party.

Yuri had learned from the ubiquitous Russian bureaucracies that the key to penetrating a bureaucracy was to keep hitting different places until a chink in the armor was found.

A security alert appeared on Miles Huxley's computer. The alert indicated the detection of a string of phone calls into Sellco regarding topics for which Miles was listed as the primary contact. The alert displayed the key words detected in each call: *teaching machine, advertising,* and *discovery.*

Miles smiled; Sellco's armor was better than outsiders knew. A semantic communications analyzer program had automatically generated the alert message with speech recognition ability. Every phone call, every e-mail, and every instant message into and out of Sellco was monitored for key words and phrases. The source, destination, time, and contents of every communication were logged, and the semantic communications analyzer looked for patterns indicating security threats and sales opportunities.

Miles clicked on the source phone number in the alert. The reverse phone number lookup showed that this was the number for Yuri Petrov. A click on *show details* indicated that he was a professor of computer science at the University of Illinois in Urbana-Champaign. The program hyperlinked to the university website that listed Yuri Petrov's research projects, several related to teaching machines. Miles became seriously worried when he read Petrov's online résumé; this professor just might have the skills to find the secrets hidden inside the teaching machines.

Rapid clicks produced Petrov's photo and credit history. Miles opened another window on his computer screen where the Sellco purchase potential profile for Petrov showed that he smoked cigarettes, purchased Persian carpets, listened to 1940s–1970s American jazz, and had every book written by Patrick O'Brian. In addition, he had received a manufacturer's rebate for skin lotion, had traveled to Russia last year, rented an apartment, and had an estimated net asset value between five and ten million dollars.

Miles double-clicked on Petrov's phone number and the phone was answered on the second ring.

"Hello, this is Miles Huxley at Sellco. A colleague of mine just talked with you and said I should call you. It sounds like you have discovered our clever advertising for teaching machines." Miles had intentionally phrased this to provoke a response if the professor had discovered the subliminal advertising, but if he had not, then Miles could easily deflect the discussion into Sellco's legitimate ads for people to buy Hewlett-Packard teaching machines.

Professor Petrov fell for the bait like a wolf grabbing fresh meat. "Clever! You think your insidious ads are clever? I think the ads are an evil deception and must be stopped."

"I'm not sure what you are talking about." Miles kept his voice casual.

"I am talking about the hidden Pepsi, Xarim, and Dexus ads that appear every thirty minutes on every teaching machine in the country. Using special test equipment in my laboratory, I have broken though the clever veil of secrecy."

"Blast!" thought Miles, alarmed at the risk of losing everything his job depended upon. He had been told that no one could ever discover Project Mercury, but there was no doubt that this professor had. Project Mercury was worth billions of dollars in revenue, and it would all be lost if the secret became known. Miles was responsible for Project Mercury; he would not allow anything to ruin his gold mine. He had to handle this himself since there were only a handful of people who were allowed to know of Project Mercury. The only other person who might be of help was his boss, who was on a ten-day safari in Africa. Miles had complete confidence in his abilities and certainly was not about to cry for help to his vacationing boss. Miles must be careful about what he said in case the conversation was secretly being recorded.

"That is quite an interesting discovery, Professor Petrov. I'd like to see this for myself."

"Are you trying to tell me that you know nothing of this evil subliminal advertising?"

"As I am sure you can understand, something of this importance should be discussed in person, face to face, so that we can best understand each other."

"Ah, yes. We must be careful, mustn't we?" Professor Petrov said scornfully. "Well, this subliminal advertising is wrong, and it must be stopped. I have no qualms about telling the world. I demand that these subliminal ads be removed permanently."

Miles had to maintain control of the situation. The best tactic was to embrace and smother the threat. "Professor Petrov, I share your concerns. This is a very serious issue, and we would not want something like this to spoil the excellent reputation of Sellco. I think that together we can address your concerns, but first would you please tell me who else has heard of your important discovery?"

"No one yet."

"No comments to a colleague, no e-mails?"

"No one. Why do you ask?"

"I'll be happy to explain this matter when we meet. The situation is more complicated than you may know. There are reasons why it's imperative that you must not mention your discovery to anyone before we have discussed this in person."

"There is even more to this abomination?"

"You may be at some risk that I can't discuss right now. Please heed my advice to keep silent until we meet." Miles was using the bigger secret ploy as a lever to get Petrov to keep quiet and to agree to meet with him.

"OK," said Professor Petrov tentatively.

"Good. I can meet you at your office at the University of Illinois, tomorrow afternoon. How about two o'clock?"

"That will be OK."

"Please give me your address and directions." Miles was looking at a map with the Coordinated Science Laboratory building highlighted, but asking for directions could help build Yuri's cooperation.

"Room 1A146, 1308 West Main Street, Urbana, Illinois. Two blocks west on Main from Goodwin Street. We face the Beckman Quad."

"I will see you Thursday at two o'clock. Please be sure to keep all of this to yourself for now. OK?"

"OK."

The moment that Miles hung up, he clicked on the Mercury Control icon, which was disguised as the PC-help icon, and entered his password. He then clicked on the menu item "EMERGENCY BROADCAST—FLUSH ALL." Within seconds, every trace of the hidden advertising program on every teaching machine in the world, including Professor Petrov's teaching machine, was deleted. Regret filled Miles, but temporarily putting the vital project out of action was necessary to ensure protection of Sellco. Miles could get Project Mercury back in operation quickly after he had dealt with Professor Petrov. None of the Platinum Program clients knew about Project Mercury, but before long the vaunted effectiveness of the Platinum Program would erode to being little better than the Gold Program.

———◆———

The next day, Miles Huxley arrived precisely on time at Professor Petrov's office and saw that the Sellco profile entry for purchasing Persian carpets was correct. To place Professor Petrov at ease, Miles had chosen to wear a smartly coordinated casual business ensemble instead of the usual power suit he wore when meeting clients. Miles extended his hand. "Miles Huxley, Sellco vice president. You must be Professor Yuri

Petrov." He had no doubt that this dwarfish man was Professor Petrov; he had studied his photograph on the University of Illinois website.

Professor Petrov stood and curtly shook the offered hand. "Yes; have a seat."

Miles remained standing and walked over to take a closer look at one of the elaborately designed carpets on the wall. "What an exotic collection, Professor Petrov. This silk carpet must be Iranian, but the other one is more difficult to identify. It is often hard to distinguish Turkmenistani carpets from western Chinese." Miles had done his homework for this meeting. The selection of short courses available on teaching machines was remarkable.

"It is from Turkmenistan."

"These are the finest carpets I have seen; you must be a true connoisseur."

"It is just a hobby."

"Well, let's get to business. Shall we? You'd mentioned during our phone call that you could display the advertising messages on some equipment in your laboratory. Could we visit your lab? I'm interested in seeing this." Miles wanted to get out of Petrov's office on the off chance that there was a recording device there.

Miles was truly impressed by Professor Petrov's large laboratory. On one side was the largest computer Miles had ever seen sitting next to what looked like a teaching machine scanner helmet on steroids. On the other side of the laboratory sat a normal teaching machine near a test bench with a stack of many types of complicated electronic equipment that Miles did not recognize, two normal-looking computers with their covers removed, and a video monitor. Multicolored wires snaked about the equipment.

"Very impressive. This is all yours?"

"Technically it belongs to the University of Illinois, but this lab is used by me and a few of my graduate students."

"Can you display the advertising messages on this teaching machine?"

"No; the circuits in the teaching machine can't function in the repetitive mode needed to make the subliminal messages visible. I will display them on this auxiliary video monitor." Petrov selected the EMULATE mode on the digital signal analyzer and ran the GLITCH-1 file as a repetitive sequence. "Drink Pepsi; it makes you sexy" appeared on the video monitor. Swift keystrokes produced the other two subliminal messages.

It was disappointing to see the images; Miles had hoped that every copy had been erased. The professor must have saved a copy of the Project Mercury files.

"Remarkable. I imagine it was difficult to find."

"It was hidden better than the tomb of the Egyptian Pharaoh Akhenaten," Professor Petrov boasted.

"As you requested, we've discontinued the advertising from the teaching machines. You can confirm this right now by examining this teaching machine in your laboratory or any other teaching machine in the world."

"Ah, so you admit that you are the source of this despicable subliminal advertising."

"This was the idea of others, not me." Technically, he was telling the truth. "I have long had reservations about it," he then lied. "As an act of good faith, we have removed the advertising from all of the teaching machines. Please inspect this machine now to confirm what I say."

As Miles watched, Petrov used the digital signal analyzer to search through the entire memory of the teaching machine for the subliminal advertising program or any fragments of the program.

"The program is gone; there is no trace of it," said Professor Petrov warily.

"You have remarkable skill, Professor Petrov. You're just the type of scientist we need for an important research project. I want to help make teaching machines more effective for their real purpose: teaching people. It would be valuable to find a way for a teaching machine to verify that the student was paying attention to the important parts of the lesson. Sellco will benefit by having better educated employees and by the corporate goodwill that comes from funding such good research." During his preparations for this meeting, Miles had read every scrap of information about Professor Petrov. His name had been included in a Coordinated Science Laboratory research proposal for integrating eye tracking into teaching machines that Susan Hebb had uploaded only a few days ago.

"A colleague and I have an idea for improving teaching machines by integrating a pair of video cameras to track the fixation points of the student's eyes," Professor Petrov said uneasily.

"Perfect. I'm prepared to fund this research for ten million dollars per year plus a personal stipend of half a million dollars a year for you for the next two years."

"That's nice, but it does not address my main concern. What assurances will I have that the subliminal advertising is permanently discontinued?"

"I'm sure a computer scientist of your skill can devise a way to automatically monitor teaching machines in many locations to confirm the absence of subliminal advertising. You would know instantly if the advertising resumed, and you'd have the evidence to prove its existence. The subliminal advertising has been suspended for now, but I need your help to end it forever." Miles had prepared an elaborate ruse to gain the professor's cooperation. "While both of us have our concerns about the practice of subliminal advertising, I'll need conclusive arguments to convince the senior executives in Sellco. Neither of us is an accredited expert in sociology or ethics. We must form a panel of such experts to investigate this issue, and you can participate in the panel as part of the research project I mentioned a moment ago. For some time now I've been planning to form this panel, and you are just the advocate we need to round it out." Miles was betting Professor Petrov would think that working within the system was far more effective than fighting from the outside.

"I want to see who will be on the panel of experts."

Miles did not have his mind-reader assistant with him, since the executive assistant was not one of the few who were permitted to know of Project Mercury. Nonetheless, Professor Petrov seemed receptive.

Miles reached into his briefcase and pulled out two sheets of paper. "As I said, I've already been laying the groundwork. Here is the list of panel members with their credentials. They've already given their preliminary agreement to participate if we form the panel. We will need to add your name to this list. What do you think?"

"I see that you are serious about this." Professor Petrov seemed impressed by the set of credentials.

Miles reached into his briefcase again and carefully selected a folder marked Version 3. "I've prepared an agreement for the research funding and the formation of the expert panel. The language is largely taken from standard research agreements that I'm sure you've seen before. I'll be happy to answer any questions you may have. Please take your time to read it carefully." Miles handed the four-page document to Professor Petrov and then pulled some other papers out of his briefcase that he kept to himself. "As you can see, it's fairly short. Take your time reading it while I catch up on some of my own work." Miles directed his attention to the papers in his hand.

Professor Petrov read the entire document. Miles had made sure the document was readable and devoid of obscure legalese. It detailed standard terms and conditions for a rather open-ended research project, the functioning of the expert panel that would produce recommendations based on the consensus of the panel, the funding as Miles had described, and a straightforward nondisclosure agreement.

"My department head usually reviews contracts," said Professor Petrov, scratching his chin. Miles became worried, but then Professor Petrov continued, "But I doubt he would have any problem with this. It seems fine."

Miles handed him a pen and tried to mask his nervousness. "Please sign and date both copies so we can get on to the work right away."

Miles was surprised when Petrov signed both copies of the contract. He had been prepared with a series of ploys to get his signature. Miles signed both copies, put one copy in his briefcase, and gave the other to Professor Petrov.

"You've made the right choice, Professor Petrov. You must know how seriously we take the nondisclosure agreement. As you can see in the language of the agreement, this prohibits any mention of the hidden messages in the teaching machines, even within the discussions of the expert panel. The panel is to investigate subliminal messaging in a generic context only. If the slightest word of the hidden messages slips out, we'll know it was you, and Sellco would have to file criminal charges."

"Criminal charges? A nondisclosure agreement is a civil matter."

"Oh, no, Professor Petrov; we checked your background and have incontrovertible evidence that you have provided classified information on neural network technology to unauthorized colleagues in Russia."

———

Yuri belatedly realized that Miles Huxley had trapped him. This devious Sellco vice president was more dangerous than Yuri had thought. Huxley was a false comrade who smiled and shook your hand while hiding a knife in the other hand. He had heard stories about other immigrants who had been deported on the slightest evidence of misdeeds. Some of his past e-mails had discussed aspects of technology beyond what was in the published literature. Yuri's only hope was to buy time by convincing Huxley that he would behave.

"I correspond about my work with colleagues in many countries, but I have never given away any secrets."

"Our evidence proves otherwise," Huxley said smugly. "You keep your secrets, Professor Petrov, and we will keep ours. Let's wait to see the conclusions of the study by the expert panel before we do anything we might regret."

"OK, I agree," said Yuri, now suspecting that Sellco would rig the expert panel. His only choice was to play along and later figure out a solution to this mess. "*S etimi padlami nado bylo derjat' uho vostro.* With these bad people, I will have to keep my ears tuned," he muttered to himself.

Huxley seemed pleased. "While your communications with your Russian colleagues are incriminating, I'm sure your intentions were good. You should not worry too much about it, since I will certainly not mention it to anyone. Let's focus on the more positive prospects of the research that Sellco will be funding you to do."

The serpent slithered out of the lab. Yuri had a lot of thinking to do and needed a cigarette.

12

"Hello, lover. I was thinking of you," said Hamilton's wife. It was the third time she had called that day.

"I was thinking of you too, dear," Hamilton von Helmholtz lied as he turned on the video screen on his phone. He usually preferred audio-only phone calls, but the video made the frequent calls from his wife more bearable.

"I'm going out for a while. Do you think I should have my nails done first and then shop for a new pair of summer shoes, or should I shop for the shoes first?"

Hamilton had learned that saying "You should decide yourself" did not work. He mentally flipped a coin. "Oh, I think you should buy the shoes first. That way there will be no worry of scuffing your nails while trying on shoes." This was one of the prices he paid for his choice of a bride. There was no question as to why Hamilton had married her; she was a stunning prize, a dazzling trophy wife. She had big bright eyes, the complexion of a baby, a smile that made any man's heart skip a beat, long blonde hair, and was perfectly proportioned in every respect. Hamilton pressed a button on the video screen to zoom in; she was one of those rare women who looked better close up. In private, she could be tedious. In public, she was alluring, and they both enjoyed playing a clandestine game of watching her irresistible effect on any man within eyesight.

She flashed a smile that would have delighted any orthodontist. "You're so clever, *cheri*. I love you."

A message flashed on his video screen. "Please excuse me, dear; I have an important call to take now."

"Bye bye, lover." She blew him a kiss.

Hamilton punched two buttons on his phone and dropped his voice an octave. "Hello, CSL, von Helmholtz."

"Hi, this is David Katz at Pharmor. We've reviewed your phase-one report on the neurological effects of Xarim. The results are inconclusive and unpromising. Frankly, some of the results are contrary to what we wanted. We've decided not to fund phase two, and we don't wish the initial research to be published."

This was a big blow to Hamilton; he despised unproductive research. He knew why Pharmor wanted the initial research buried, and this gave him leverage. "Susan Hebb did some fine work on that project and deserves to be published. Read your research contract; we can publish without your approval. I wouldn't ask Susan to throw away so much work unless we saw some serious quid pro quo."

"What the hell are you playing at, Helmholtz? You know what we need." Katz sounded surprised.

"I think you need two things. First, you need to fund a new, major research project at CSL on a safe topic that will look sexy when we publish. Second, you need us to erase all the results from the Xarim project."

There was a long pause. Hamilton figured that Katz had little choice. Katz relented. "OK, how about a five-million-dollar study of memory enhancement by stimulating protein kinase C?"

"Perfect. I'll have a contract sent to you today."

"And the Xarim project files?"

"They will be deleted after we have a signed contract for the new work."

"OK, but this time any publication must have our approval."

———

Cigarette-enhanced contemplation had solidified Yuri's conclusion. The Sellco expert panel would be a sham. He had already checked several teaching machines to confirm that the subliminal advertising program had been removed from all of them. He knew that Miles Huxley had done this to remove the evidence of Sellco's activities, not to satisfy Yuri's demands. Sellco would resume the subliminal advertising once they felt it was safe. He needed to find out what Sellco was really planning and hopefully uncover the necessary evidence. No one would believe the paranoid claims of an old-school Russian immigrant who could be charged with espionage. The GLITCH files that were still stored in his digital signal analyzer would be dismissed as Yuri's invention. He needed hard evidence that could not be mistaken.

Yuri knew of a way to find out more about Sellco's activities, but it had risks. However, doing nothing had risks too. He wanted to know what was going on, so he programmed his computer to start at an arbitrary IP address and ping sequential IP addresses on the Internet until he got a response from a computer that lacked security software. After just four seconds of trolling through IP addresses, he found a computer in Sacramento, California that was naked to the world. It was amazing how many people still did not bother to put firewalls on their computers.

Yuri thought back to his undergraduate days when he and Dmitri hacked computers in their spare time. "There are corrupt commissars here too, Dmitri," Yuri muttered under his breath, nervously looking up from his keyboard to be sure he was alone in his laboratory.

With trepidation, he hijacked the computer in Sacramento and loaded a password cracker program onto it. He then instructed it to go to the Sellco corporate server and start trying one password after another until it found one that worked. This was a common form of attack that Sellco servers were surely designed to rebuff. The attack was not intended to succeed; it was intended to attract the attention of the Sellco computer security staff. Since the diversionary attack came from Sacramento, they would not know its true source.

Next, Yuri used the administrative access code for the University of Illinois campus computing network that he had obtained while helping Takashi fix the virus problem. He loaded a Trojan horse program onto nearly every computer on the campus network. The Trojan horse hid in the background; it exhibited no sign of its existence on the three thousand computers. The purpose of the Trojan horse was not to crack the password; it was to destroy the Sellco software firewall by overwhelming the packet filter buffers with a torrent of IP packets. Nearly every computer at the University of Illinois had been transformed into robot hackers; the Sellco computer defenses had no chance against the army of three thousand attackers. The firewall crashed down in thirty seconds.

As soon as Yuri entered the Sellco corporate computers, he found a good hiding place in one of the servers and uploaded a program that would be useful later. He then quickly searched for information about the subliminal advertising program. He found references to Project Mercury and a list of its clients including Alfred Grossberg, White House chief of staff. Project Mercury was shown on "temporary hold" with a list of messages queued to be sent next: "Slaughter is the right choice,"

"Subliminal messages are harmless; what you can't see can't hurt you," and "Xarim makes you fit and trim."

He was astounded. Sellco planned to conduct subliminal political advertising to gain confirmation of Robert Slaughter to the Supreme Court, and they also planned to neutralize the threat of future exposure of subliminal advertising. It was clear that Sellco intended to resume the subliminal advertising as soon as the risk of exposure was removed.

———

At the Sellco corporate network management center, Alice was on the phone with a Sellco manager who claimed that his access to an Internet pornography site was being blocked. The manager explained that he needed access to the site to see if Sellco's advertising was displayed correctly. The records confirmed what he said, so Alice entered the website as an exception in the access control subsystem. Five computer monitors sat at her network management workstation; one of them showed the status of every major part of the Sellco corporate computer network. Alice saw the block on the screen labeled "gateway router" go from green to yellow, and a message said "FILTER BUFFER FAILOVER TO VIRTUAL MEMORY." She was busy and would deal with it later.

Thirty seconds later the block on the screen changed to red, displaying the message "FIREWALL FAILURE— AUTORESTART," and an incessant beeping began. This demanded immediate attention. Was it related to the access exception she had just performed? That was unlikely; she had done that hundreds of times without a hiccup.

Harry, sitting nearby, saw the firewall failure too. "What's going on? The firewall's down, the filter buffer is full, and traffic is spilling into our network without inspection," complained Harry.

Alice had not seen anything like this. She opened the firewall management screen and confirmed what Harry had just told her. It would be three minutes before the autorestart would be completed, and until then, the Sellco network was unprotected. The system was not designed for the unprecedented overload. What could have caused it?

"Check the firewall event log before the filter buffer failover," suggested Alice.

"Hah!" exclaimed Harry. "There was a password cracker attack just seconds before. Hold on—I have the IP address for the source, and I'm checking to see if it has been reassigned since then. Here it is. We're in luck; it is still assigned. I'm looking it up. It's assigned to a pet food store in Sacramento, California. Do you want me to give them a call?"

Harry's actions had distracted Alice for a while, but she soon realized the true threat, quickly accessed the gateway router management systems, and clicked on HARD STOP. The system responded, "ARE YOU SURE?" and she clicked YES. She looked heavenward for forgiveness, hoping her drastic act was justified.

Not aware of Alice's actions, Harry yelped, "Cripes, now the gateway router is down too."

"I shut it down."

"You shut it down! Why? It'll take at least fifteen minutes to get it running again." Meanwhile, the entire Sellco computer network was down. Her job was to keep the network running, but she dared not let it run unsecured. Had she done the right thing? Her boss would demand an explanation for unplugging the entire corporation.

Alice had acted purely on intuition. The firewall problem did not feel like a random failure and was surely not caused by a password cracker. She hoped that she was right because everyone in Sellco would feel the results of what she had done.

The ceaseless flow of data within Sellco took its first pause in years. Over five thousand computers came to a stop. The phones at their workstations started ringing in fifteen seconds; they ignored the phones.

"I can't believe you had the balls to do that." Harry looked dumbstruck.

"You have your genders confused, Harry." Alice laughed. She was feeling better as she inspected what remained of the packet filter buffer. The overload had badly fragmented the linked list, but there were enough intact packets to show a clear pattern in the source addresses of the packets. The brute-force attack on Sellco's defenses had been effective, but it lacked stealth. Alice's rapid and bold action had saved the packet filter buffer before the database could be totally trashed.

"Look at these IP addresses," observed Alice. "There are thousands of different IP addresses, but they all come from a block of addresses assigned to the University of Illinois in Urbana-Champaign. It's a swarm attack."

Harry nodded. "I've got to hand it to you, Alice. You made the right call. Someone had their hand in the cookie jar, and you slammed the lid shut before they got very far."

After fifteen minutes, the Sellco network was back to normal. Alice sent a broadcast message to all accounts. "The network administration department apologizes for the recent network outage. All systems have been restored, and the only data lost were messages in transit at the start of the outage. The network was forced down due to a swarm attack originating at the University of Illinois in Urbana-Champaign. Our files were exposed for about one minute, so any stolen data should be minimal. We are investigating the situation and will take action to prevent any recurrence. Thank you."

Yuri's access to the Sellco computers had been severed more quickly than he had expected. He had been distracted by the shocking revelation that Sellco was performing secret lobbying for the Sherrington administration and planned to resume subliminal advertising. He had not copied any of the Sellco files before he suddenly lost his access. He knew that another attack like this would not succeed. Sellco would fix the hole in their defenses. Yuri sent messages to all of the computers in the University of Illinois campus network to remove all traces of the Trojan horse program except for one part. The subroutine was so small and so well hidden that it would never be found.

13

———

When Miles Huxley saw the broadcast message from the Sellco computer system administrator about the computer attack from the University of Illinois, he suspected that Professor Petrov was behind it. After all, Petrov had the computer skills. To make sure, he called Sellco's computer network department. After ten rings, Alice finally answered her phone.

"What have you learned about who was behind today's computer attack?" asked Miles.

"We talked to Mr. Fujikawa," Alice replied, "at the University of Illinois computer network department. He was very helpful. Between the transaction records he found on his end and what we have, it seems that every computer at the university was involved except the six computers assigned to a Professor Yuri Petrov in the computer science department and the four computers assigned to Mr. Fujikawa We're not sure what to make of that."

For Miles, that was proof enough that Professor Petrov was the perpetrator of the attack. This professor knew about the subliminal advertising and now he had gone rogue. Miles thought, "Lord knows what he found when he broke into

Sellco's network." Stronger measures were needed. Miles had to act quickly before Professor Petrov did real damage.

A Sellco attorney joined Miles for an impromptu meeting with agents from the local FBI office. The Sellco attorney presented evidence of the recent computer attack and the evidence of Petrov's sending classified information to colleagues in Russia. Given the prevailing attitude in the country about foreigners, it did not take much to get the FBI to act. Miles emphasized the need to quickly confine Professor Petrov before he gave away more national secrets and explained that Petrov was aware that Sellco had reported his nefarious activities to the FBI. As a result, the professor might try to get even with Sellco by making up ridiculous stories about them. The Sellco attorney went further, saying that Petrov could also be in violation of a nondisclosure agreement and that anything he said might be used in a civil suit by Sellco. As a result, the Sellco attorney asked that the FBI agents keep anything they heard from Professor Petrov to themselves and limit his exposure to a minimum number of people. Most importantly, anything the professor said had no credibility.

Miles was allowed to remain while the New Jersey FBI office called the Illinois FBI office, and he made sure all of the instructions were passed along to the agents in Illinois.

———

Only a few hours after the attack on the Sellco computers, FBI agents Edgar and Dover from the Illinois office arrived at the Coordinated Science Laboratory with a warrant for Petrov's arrest. Agent Edgar had received a rushed briefing and the necessary warrants for arrest and search. Yuri Petrov was an old-schooler, and it was well known that these people were prone to criminal activity. Agent Edgar was eager for any excuse to capture one of these strange people who threatened modern society. Professor Petrov was not in his office, but someone else stepped in while they were looking about for signs of where he might be.

Agent Edgar showed his badge. "I'm FBI Agent Edgar and this is Agent Dover. Who are you?"

"I'm Takashi Fujikawa; I work here at the university. Where is Yuri?"

"That's what we want to know. We have a warrant for Yuri Petrov's arrest on a charge of espionage. Can you help us find him?"

"Yuri? Espionage? Wow! I would have never guessed." Mr. Fujikawa seemed sincere. "Follow me. Maybe he's in his lab."

"We also have a search warrant for Dr. Petrov's office and residence. We'll need to copy everything from his computer. Who should we talk to concerning access to his computer?" inquired Agent Edgar as they walked to the lab.

"I'm the campus computer network administrator, so I can help you. But first I must check with the head of the Coordinated Science Lab, Hamilton von Helmholtz."

"Do you know anything about an attack conducted this morning upon the Sellco network by all of the computers here at the University of Illinois?" asked Agent Dover.

"I got a call from the Sellco folks this morning," replied Mr. Fujikawa. "I helped them isolate the source to the computers on our network. It seemed to come from every computer on the campus except Yuri's and mine. Whoever did it was slick; there was nothing left behind to examine." With reluctance, he continued, "Yuri is one of the few people I know with the talent to pull off a swarm attack like that."

"We'll want to talk to you further at a later time," said Agent Dover.

They entered Professor Petrov's lab, but he was not there.

"Yuri works with Susan Hebb a lot; let's see if she knows where he is," suggested Mr. Fujikawa.

Susan was not in her office. After looking in a couple of other places with no luck, they thanked Mr. Fujikawa for his help and said they would return later. Agents Edgar and Dover went to see if Professor Petrov was at his apartment on the other side of campus.

———

Yuri had been sitting at his desk for just a moment when Takashi walked in drinking a can of Pepsi. Takashi seemed astonished to see Yuri sitting there.

"Where were you?" asked Takashi.

"I stepped out for a smoke," explained Yuri.

"Two FBI agents were just here looking for you. They were here to arrest you for espionage! Yuri, what have you been up to?"

Yuri knew that Takashi joked around sometimes, but he seemed serious and very worried. Yuri instantly made the connection to his attack on the Sellco computer and the espionage threat made by Miles Huxley with the FBI agents. Yuri was becoming worried too.

"I haven't done anything wrong. I think it is a misunderstanding."

Takashi's eyes narrowed with suspicion, "Does this misunderstanding have anything to do with computers here at the university crashing the firewall at Sellco this morning? The FBI agents were asking about that. You weren't involved with that, were you?"

"Don't worry. There is no truth in this talk of espionage." Yuri would rather tell a white lie than possibly expose Takashi to risk too. Sellco would play hardball with anyone they thought might threaten their dirty secret.

"Yuri, they were FBI agents complete with badges, guns, an arrest warrant, and a search warrant. Espionage carries the death penalty. You should be worried even if you are innocent."

"Well, I am innocent, and the worst they would do is lock me away for a few years."

"Don't you remember the Chang espionage case last year? They executed both the husband and wife." Takashi was right, and Yuri became concerned. The death penalty had become common for espionage, especially for foreigners.

Susan walked cheerily into Yuri's office. "Hi, Takashi. Hey, Yuri, you're late for our chess game again."

"I think Yuri will be playing with the FBI," Takashi said darkly. Just then the cell phone on Takashi's belt yelped with the RED ALERT sound effect from the original Star Trek TV series. Yuri had heard Takashi's cell phone play this sound effect before, and Takashi always went running when it sounded. The RED ALERT meant that the network management software that monitored the campus data network had detected a critical problem and had sent a special message to Takashi's phone to call for help. The first time Yuri had seen Takashi go running in response to the automated call from the network management system, he had wondered who was the master and who was the slave: man or machine?

"If you're innocent, you should turn yourself in," suggested Takashi, dashing out the door.

Perplexed, Susan asked Yuri, "What's Takashi talking about?"

More than anything, he did not want to place Susan at risk. If he told her about it, then she could be considered an accomplice to the false espionage charge and his attack on the Sellco network. He could not tell anyone about Sellco's subliminal advertising. He must not expose others to the same risk he carried. Being careful, he said, "Takashi tells me that FBI agents were here to arrest me for espionage. I am innocent, but you know how foreigners are treated." He looked her straight in her good eye. "Please trust me, Susan."

Susan's cheery mood had changed to dire concern. "There must be some reason why they think you are a spy. What is going on, Yuri?"

Yuri was reminded of Dmitri dying as a result of Yuri's misadventures. After all these years, guilt still plagued him. Susan was the last person he wished to be hurt as a result of his foolishness.

"I have discovered something despicable being done by others. It is a great evil that I cannot tell you about because it could place you in danger. All I can say is that I am innocent, and I am trying to stop it. You and I and many others are the victims." Yuri thought further and added, "There is one thing I can tell you. From my research on brain scan analysis, I think it might be possible to develop a lie detector that could also detect if a person is trying to hide something. So anything I tell you might be discovered. Please do not tell anyone of my theory."

Yuri was understating what he knew. In fact, he had written an experimental lie detector program for teaching machines and performed some veiled experiments on graduate students. He had told the students he was studying the recall latency of the brain, so they would not know the true purpose of the experiments. After confirming the effectiveness of the experimental lie detector program, Yuri decided that the technology would likely do more harm than good, so he had buried the program in his private archive and never told anyone of his discovery.

Susan's face showed confusion and concern. Stepping closer to Yuri, she looked deep into his eyes. They were good friends, but Yuri was pleasantly surprised and delighted when she took his arm and held it softly. His pulse quickened; had his fantasies of Susan come true? He could smell her perfume and was about to say that he liked the scent when Susan spoke first. "Irises dilated. Pulse fast, about ninety," she reported clinically. "Come to my lab. I want to take your blood pressure."

Yuri's disappointment turned to anger. "What are you doing?"

"Oh, I've begun some research on the effects of stress on the sensory process. Do you notice any color shift in your vision?"

"Yes, I am seeing red! I am not one of your lab monkeys," growled Yuri. Susan's blindness to his feelings was infuriating.

"Irritability. Another symptom of stress."

"*Vse ravno chto gluhomu stihi chitat'*. This is like reading a poem to a deaf man," he said to himself as he tried to calm down. "Susan, did you hear what I just told you? This is not one of Takashi's sick jokes. There really are FBI agents looking to arrest me for espionage. Espionage carries the death penalty. I am innocent, and I am trying to stop some people who are dangerously deceiving everyone, including our government. I must stop them, but I can't endanger you by telling you more."

Finally, Susan seemed to understand and showed compassion. "I'm sorry. I've been thinking all day about a theory that stress accelerates aging, and I was concerned about the effects of this stress on you. So, are you going to turn yourself in to the FBI?"

"Never." Even in America, the police could not be trusted. "That would put an end to my efforts to stop the massive deception, and I would be put on trial for espionage with fake evidence that might be hard to discredit. I must avoid the FBI agents until I have the evidence to prove what is really happening. I will hide until I figure out how to get the evidence I need and to clear myself from the false charges."

"Where will you hide?"

"Susan, I can't tell you. You might be questioned."

"Right. Is there anything I can do to help?"

"I don't want to expose you to assisting someone charged with espionage. If I think of something later, I might contact you." As he was talking, Yuri was searching his office and putting things in a backpack. This included cigarettes, a radio-frequency detecting probe, a Swiss Army knife, and when Susan glanced away, the postcard from Julie. He turned off his mobile phone. He would never again turn on the wireless functions since it would give away his position to the authorities. Without the wireless functions, he would feel disconnected from the world, but at least the annoying advertisements that periodically popped up on the screen of his mobile phone would cease. He felt that his withdrawal from cyberspace would be difficult, but it was necessary to evade dataveillance by the FBI.

"Those FBI agents could return at any moment; you'd better get going. I know you couldn't have done anything bad. You are the one person around here that I trust. If there is anything I can do, call me."

"I will." He felt better when Susan showed kindness toward him.

"Good luck, Yuri. I hope you succeed." Susan gave him a good-luck kiss on the cheek. Yuri's cheek tingled, and the tingling radiated throughout his body.

"Thanks. We'll play chess again as soon as I fix this mess." He walked out the back door of the Coordinated Science Laboratory feeling silly wearing sunglasses and a hat on a cloudy day. He knew it was a poor disguise.

His apartment was number one on the list of places he could not go. He rode his bicycle directly to his bank. The bank might be risky too, but it was necessary. Thankfully, the bank was nearly deserted. He hoped that he was one step ahead of the FBI as he took off the hat and sunglasses and walked up to a teller window. Hiding his unease, he tried to act normal as he asked to withdraw all the funds from his account. The teller called for a bank vice president, whose only concern was to be assured that Yuri was not under duress and that he could state his mother's maiden name. Yuri was presented with an impressive stack of currency. The fifty-dollar bills were printed with a border advertising the Bank of USA, the hundred-dollar bills were framed with J. P. Jones Bank, and the five-hundred-dollar bills had City Bank. The heft of the thick stack of bills made Yuri feel better. Next he visited the safe deposit vault where he added his passport and a collection of gold coins to his backpack. He rode his bike a few blocks and locked it in a rack with other bikes. From there it was a six-block walk to the train station.

The next train to Milwaukee would depart in an hour and a half. Yuri bought a second-class ticket with cash from a ticket vending machine; he knew to not leave a trail of credit card purchases. Instead of waiting in the station, he walked to the stores nearby. Like many city centers, downtown Champaign had eventually learned to compete with the shopping malls on the outskirts of town. At a drug store, Yuri bought a shaver, a toothbrush, and some other basic supplies. At another store, he abandoned his conspicuous all-black clothes and bought two pairs of denim jeans, three light-colored polo shirts, socks, and underwear. He knew the new clothes helped him to blend in, but he felt odd.

—•—

Agents Edgar and Dover returned to Professor Petrov's empty office. Agent Edgar's trained eyes noticed that a backpack and notebook computer were no longer there. Professor Petrov had slipped past them. Professor Petrov's laboratory and Susan Hebb's office were still empty. The two agents finally found someone in their office. Hamilton von Helmholtz did not seem to know anything, but he agreed to their request to keep

Professor Petrov's office and laboratory locked. Helmholtz's administrative assistant provided Agent Edgar with the lock codes for both doors, so he could return to examine the rooms later. Signs would be posted on both doors forbidding entry.

Next, the two agents visited Takashi Fujikawa's office. He was busy dealing with a minor crisis on his computer, but told them that he had seen Professor Petrov about an hour ago and advised the professor that he should turn himself in to the FBI. Agent Edgar realized that they had made the mistake of not giving Mr. Fujikawa their business cards when they had first met. This time he made sure that Mr. Fujikawa and everyone else they met were given business cards with the request to call immediately if they learned Professor Petrov's whereabouts.

With every minute, it would become harder to find Professor Petrov. It was clear that he had run. The standard FBI procedure was to first rely on the network of a million traffic cameras in every state of the union. Each camera took photographs of traffic violators, and an optical character recognition program recorded their license plate numbers. Originally, photographs were taken only of traffic violators such as speeders or people who ran red lights. Later, after all of the traffic cameras had been connected to a nationwide network, the practice expanded beyond recording only traffic violators. The license plate of every car on the road was recorded.

To protect the privacy of citizens, the traffic records could only be accessed when a court order had been issued for due cause to search for a specific license plate. The system enjoyed support from much of the public because of the ample publicity whenever an abducted child was saved by the system. Now it was difficult to drive more than ten minutes without seeing a traffic camera. The vast network of traffic cameras cost less than the many thousands of police cars they replaced, and they were far more effective in enforcing traffic laws. The traffic camera network was a powerful tool for the local police and the FBI, and there was rarely any question about rapidly getting a court order to search for a license plate.

The two FBI agents returned to Professor Petrov's office with cell phones to their ears. Agent Dover was asking his office to find the car and license registered to Yuri Petrov, but the search was taking a long time. Agent Edgar was talking with the nearby Willard Airport, asking if anyone matching Professor Petrov's description had been seen or if he had purchased an airplane ticket. Willard Airport was relatively small, but it was taking a while to check with everyone there.

"They can't find a car registered to Petrov," said Agent Dover.

"Check for rental cars and stolen cars in the past two hours," suggested Agent Edgar.

After ten more phone calls Agent Dover reported, "No recently stolen cars and only one recently rented car to a twenty-five-year-old woman."

Agent Edgar was still busy with people at the airport and told Agent Dover, "Get the license for the rented car and a court order to track it. A friend might have rented the car for Petrov. See if you can find his friend, Susan Hebb, to find if she knows anything and whether she loaned her car to Petrov."

While Agent Dover was talking with Susan Hebb and getting a court order for the rental car license search, Agent Edgar had finished with the airport and was now busily calling used car dealers. That took a lot of time because the used car dealers loved to talk.

Agent Dover returned, frustrated with the lack of progress. "Susan Hebb mentioned that she talked with Petrov, who left over an hour ago. He didn't tell her much except that he claimed innocence and that he was fighting an evil plot of some sort. Her car is parked next to this building."

Agent Edgar was still talking to chatty used-car dealers, but he put the phone aside and said, "Call the bus and train stations."

The people at the bus station had seen no one matching the description. The agent at the train station reported the same and that the train for Chicago and Milwaukee had just departed.

Agent Edgar was still talking to an especially loquacious used-car dealer when Agent Dover reported no useful news. Agent Edgar put the phone aside and said, "Check on his driver's license."

Agent Dover made the call and reported in astonishment, "Yuri Petrov has no driver's license."

Agent Edgar hung up on the dealer, bellowing "No driver's license! I hate these old-school people. What kind of weirdo is he?"

14

First-class food service on the airlines paled in comparison to the second-class dining car on the Electroliner train. Yuri sat back and consciously willed himself to relax as he made his escape from Champaign. He tried to concentrate on the menu listing thirty choices of meals freshly cooked in the train's galley. He chose comfort food: meatloaf with mashed potatoes and gravy, green beans, and milk. The dining and lounge cars offered video screens showing the current position of the train, speed, estimated time of arrival, and information about upcoming sights as well as the next destination. Of course, the video was peppered with advertisements.

After the satisfying dinner, Yuri used one of the free public Internet terminals in the lounge car to look up some information that he would soon need. He was comforted to see that there was no word of his arrest warrant in the news. He expected that Sellco would seek to keep a low profile on this case. The meal and the news reduced his anxiety to a tolerable level of paranoia.

Yuri took the radio frequency detecting probe from his bag and methodically scanned everything he had. Using his Swiss

Army knife, he cut an RFID chip from his belt. The person in the seat across from Yuri stared at the strange behavior, so Yuri retired to the privacy of the washroom. He cut the RFID chips out of every item of clothing, his computer, a mini-flashlight, his cell phone, an umbrella, and even the bag that held everything. The one thing he could not scan was the RF probe itself, but by visual inspection he found the chip hidden in the battery compartment of the probe. Everything he had with him now had little holes, but at least he was free of the chips that might give away his position.

The Electroliner train ran from New Orleans to Milwaukee at a top speed of 330 kilometers per hour. This was actually the second incarnation of the Electroliner. The original Electroliner had run on the same route until it was retired from service in 1963 due to competition from the airlines. The steadily rising price of petroleum had turned the tide, and American passenger train service had come back into fashion with increased funding from Congress. Now that passenger train service on main routes had priority over freight trains, the passenger train on-time record was better than airlines. The second-class lounge seats were more comfortable and offered more leg room than first class on most airplanes.

The large population of senior citizens had spawned the resurrection of an old idea in rail travel, the rail cruise. Certain trains were configured with cars containing compact staterooms complete with bunk beds, a full private bathroom, private seating, ample storage space, and steward service on call. These trains contained public observation lounge cars, deluxe dining cars, and a health spa complete with a Jacuzzi. The rail cruise trains typically provided a ten-day tour of the country with half-day stops at selected cities. Organized tours were available at each stop. Yuri had been sure to book an intercity train and not the more expensive rail cruise.

He would have preferred to give his boss a little more time to settle in after his return from his African safari vacation, but Miles Huxley knew that Kent Fechner would want to hear immediately about the trouble with Project Mercury.

"Welcome back. How was Africa?" said Miles, entering his boss's office. As always, Fechner's suit was elegantly styled with a subtly avant-garde variation on the traditional British business suit. His suits were custom tailored in Milan, Italy to precisely fit his tall, aristocratic form.

"The scenery was a spiritual experience, but the poverty was unimaginable. I tried to ignore the wretched natives, but they kept getting in the way when I was taking photographs." Fechner lacked any semblance of compassion, and Miles had the amusing mental image of Fechner tossing a few coins in the street, not from charity, but so that the poor people would run out of Fechner's view. Kent Fechner did not appear the least bit relaxed from his vacation.

"Sorry to hit you with bad news as soon as you return, but there has been trouble with Project Mercury."

"Please sit down and give me a full briefing." Fechner appeared to take this well, pressing a button at his desk to close the door to his office.

"A computer science professor at the University of Illinois found our subliminal advertising program in the teaching machines and can read the hidden messages. The good news is that I met with him and got him to sign a nondisclosure agreement and a commitment to work with us before he told anyone else about it. I reinforced this by threatening him with espionage charges based on some fake evidence we brewed up. I was able to perform the FLUSH-ALL broadcast before anyone could get a copy of the program."

"So Project Mercury is on hold for now?"

"Yes."

"Smart move, Miles. With the evidence gone, no one can prove anything."

"The bad news is that Professor Petrov later went rogue and hacked into the Sellco computer network. The whole network was down for fifteen minutes, and there's no telling what he found in our computers. Our computer experts say that this professor is remarkably adept. He is outraged about the subliminal advertising and is determined to stop it. He is dangerous.

"So I contacted the FBI with our evidence of espionage and computer hacking. They sent agents to arrest him, and I made sure that they knew to keep a lid on it and to not believe anything he said. Unfortunately, the FBI sent Laurel and Hardy to perform the arrest and they bungled it. Now Professor Petrov is on the run. The FBI says that he has told his friends that he can't tell them anything about the situation. He seems to understand that he must not expose anyone else to the trouble he is in. I think the cork is still in the bottle thus far."

"Do we know where to find Professor Petrov?"

"No; it seems the FBI agents scared him away. The FBI says that they hope to find him soon, but their performance thus far does not instill much confidence." Miles was putting as much positive spin as he dared on his report to counteract Fechner's tendency to see the negative side of everything.

"Has anyone at the FBI heard anything about Project Mercury?"

"No."

"Good," said Fechner, casually popping a mint candy in his mouth. Thus far, Fechner seemed to be taking this better than Miles had expected.

The antacid mint did little to quell Kent's churning stomach. Kent forced his frenzied mind to calm down and think methodically. Miles did not know how badly he had bungled the situation or the full magnitude of the threat to Sellco's future. Kent decided to go easy on Miles because he had done what seemed appropriate given what Miles knew. Reprimanding Miles would just make him defensive, and Kent had no time to waste listening to excuses.

Miles knew a lot about Project Mercury, but Kent had never told him that one of the clients was Alfred Grossberg, the president's chief of staff. He knew nothing of the political lobbying messages that had been sent via Project Mercury on several occasions. Miles was unaware of the extreme political ramifications that would result from the exposure of Project Mercury or the vital relationship between Sellco and the Sherrington administration.

Kent's relationship with Grossberg and Sherrington went back many years to when Senator Sherrington had sponsored a bill that would not allow local ordinances to restrict advertising such as billboards. Sherrington had masterfully finessed approval of the bill with arguments based on freedom of speech.

Most importantly, Miles was unaware that the importance of Project Mercury went beyond generating billions in profit for Sellco. Project Mercury was an irreplaceable tool that was essential to the Sherrington administration's strategy to defend the United States from many threats, both internal and external. Kent Fechner saw eye to eye with Alfred Grossberg about the United States' precarious position as king of the hill. Project Mercury was a life-or-death issue for Kent Fechner, Sellco, and the United States. Involving the FBI was a dangerous step. If the FBI captured Professor Petrov, they would question him, and despite Miles's requests, the story would get out. At least the secret was safe thus far.

Kent knew what must be done, and it must be kept secret. The only way to keep a secret is to tell no one. Kent must do this himself. Professor Petrov had poked a hornet's nest and was about to get stung.

"Project Mercury is more important than you know," said Kent. "There are aspects of the project that you have not been told. If you had known the full story, you would have done things differently." Kent saw Miles's defensive reaction. "I don't blame you, Miles. You reacted quickly, and given what you knew, you acted well. If there is blame, then it lies with me for not telling you more. There are dangers here that you don't know, so I am going to take it from here. You are to fully disengage and leave it to me. If anyone contacts you, send them to me." Miles was looking glum. "You've kept this from spinning out of control, Miles. You did a good job. Now it's my turn. I'll get Project Mercury going again."

Miles seemed relieved as he left.

In Kent Fechner's opinion, the laws and rules of society existed to help people with simpler minds to stay out of trouble. Special people like Kent operated by their own set of rules that were appropriate for their intelligence. He was smart enough to look out for himself without the needless restrictions that applied to most people.

As soon as Miles had left his office, Kent closed the door and picked up his phone. The phones at Sellco headquarters had the traditional dial tone, unlike every other phone in the country, which played advertising jingles instead. Alfred Grossberg was not in Washington, DC, so he could not call the secure phone in Alfred's office. The next best thing was a secure version of instant text messaging sent from Kent's computer to Alfred's cell phone.

"*We need to talk now! Where are you?*" messaged Kent.

After a few minutes, Alfred replied with a text message: "*I just stepped out of a meeting. It was a waste of time anyway. Can't say where I am, will be away from DC a few days. No secure phone here. Use secure text messaging.*"

"*Project Mercury on hold,*" Kent messaged. "*Unable to send your message to support Slaughter. A professor, Yuri Petrov, discovered everything about Project Mercury; may include your role. FBI issued warrant for his arrest for espionage based on evidence from us. We believe Petrov has not told anyone what he knows. If FBI questions him, this might be disclosed. FBI needs to find but not arrest Petrov; only tell you when they learn where he is.*"

"*You know how important Mercury is. What do you plan?*" Alfred responded.

"*You give me Petrov's location; I will eliminate the threat permanently, myself.*"

"*I don't want to know the details of how you will silence him.*"

"*Do you have any better ideas?*"

"*No. Do it fast; the confirmation of Slaughter is soon. We need help from Mercury.*"

"*I will move fast when I get Petrov's location.*"

"*OK. I will contact Zack Broca at the FBI today.*"

"*Bye.*"

———

Alfred Grossberg's loyalty to President Sherrington went beyond doing what he was told. As the president's chief of staff, Alfred protected President Sherrington from potential risks and did whatever it took to implement Sherrington's vision for a stronger America. Sherrington had an instinctive understanding of political strategy, brilliant vision, and the most powerful charisma that Alfred had ever witnessed. Anyone who met

Sherrington was instantly charmed. Even the sophisticated Alfred Grossberg had fallen victim to Sherrington's charisma. However, Alfred knew Sherrington's limits, and foremost of these was a disinterest in the details of executing his strategies. Execution was Alfred's forte.

Zack Broca, director of the FBI, was part of the Sherrington machine, a group of department heads handpicked for their loyalty to the president. Zack received a phone call from Alfred Grossberg.

"Hi, Zack," said Alfred, "I have a favor to ask." When he said the word "favor," he knew Zack would take it as an order.

"You want me to fix a parking ticket?"

Alfred did not laugh. "Your agents in Illinois are attempting to arrest a professor, Yuri Petrov, on a charge of espionage."

"Yeah?" Zack sounded like he did not already know about it.

"It's urgent to find Petrov before he spreads dangerous misinformation. Frankly, the agents who have been acting on the Petrov case haven't accomplished much. Could you get some more agents on the case?"

"This sounds important. I'll make sure that we make the arrest ASAP."

"This case has diplomatic complications, so we are asking that your agents hold off on the arrest until the time is right. Locate Petrov quickly, but keep your agents at a discreet distance. Petrov and others near him must not know we have found him. Give me a call the instant you know where Petrov is, and then we will have the right people defuse the diplomatic angles."

"Lord, Alfred, you're a great one for playing your cards close to the chest. We will do as you ask, but it would help if you let us know the big picture."

"I'll let you know more when I can, Zack. I really appreciate your help. Please make sure all your agents understand the rules of engagement: Locate Petrov, but stay away. Treat this case as need-to-know."

"We always do. I assume you want me to call you directly at any time, day or night?"

"Right. Thanks, Zack."

Within minutes, two senior agents and four specialists had taken over the Petrov case. Agents Edgar and Dover were still helping in Champaign, but they were now on a short leash. There were no indications of where Yuri Petrov was, but the FBI had spread its net, and Zack Broca knew it would not be long before the suspect made a mistake.

15

Yuri passed up the taxi stand at the Milwaukee train station and walked four blocks to a hotel where he found a taxi waiting. With his hat on and head held down as if Yuri were reading something in his lap, the driver could not see Yuri's face for the entire thirty-minute drive to the Lakewood Bed and Breakfast Inn just south of Port Washington, Wisconsin. Yuri said little and gave the driver a tip that would not be remembered as being large or small. Yuri walked toward the Lakewood Inn, but as soon as the taxi left, he turned and walked down the road, glancing at a map he had handwritten while he was at the Internet terminal on the train. He walked nearly a mile before he rang the doorbell on a well-kept ranch-style house with large picture windows shaded by a pair of majestic maple trees.

"Yuriii!" shrieked Julie when she opened the door. "My goodness, I didn't know you were coming." She seemed happy, but her excitement made it hard to be sure.

"Your postcard said 'come any time.' I hope this is a good time."

"Sure. Come in, come in."

"I guess I should have called ahead to let you know I wanted to visit."

"Now is fine, but why the surprise visit?"

"I suddenly realized that the next two weeks are the only openings on my calendar to use up my remaining vacation days for the year. Helmholtz does not allow us to carry over unused vacation days, so it's use 'em or lose 'em. Port Washington looks so nice in your postcard that I decided to come here. If this is inconvenient, I could stay at an inn nearby."

"Oh, no. I wouldn't have my savior staying anywhere else. It'll be fun to explore the local sights with you and cook for you. Oh, Yuri. I shall feed you until you beg for mercy." Julie's emotions seemed to be racing ahead, and Yuri hoped she would not misinterpret his intentions.

"So it will be a contest of my stomach against your culinary skills. Perhaps I should surrender now?"

"I'm working six days a week, so you'll be on your own a lot."

"That's fine; I brought my notebook computer. I have begun a new project and will need much time for work."

"You're a workaholic, Yuri. You're on vacation. Remember?"

"Well, this is not official work; it is more like hobby work."

"You're hopeless. Sometimes I think you are half computer. We must celebrate your visit."

Julie sat him down at the kitchen table and told him about her adventures as a chef at the fine restaurant while she prepared a Champagne Flamingo cocktail by mixing chilled champagne, vodka, and campari. She continued to chat as she pulled out a large skillet and a mixing bowl.

"I already had dinner. Please don't bother cooking anything," urged Yuri.

"Did you have dessert?" she said temptingly.

"No, but this champagne cocktail is fine."

"Well, I need some dessert, and I bet you can't say no to chocolate hazelnut-filled crêpes." She was right; Yuri could not say no.

They ate in the family room, and Yuri noticed the teaching machine was paused in the middle of a program. Yuri gestured toward the teaching machine. "Did I interrupt a lesson?"

"No—well, I was just playing an adventure game." Julie laughed lightly to herself. "I play the head chef in the court of King Louis XVI of France."

"You spend too much time with teaching machines. You need the company of real people."

Julie shook her head. "You're the same old Yuri, always speaking of the evils of teaching machines. Why do you work on the technology if you think it's so bad?"

"My concern is the loss of human interaction," lectured Yuri. "Teaching machines have greatly improved education, but they are overused. The technology offers many benefits if used properly. For example, it has improved public health while reducing the cost of healthcare. The brain scans not only detect and diagnose brain disorders, but also a large number of maladies throughout the body are detectable via their influence on the nervous system. Everyone has an extensive monthly medical exam performed simply by running a diagnostic program on their teaching machine at home or a nearby clinic. The treatments of some conditions, such as diabetes, are greatly aided by daily monitoring and behavioral training with a teaching machine."

"Don't forget, with the exception of a rare handful of people..." Julie gave Yuri a piercing look "...virtual hypnosis has eliminated the public health menaces of smoking, drug abuse, and alcoholism."

"With the amount of champagne we are drinking, we both may need help," quipped Yuri.

Julie chuckled and then continued, "Don't worry, I have a medkit." She pointed to a green box near the door of her home. Like most homes, the medkit contained an electronic defibrillator, emergency drugs, bandages, and oxygen. "Have you taken the emergency medical course on a teaching machine?"

"Not yet. I really should get to it." For someone who worked so much on the technology, Yuri had an ironic lack of interest in using teaching machines himself.

"Yes, you should. I took my emergency medical procedures refresher course just last week."

After Julie showed Yuri around the house and where his bedroom was, he slipped out to the backyard for a relaxing cigarette in the cool night. He was getting low on cigarettes and would need to buy more tomorrow. The backyard patio offered a serene view of Lake Michigan where a sailboat was headed toward Port Washington.

———

They spoke in intimate whispers about what they would do the next day. There were shopping and simple cleaning chores that he gladly volunteered to do. She lay next to him, soft, warm, willing, and familiar. Her little squeaks and purring sounds told him that he pleased her. He never ceased to be amazed that such a wonderful woman would find him attractive. She accepted him as he was: a short, overweight, nerdy professor who smoked. She was a refuge from a world that treated him as an outcast. He wrapped an arm around her, but as he pulled her closer, there was something wrong. She was as pleasant as ever, but he did not feel right. She was perfect, but there was something wrong with him. What could be wrong when he was holding her in his arms? He had been here before, but this time it was not real; something was false. Why could he not enjoy being with her?

Yuri woke in a cold sweat alone in bed and realized that he had been dreaming of his dead wife again. It hurt as much as ever.

———

The Coordinated Science Lab was abuzz about Yuri. Susan Hebb was disturbed by all of the talk about FBI agents, espionage, and reports that Yuri had crashed the Sellco computer network. These bigots took any opportunity to show their superiority over old-school people. Yuri's guarded talk of a widespread evil plot sparked Susan's curiosity. What did Yuri know about this plot, and what had he found in the Sellco computers? Where was Yuri and what was he planning to do? Since they had worked together, Susan had the door lock codes for Yuri's office and laboratory. Her search of Yuri's laboratory yielded nothing. Her limited computer skills and Yuri's habitual tight security on all of his computers kept her out of them. In Yuri's desk she found a copy of the research contract Yuri had recently signed with Sellco. The contract, worded in general terms such as "confidential computer-based advertising techniques," provided little insight. The terms for nondisclosure and an expert panel to study advertising ethics raised more questions but provided fewer answers. It seemed that Yuri had been secretly working with Sellco, but had the deal gone sour?

As she searched his office, she noticed the magnet sitting in an empty space on the cabinet and recalled the postcard from Julie.

———

"How long will you be here?" asked Julie, as she prepared a mushroom and cheddar omelet for breakfast.

"About ten days, but if that is inconvenient, please let me know. I could stay elsewhere," said Yuri, nibbling a warm, freshly baked scone spread with lemon cream.

"You're welcome to stay as long as you want. Feel free to come and go as you wish," she offered, handing him a spare key to the house. "I work from two to eleven most days, but I have Wednesday off this week. We could charter a boat to go sailing on the lake."

Yuri was more interested in staying out of sight and devising plans, but he knew that he must maintain the appearance of being on vacation. "No sailing for me, thank you. I get seasick easily. Maybe a simple tour by car is better for me."

Yuri insisted on cleaning the dishes after breakfast. He had to do something in return for Julie's extraordinary hospitality. Julie said good-bye and drove to work.

Now that he was safe, Yuri could concentrate on his dilemma. He was on his own since he refused to place anyone else at risk of aiding a person wanted by the FBI. He regretted keeping the true purpose of his visit secret from Julie, but he had no choice. All of his thoughts revolved around developing a plan to expose Sellco's subliminal advertising and its use by the White House to turn the United States into an oligarchy. He was sure that Sellco and the White House had covered up any evidence.

Yuri recognized the situation from the game of chess. This was a stalemate, and he needed to force his opponent to make a bad move. Since they knew he was the only one aware of their secret, the only solution was to fake his own death. Then they would feel safe enough to resume the subliminal advertising and thus expose the evidence he needed. Yuri went through several cigarettes contemplating how to convincingly fake his own death and how to remain undercover afterward. The cigarettes calmed him better than anything else.

As the number of cigarettes in his last pack diminished, Yuri's anxiety grew and so did his need for another smoke. Using Julie's computer, he ordered six cartons of cigarettes from his web merchant for express delivery tomorrow afternoon. Meanwhile, he kept out of sight and began growing a beard to make him harder to recognize.

Julie's suggestion that morning of sailing on Lake Michigan had meandered through Yuri's brain and eventually blossomed into a plan to fake his death by leaving a suicide note and making it appear that he had jumped overboard while taking a ferry across Lake Michigan. He found on the Internet where he could buy a mannequin and a rubber mask made to match a set of photographs. The mannequin would be weighted to sink in the water, and he would arrange for a witness to see the fake Yuri fall off the ferry. Any investigation of the death should not find the connection to the company that made the custom face mask, since the company was located in Mexico. Yuri was not entirely pleased with his plan, but it was the best he had for now, and he might come up with something better after more thought. He had yet to work out the more difficult part of the plan, including where to remain hidden long-term and how to take legal action against Sellco and the White House administration while supposedly dead.

He spent much of the day on the Internet learning about aspects of the law pertaining to espionage, wills, and estates. He used Julie's computer, since he was taking no chance of his computer's identity being detected on the Internet.

—■—

After Kent Fechner received the text message from Alfred Grossberg relaying Yuri Petrov's location, he called Sellco flight operations and asked for a corporate jet to prepare for flight. Professor Petrov had made the mistake of ordering cigarettes using his web merchant account and providing an address for delivery. Kent had developed a flawless plan to eliminate Yuri Petrov and was ready to act the instant he received the message from Alfred Grossberg. Secrecy was vital to the plan. According to Kent's own rules of conduct, anything was allowed if one was not caught. He would not be caught if no one knew, and the only way to ensure that no one knew was to do the job himself.

Once the Sellco jet reached cruising altitude, Kent sipped a glass of chilled Perrier water with a slice of lime and no ice. He reveled in the relaxing absence of the advertising that annoyed passengers on commercial flights. While the word *commercial* supposedly meant that the seats on the flights were for sale to the public, the word could also describe the ceaseless onslaught of audio and video commercials that passengers had no choice but to view as they were strapped into their cramped seats.

Kent ordered the copilot to reserve a rental car at their destination airport. He made sure that the car was reserved in the copilot's name, not his. As another degree of anonymity, the jet was reserved in the name of Miles Huxley. As part of his plan, Kent had prepared a "ready bag" with everything he would need. He was filled with calm anticipation as he contemplated his plan to kill the meddlesome professor. After taking another sip of water, he napped as the jet streaked toward Milwaukee. Upon arrival in Milwaukee, the copilot picked up the rental car and handed it over to him at the terminal.

The FBI report forwarded by Alfred Grossberg had been quite thorough. It gave the address of Julie Mountcastle's parents' summer home where she now lived, where she worked, and what hours she worked. Kent slowly drove by the house twice to get a good view of the area and then found an inconspicuous place to park less than a block away that offered a clear view of the house. As requested, there was no sign of FBI agents in the area. His parking place was near a public park, so no one would question someone sitting in a parked car reading a newspaper. Still, Kent was glad that he did not have to keep up the ruse of reading the paper for too long. He observed a young woman in a car leave the house a little over an hour before the time the FBI report stated that she started work. She would be gone for the rest of the day, and Yuri Petrov would be alone. To be sure to catch Petrov before he might go on some errand, Kent went to the house as soon as Miss Mountcastle had left for work.

Kent wore uncharacteristically common clothes and a large badge saying "Computer World Tech Team—my name is KENT," as he rang the doorbell. Professor Petrov opened the door and gazed up. Kent glanced at a paper in his hands and did his best to impersonate a simpleminded hourly worker. "Is Julie Mountcastle home?"

"No, she just left for work," rebuffed Professor Petrov, blocking entry to the house.

He showed the paper to Petrov. "She has a service contract with Computer World, and I'm here to install a software update on her computer. Would you show me where her computer is?"

"Can't you do software maintenance remotely via the Internet?"

Kent improvised. "Yeah, I tried, but it seems there is something connected to the computer that's interfering with the update." Professor Petrov still seemed reluctant. "I will be out of town for the next few days, so it would be great if I could do it now."

Hesitantly, Professor Petrov let him in and led the way to the computer in the family room. Kent followed him, reaching into a pocket. Petrov turned around and gasped in shock at seeing a nine-millimeter pistol pointed between his eyes.

"Sit down in that chair, now," Kent ordered firmly, gesturing to a chair next to a teaching machine.

The color drained from Petrov's face as he sat down.

"If you stand up, I'll kill you without hesitation," Kent said coldly.

———

Yuri was a man of methodical plans, not reckless action. He sat down with his eyes fixed on the gun. Reflex-driven surprise gave way to gut-churning fear. He forced his eyes to scan the room, desperately looking for an escape route, a weapon, or an inspiration. The only thing within reach was an afghan-style blanket, which was worthless both tactically and artistically. The intruder's tone of voice and manners left no doubt that the man holding the gun was dangerous.

The man reached into his duffel bag. He did not look like a person who could be outwitted easily and certainly was not acting like a FBI agent. In fact, he seemed to be quite intelligent and to know exactly what he was doing. He was wearing expensive leather gloves, which scared Yuri more than the gun pointed at his head. The gloves meant that this man was prepared to use the gun and leave no fingerprints. The man's steel-gray eyes showed confidence and enjoyment, which deeply disturbed Yuri.

"Who are you and what are you doing here?"

"I shall be asking the questions, Professor Petrov. You know too much already."

This man knew his name. This was not a random robbery; the man had come specifically for Yuri. Had he come to kill him? "Are you from Sellco?"

"You're a curious one, aren't you? I must give you credit for cracking our subliminal advertising program. We had two top experts try for six months to crack that system, and they never got close. Also, you hacked into the Sellco corporate network. Our network managers said it was an artful bit of hacking. You have great skill, Professor Petrov, but you lack the judgment to keep your nose out of other people's business."

"You have great power, but you lack the ethics to use it wisely," Yuri sneered.

"I have the power to solve your problems and mine. You know too much, but I can fix this." The man inserted a memory card into the teaching machine and executed a program. "Put the teaching machine helmet on and I'll ask you some questions to find out how much you know. Then we can erase the secrets and our problems will be solved."

As he put on the helmet, Yuri wondered how the secrets could be erased. Then he noticed the program running on the teaching machine. The display format of the program was identical to the lie detector program that Yuri had mothballed two years ago. However, he had used the same standard graphic display software tools that anyone else would have used. The display of all programs that used the standard software tools tended to look the same.

"Is that a lie detector program?" asked Yuri.

"Yes, it is, so tell the truth." The man emphasized his point by centering the gun between Yuri's eyes.

"Where did you get that program?" asked Yuri, doubting he would receive an answer. He needed a strategy to gain control of the situation. He needed something better than asking dead-end questions.

The gun callously pointed at his head dispelled Yuri's usual self-assurance. In the next critical moment, he could lose his life or he could grasp victory against Sellco. Heroic action was needed, but what could he do? He had no experience with martial arts, and even if he had, it would be hopeless. The man was staying too far away for Yuri to grab the gun. Yuri worried that his fear had made him too scatterbrained to find a solution. Playing along to buy time was the only course he could think of.

"I'm asking the questions today," insisted the man, looking down his nose at Yuri. "Have you told anyone about the subliminal programming?"

"No." The man glanced at the teaching machine's display, and the program indicated truth.

"Have you left any notes about the subliminal advertising or sent messages to anyone about it?"

"No; I didn't want to get anyone else in trouble."

"Smart move, professor."

"Do you know of any way that someone else might learn of Sellco's subliminal advertising activities?"

"No. The most likely risk to your program is that you will overuse it, and someone will investigate why certain products sell so well."

"Yes," the man said dismissively, glancing at the teaching machine. "We're well aware of that risk. What did you learn when you hacked into the Sellco network?"

"I confirmed that Sellco was behind the subliminal advertising. You have removed all traces of the advertising for now, but you plan to resume with messages that say subliminal advertising is harmless. You also plan to run ads to help the Sherrington administration to gain approval for its nominee to the Supreme Court. You are aiding the destruction of democracy in America." Yuri suppressed his anger at Sellco and focused his consciousness on the words he spoke to keep his mind from wandering into what he had not said. He knew that a person could hide information from the lie detector program he had developed. If one kept one's thoughts away from the hidden information, the lie detector program indicated truth with some minor instability in the secondary indicators. This program was behaving exactly like Yuri's program; this made him more suspicious than ever that the man from Sellco had somehow obtained a copy of the program that Yuri had placed in his private archive.

"Another mistake, professor," the man said pompously. "With my help, the Sherrington administration is doing what's necessary to protect our country." The man sneered, "Of course, an old-school person like you wouldn't understand." He pulled a bottle with a clear liquid and a glass out of his bag. "The solution to our problems is in this bottle. This will alter your brain chemistry so that you will permanently forget each memory that I trigger with my questions during the next hour. Drink this, and then I will ask you a series of questions to make sure you forget."

Yuri had never heard of such a "forgetting drug," but Sellco seemed to have access to the most advanced science. "I won't drink it. I don't trust you."

"You can trust me to make you forget one way or another." The man moved the gun a bit closer. "I have no qualms about shooting you right now. There will be no further discussion; pour the solution into the glass and drink it now."

Yuri was afraid of the damage the chemical solution might do to his brain. The man's finger tightened on the trigger, and it looked like he was going to fire. Frightened into action, Yuri decided that drinking the solution was better than a bullet in the head. He poured the liquid into the glass and tasted it. "This tastes like vodka; what is it?"

"Drink it all. No more discussion."

It was top-grade vodka; Yuri drank it all.

"Let me remind you to remain seated. Take the helmet off." The man remained at a safe distance with the gun pointed at Yuri.

Yuri took off the helmet and noticed that he felt a bit woozy. This was odd because Yuri usually held his liquor well. The man glanced at his watch and then a smug, satisfied look grew as he silently gazed at Yuri.

"So when are you going to ask me the questions?" asked Yuri, his voice slurred.

The man glanced at his watch again and smiled briefly. "Since you are a Russian, I thought you would appreciate the finest vodka." He took the empty bottle from the table, stowed it in his bag, and replaced it with a partly empty bottle of vodka from his bag. "Have some more vodka. I insist."

Yuri was groggy, dizzy, and not thinking clearly. He poured the vodka into the glass, spilling some in the process. His head lolled as he wondered why he felt so sleepy.

———

Kent looked down at the foolish, weak professor. This had been so easy; he had expected there to be more sport to it. He took a bottle of Valium from his bag and placed it next to the vodka. "The cocktail you enjoyed was a mixture of Valium and vodka. It's interesting that an overdose of Valium is harmless, but it is quite lethal mixed with alcohol as in the mixture you just drank."

Once Petrov passed out, Kent took the bottle of Valium and pressed Petrov's fingers on it. Now only Petrov's fingerprints were on the glass, vodka, and Valium.

Kent had decided to not attempt a fake suicide note. It was best to keep it simple. He looked about the room to assure that everything was where it should be. He noticed that he had almost forgotten to retrieve the memory card attached to the teaching machine; that went into his bag. He waited a few minutes and looked at his watch. According to his research, Petrov should be dead by now. Kent observed no sign of life; it was time to leave. He had never killed before and was exhilarated by the feeling of power it gave him. He leaned closer and heard no breathing, but to his horror he did hear a deep rumbling sound coming from the garage. The garage door opener was operating, which could only mean that the owner was returning home much earlier than expected.

Kent had accomplished what was needed and realized that he could quickly slip out the front door while the owner entered from the garage. He grabbed his bag and timed his escape perfectly. Relieved, he drove directly to the airport for his return home.

16

Julie had stopped at a store on the way to work to buy a pair of shoes when her cell phone rang. To avoid the cost of a failed delivery attempt, FedEx always called the customer's cell phone before attempting to make a delivery that required a signature. She was only ten minutes from home, so she told FedEx to go ahead with the delivery. There was no answer when she tried to call Yuri's mobile phone, so she zipped home to meet the delivery truck.

At first she thought that Yuri had fallen asleep, but then she noticed the vodka bottle, the Valium pills, and the spilled liquor. She saw that Yuri was not breathing and his skin was deathly white. Yuri had killed himself. Why?

After a moment of shock, Julie's emergency medical training kicked in. There was no pulse at the wrist. In desperation she checked the neck and thought she felt a faint pulse. Yes, there was a pulse. She put her ear right next to his nose. She detected the hint of a shallow breath, but then it stopped.

Julie had taken the emergency medical refresher course on the teaching machine only a week ago. The standard procedure in this situation called for a dextrose intravenous drip in case the person was in diabetic shock. She did not recall Yuri being diabetic and did not have dextrose solution at hand anyway. The second step in the standard procedure called for an intravenous injection of Narcan to counteract a possible narcotic overdose. Julie ran to get the medkit, which contained a single-use syringe of Narcan, but before she injected the Narcan, she glanced again at the bottle of Valium. Yuri would be dead in seconds. There was no time for the standard treatment protocol, and there certainly was no time to call for an ambulance. She grabbed the syringe of Romazicon and prayed that Yuri really had taken a depressant overdose as she injected him. Julie dragged Yuri to the floor and desperately began to perform CPR.

The Romazicon acted quickly, and Yuri woke when Julie's mouth was firmly pressed against his.

"You just can't resist kissing me," said Yuri, his voice slurred.

"I thought you were dead," said Julie, exasperated. Then she did kiss him.

"I feel terrible. What happened?"

"You tell me, Yuri," replied Julie, perplexed. Pointing at the vodka and Valium, she asked incredulously, "Did you try to kill yourself?"

Yuri swayed as he tried to sit up. He seemed groggy as he spoke slowly. "I have not been open with you, Julie. I came here to hide from some bad people. One of them found me and forced me to drink the vodka and Valium to make it look like I had killed myself." He shook his head to clear his thoughts, but it just made him dizzy. "I didn't want you to become involved with these bad people, so I had to keep this from you. How did you revive me?"

"I got a call from FedEx about the delivery of your cigarettes, so I came home to meet the delivery truck. I found you nearly dead and gave you a shot of Romazicon from the emergency medkit. Who are these bad people?"

"It would be dangerous for you to know more," warned Yuri, seeming more alert. "Just know that I am innocent and that I must leave right now before they come back. Please help me pack my bag and get it in the car."

Julie tried to tell Yuri that he should see a doctor and call the police, but there was no dissuading Yuri from his insistence that he leave immediately. He was still dizzy when he got into the car, and Julie put the bag in the trunk. As Julie pulled out of the driveway, she saw the FedEx truck pulling up to the house.

Yuri looked at the truck. "That must be delivering the cigarettes I ordered."

Julie stopped the car. "It'll take just a minute to get your package."

"No, don't stop. We must go to downtown Port Washington right now," he urged with excruciating regret.

If there had been any doubt, now Julie knew how scared Yuri was. Yuri cast a longing look at the truck as they drove off.

"We should report this to the police," repeated Julie.

"Can I ask a favor of you? Could you please wait until tonight before talking to the police? I do not trust the police, so I need a little time to get away. You could say that you suspected it was a suicide attempt, but I told a doubtful story about a murder attempt by someone you never saw. After you had thought about it for a few hours, you decided that you should contact the police. I am not asking you to lie, just think about it for a few hours."

"OK." Julie was worried, but she trusted Yuri.

———

Yuri asked Julie to drop him at a used-car dealer in downtown Port Washington. He thanked her profusely for everything and told her that for her safety he could not tell her anything and that she should go to work before she was late. It took some convincing, but eventually she left him. He was still a bit foggy but feeling a little stronger.

A salesman was eagerly eyeing him from the used-car dealer's office, but Yuri was in no mood to talk with him. As soon as Julie was out of sight, he slowly and unsteadily walked down the sidewalk with the wheeled bag following behind him. He lit up his last cigarette and felt better. Tossing the empty cigarette package in a trash can, he savored every puff; there was no telling when he would find another smoke.

The depth of the problem was sinking in. Not only was the FBI searching for him, but also the man from Sellco meant to kill him. How had they found his hiding place?

Near the harbor, he asked a woman sitting on a bench about chartering a boat. She did not know about chartering boats but suggested he talk to the people who were busy on a large sailboat a few slips down the pier. A man in his mid-seventies and a girl about fifteen were on the boat; it looked like they were getting ready for departure. The man's full head of flowing white hair was a sharp contrast to his dark, weathered complexion. He was fit and trim—no doubt he used Xarim.

Yuri walked up to the sailboat and called out, "Hello! Can you tell me where I can charter a boat?"

The old man stepped closer and put a hand to one ear. "My hearing isn't what it used to be."

Yuri repeated his question more loudly.

"You want to go fishing or just a sightseeing tour?" the old man asked kindly.

"I would like go south. Maybe Milwaukee."

The old man nodded as he considered this. "I was just about to take my granddaughter out for a couple of days to teach her about sailing. We were fixin' to sail to Chicago, where I'll show my granddaughter some places I know."

"Yes, Chicago would be fine for me."

"Can you afford fifty dollars for the trip?"

"Yes. I can pay cash." Yuri would have gladly paid much more for transportation that would never be traced.

"My name is Larry, and this is my granddaughter Nicole. Come aboard."

"Thank you; I am Peter." Peter was close to Yuri's father's name, Pyotr.

Larry helped Yuri to haul his bag on board and stowed it in the cabin. "Have you sailed much?" asked Larry.

"No. I have never been sailing. It will be nice to see what it is like to calmly float along with the wind."

"This is nothing like a hot-air balloon, mate. It'll be a good deal more exciting. There is a stiff wind today that'll make for fast sailing. Have a seat right over there." Larry pointed to a place near the aft of the cockpit, close to where Larry was sitting at the stern. "Stay seated. We wouldn't want you to fall overboard when we come about."

Before Yuri could have second thoughts about his mode of transport, Larry called out to Nicole to let go of the lines and haul in the fenders. They moved slowly away from the dock and through the calm waters of the harbor powered by an electric motor driving the propeller. With the high price of fuel, sailing had become more popular. Power boating was reserved for people who needed to prove that they had money to burn. Like most modern sailboats, Larry's craft had solar cells to recharge a large electric battery for the electric motor, lights, and electronics on board.

The waves grew as they left the harbor. Larry sat at the stern of the boat, which formed a broad curved arch that allowed the helmsman to remain seated while the boat heeled. The large wheel before Larry controlled the rudder. Many controls were within easy reach of the helmsman, including the stereo where

Larry turned up the volume to better hear AC/DC playing "Overdose."

The waves hit as they left the harbor. The boat rocked and rolled. Larry shouted directions to Nicole, who seemed to enjoy darting about working the rigging to trim the mainsail and the jib. She had clearly done this before.

Yuri held on as the sloop wildly moved about every axis of rotation in seemingly random movements. Sailing was nothing like he had expected, and Yuri's sixth sense was disturbed. The vestibular system in his inner ear was reeling from the relentless rocking of the boat. Waves of nausea flowed through him. He took deep, steady breaths and focused on the horizon. "*Nu kogda je eto konchitsa eta chertova boltanka?* When will this damn rocking end?" grumbled Yuri. Yuri was losing the battle against the tossing motion and the aftereffects of the drugs. His stomach was lurching. He leaned over the side and retched.

"Sorry, I have trouble with motion sickness," Yuri apologized.

"That's OK," replied Larry kindly. "It is kind of rough today. Don't worry; the boat will settle down once we get up to speed on a steady course." Larry reached into a cooler and handed a beer to Yuri. "Here, this'll help to get the taste out of your mouth."

After the vodka, the Valium, the drug injected by Julie, and the seasickness, Yuri had no desire for a beer. "Would you have something without alcohol?"

"Sure; I brought Pepsi for Nicole."

As Yuri took the Pepsi, his mind wandered back to the subliminal advertisement, "Pepsi makes you sexy." Right now Yuri did not feel sexy.

Larry instructed Nicole to adjust the sails for beam reaching, and then he showed her how to read the rows of telltales on the jib to adjust the sails for maximum speed. They were moving fast through the waves. As Larry had promised, the motion of the boat changed to a more tolerable steady rocking. As the bow punched through a large wave, a fine spray flew back to the cockpit. They raced before the freshening wind as the waves grew larger. Six smaller sailboats, headed for Port Washington's harbor, passed by them going the opposite direction.

Larry pointed at the smaller sailboats. "They are headed for the harbor because the weather service just issued a near-shore small craft advisory." He added derisively, "Those auto-sailboats can't handle these conditions."

Yuri looked up at the sails stretched drum-tight in the strong wind, wondering if they might rip. The fearsome forces at work astonished him. He could see the mast flex with the gusts of wind. The sailboat was moving even faster, and he could feel the pounding impact on his rump as each large wave slammed into the hull. Could the hull withstand this punishment?

To adjust the weight in the boat, Larry asked Yuri to move to the starboard side. With the boat leaning, Yuri awkwardly crawled to the other side. Larry shouted to Nicole, "Coming about." Then he spun the wheel and the boom suddenly swung over, missing Yuri's head by a few centimeters. Yuri clung to the side of the boat as it heeled over hard and seemed to be on the verge of tipping over. Would one of the larger waves capsize the boat? The seasickness was gone, replaced by the mortal fear that the boat would be torn apart. Inexplicably, Larry seemed to relish the experience as he nodded in time to the pounding music.

"Can the sails and hull withstand these conditions?" asked Yuri, on the verge of terror.

"Don't worry about *Reincarnation*," Larry chuckled. "She hasn't even worked up a sweat yet." Yuri had noticed the name *Reincarnation* on the back of the boat before he had boarded. "The hull and mast are continuous carbon nanotube; it's inde-structible. The sails are Kyzan. They can take much worse than this." Yuri looked up again at the brilliantly white billowing sails. One-meter tall red letters proclaimed, "Kyzan fabric from Dupont." Dupont Corporation had contributed yet another word to the English language.

Larry continued, "These conditions are what *Reincarnation* was built for—real sailing. She has a deeper draft and broader beam than those auto-sailboats, which have to turn tail just when the sailing gets fun."

The sailboat continued to furiously plow through the waves as Yuri asked, "What are the auto-sailboats good for?"

"They are for young folks who used to have power boats but can't afford the gas anymore. The auto-sailboats have computer-controlled servomotors to adjust all of the lines. You never have to touch a sail, a line, or even the tiller. It's a sailboat for folks who don't know how to sail. Everything's controlled by a computer. You just enter a destination into the navigation system, and the computer figures out how to trim the sails and steer the rudder to get you there. An anemometer tells the computer the wind speed and direction. It uses GPS navigation and radar to avoid other boats. The computer will use the hybrid electric/gas motor when necessary. The auto-sailboats are even programmed to return to port when a radio warning is issued by the weather service. They're designed for speed in moderate conditions, but they're useless when there is enough wind for serious sailing."

Having concluded that the boat was not about to tear itself apart, Yuri felt better. "Where does the name *Reincarnation* come from?"

"When I die," Larry said wistfully, "I want to come back as a sailboat. A real sailboat like this one, sailed by someone who lets her stretch her legs."

After a while, Yuri noticed something a great distance away. "What is that on the horizon?"

Larry squinted. "I can't see like I could when I was young. I don't recommend getting old. Even my sense of taste has gone flat." Larry took a swig of beer, glanced at the navigation system, and pointed. "Chicago is about forty kilometers that way. I bet that's what you see." Larry must have noticed Yuri's accent; he asked, "What country are you from?"

"Russia."

"Why did you come here?"

"Five hundred billion dollars is hard to resist."

Larry arched his eyebrows. "Maybe I should charge you more for the ride to Chicago."

"Five hundred billion dollars is the combined amount of the endowment funds for all of the universities in the United States. No other country has even a tenth of this amount. When teaching machines put teachers and classrooms out of business, most of that money was put to work funding university research. The research funds created a second renaissance that attracts the brightest minds of the world to America, where they have the best facilities and the greatest academic freedom in the world."

"So how much of that five hundred billion did you get?"

"This year, my research budget is about two million dollars. My university salary is modest, but I have no complaints."

"Are you machine-taught or an old-schooler like me?"

"I was taught by humans. There are no teaching machines in Russia."

"I'm not sure these teaching machines are as great as most people think. That's why I spend much of my time teaching my grandchildren about my two hobbies: sailing and art. These youngsters benefit from some real teaching and getting away from those teaching machines."

"I think you are correct. Teaching machines are useful, but they are used too much. Children learn social skills and creativity from interacting with other children and human teachers."

"The younger generation is too selfish and they lack good principles. I wonder if they get this from the teaching machines." Larry turned to Nicole and said consolingly, "I'm not talking about you, dear. Your parents are raising you right, making sure you get some real teaching."

"Yeah," agreed Nicole, "Mom's told me a zillion times how lucky I am for the time you spend with me. I like how you spoil me."

Larry winked at Nicole. "Ah, but there are some important lessons hiding under the sugar coating."

Yuri was pondering the poor ethics exhibited by Hamilton von Helmholtz and the people at Sellco when Larry turned to him. "We see a lack of principles in the power-hungry government in Washington. They talk about defending democracy as they undermine it. They are making our country a police state, and yet the people show no concern. Why are the voters so blind?"

Yuri thought he knew the answer, but he only dared to say, "The politicians are very skillful, are they not?"

"You and I think very differently than the young folks. You see how they treat old-school people like dangerous aliens. They don't trust us because we don't fit into their homogeneous society."

"Hey, Gramps," Nicole shouted from the front of the boat. "There's a boat coming this way fast."

Larry shielded his eyes with one hand, squinting. "Looks like a big power boat. Don't see many of those anymore. What kinda boat is it?"

"It's a coast guard patrol boat; it'll be here in a minute."

Yuri's pulse quickened. Were they looking for him? To hide from view, he leaned over and put his head between his legs.

"Feeling sick again?" asked Larry.

Yuri was sick with worry, not seasick. He groaned and waved off Larry with his head still held low. The coast guard boat roared past without slowing and quickly went away. The sailboat rocked wildly in the wake of the other boat and Yuri was nearly seasick again. Yuri looked up and was relieved to see the coast guard boat far away.

"I wonder," said Larry, getting back to their conversation, "if the US government paid for the development of the teaching machines."

"Yes," answered Yuri. "It was funded by DARPA."

"DARPA?" asked Nicole, sitting down cross-legged on the deck between Yuri and Larry. It had been a long time since Yuri had had the flexibility to sit like that.

"DARPA," Yuri lectured, "is the US government's Defense Advanced Research Projects Agency. Long ago, DARPA also funded the early research that originally led to the creation of the Internet. In that case, DARPA was looking for a resilient nationwide communications network that would keep working even if half of the network nodes were destroyed during a thermonuclear war. In the case of teaching machines, DARPA was looking for a better way to train soldiers. Like the Internet, it worked out better than they had imagined."

"Yeah," said Larry, taking over the lecture. "The new teaching machines were first used by the US military to train soldiers to operate any weapons system and use any tactics. The soldiers are competent, loyal, and fearsome warriors. The United States' armed forces are the best trained and disciplined in the world. It's a huge strategic advantage, and unlike some advanced weapon systems, this advantage is politically safe to use. Of course, there were detractors who claimed that the new military training was brainwashing the soldiers to become mindless androids. The military countered with a brilliant advertising campaign showing how compassionate, thoughtful, and happy the soldiers are."

"Wow, that's great," said Nicole.

"That depends on where you live," warned Yuri. "Since the use of teaching machines proved to be a strategic military advantage, export of the teaching machines and the related technology is strictly prohibited. To prevent software piracy and to protect against illegal export of the teaching machines, critical software modules are not located in the teaching machine; they reside in a secure server located in Richardson, Texas. A teaching machine must be connected to the Internet and have an authorized registration to access the software. While the US experienced its revolution in education and the related secondary benefits such as increased funding for research and reduced unemployment, other nations were quickly falling behind economically and politically."

"So what's the problem?" asked Nicole.

"The brightest minds in the world are irresistibly attracted to the 'land of opportunity.' The standard of living in the US continues to improve, while in most countries it grows worse each year. The growing disparity between the 'haves' and the 'have-nots' will eventually lead to a war of desperation with adversaries who have nothing to lose."

"What should we do?" asked Nicole.

"I wish I knew," lamented Yuri. "I do know that the Sherrington administration's solution of building stronger walls around the US will fail eventually."

"A sobering lesson, dear," agreed Larry, finishing a bottle of beer. "In sailing you learn that the only solution to being on the leeward side of a shoal in a gale is to not be there in the first place."

The imperial skyline of Chicago loomed before them. "We will moor at Montrose Harbor until tomorrow afternoon," said Larry. "Do you need a place to sleep overnight?"

Yuri had planned to ask a professor he knew at Northwestern University in Chicago if he could stay at his house. However, he was rapidly becoming less sanguine about visiting known friends. "I had made no reservations. Will you stay overnight in this boat?"

"Yes. We have two cabins below. There are two bunks in the cabin where I'll sleep, so you are welcome to stay overnight if you can tolerate my snoring." It seemed that Larry would be pleased to have more time with a fellow old-schooler.

"That would be very nice. How long will you be in Chicago?"

"We'll leave tomorrow, right after lunch. I know a nice restaurant near Montrose Harbor. Would you like to join us for dinner?"

"Yes, if you will allow me to pay for dinner for you and your granddaughter."

"A fair deal."

They dropped the sails and entered Montrose Harbor. As soon as the sailboat passed the breakwater, the rocking subsided and Yuri relaxed his grip on the boat's coaming. They moored at a place that Larry had reserved when he had called the harbormaster earlier. The harbor tender took them to the shore, and Yuri resisted the temptation to kiss the ground as he stepped upon the steady shore.

———

The *Dockside Diner* overlooked Montrose Harbor. Its nautical theme, good food, and reasonable prices attracted many people from the harbor, though it was not elegant. The menus featured a large advertisement for Coke, the paper napkins were printed with an advertisement for Budweiser, and each table consisted of a large video panel with a glass top, showing a series of advertisements with occasional one-minute news or weather briefs.

They sat down in a booth, and Nicole gave a disapproving shake of her head as both Yuri and Larry simultaneously spread out several paper napkins on the tabletop, unprinted side up, to cover up the frenetic video advertisements. The waiter seemed to recognize Larry and gave a friendly wave.

They ordered hamburgers, which arrived with laser-inscribed buns proclaiming, "Make it a Buddy Burger with Buddy Ketchup."

During dinner, Yuri's craving for a cigarette became stronger than ever. Yuri mentioned that he smoked and had run out of cigarettes, half hoping that Larry might be a one-in-a-million smoker too.

"I quit smoking ten years ago," said Larry. "Just as well; nobody sells cigarettes anymore. The only time I used a teaching machine was when my doctor told me to use the virtual hypnosis program. That program was downright scary; it brainwashed me right into never wanting a cigarette again. If it can do that, it makes you wonder what else those teaching machines could make people believe. After that, I never trusted teaching machines."

The discussion of smoking was not helping Yuri's craving, so he changed the topic. "Have you spent much time in Chicago?"

"I lived in Chicago and worked as a stock trader at the Chicago Board of Trade for twenty years. It was an exciting job, and I made enough to comfortably retire at age forty-five. Then I was free to pursue my hobbies. I taught painting at the School of the Art Institute for twenty years. I was amazed how much I learned from my students. It is one of the few schools in America that continue to this day to have human teachers in every subject. They make only limited use of teaching machines."

"That is the way teaching machines should be used: as an aid to a primarily human-taught classroom," interjected Yuri.

"I plan to show Nicole around the Art Institute tomorrow morning. Would'ya like to join us?"

Yuri had more pressing matters on his mind, but politeness demanded that he accept the offer from his host. "Yes, I would enjoy that."

"Grandpa, can I have a hot fudge sundae for desert?" pleaded Nicole.

"Sure." Larry looked around for the waiter and spotted a tall man who had just walked into the diner. Larry waved at the man as the waiter arrived. He told the waiter, "A hot fudge sundae for her with extra whipped cream, please."

The tall man walked over; he was nearly Larry's age. "Spoiling your granddaughter again, Larry?"

"Since her parents don't do it," confided Larry with a mock-serious tone, "it's my duty to see that she experiences all the joys of childhood." Larry pointed to Yuri. "Eugene, this is Peter. He's staying with us tonight and will be looking for a place to stay in Chicago."

Eugene reached over and shook hands with "Peter." "Hello. How long will you need a place to stay?" As he spoke, Eugene gave a quizzical glance at Larry, who responded with a nodding approval.

"Three weeks, maybe more," replied Yuri.

"My brother is in Europe on business for a couple of months," explained Eugene, "and he's looking to rent his boat in Burnham Harbor. It would be only for boarding, not for cruising."

Yuri was surprised by the good fortune. This was far better than his original plan of asking to stay with his professional colleague in Chicago or staying at a hotel where there was a risk of being found by the FBI. "That would be great. Could I stay there tomorrow?"

"Sure. I can meet you at dock thirty-one of Burnham Harbor tomorrow. How about I meet you there at four o'clock?"

"That will be fine. Thank you."

They discussed the details, and Yuri was pleased that the price to stay in the boat would be less than the price of a cheap hotel in Chicago. After dinner, Larry, Nicole, and Yuri returned to *Reincarnation* for the night. Yuri was exhausted and quickly drifted off to sleep in the gently rocking boat. He dreamed of smoking.

Larry served as their guide through the Art Institute proclaiming repeatedly that it was one of the finest art museums of the world. The museum's Beaux-Arts architecture was a work of art unto itself. First, they visited the collection of impressionists, post-impressionists, and American oil paintings. The artists of the paintings read like the Who's Who of art: Monet, Renoir, Degas, Caillebotte, Seurat, Van Gogh, Gauguin, Toulouse-Lautrec, Cézanne, Picasso, Matisse, Rembrandt, Magritte, Remington, Wood, and Hopper. Larry reverently discussed the distinctive technique and style of each artist.

Inexplicably, Yuri found a painting depicting the resurrection of Christ particularly interesting. Throughout history, man has dreamed of life after death, and in effect this was reflected in his plan to resurrect himself after faking his suicide.

"This is a most impressive collection," marveled Yuri with sincerity.

"Few know that this collection of paintings could have been even larger," confided Larry with a tone of regret, "if it weren't for the relocation of more than fifty fine European paintings in the early 1950s. The Chester Dale collection of paintings by Picasso and other masters was on permanent loan at the Art Institute until there was a disagreement. The owner of the paintings moved the collection to the National Gallery in

Washington, DC after the Art Institute refused to permanently display the entire collection. It was a needless loss for Chicago."

"This reminds me of the exquisite jewel-decorated eggs made by Peter Carl Fabergé for the tsars of Russia. The Fabergé eggs have been scattered around the world, and only a few remain in Russia."

Nicole seemed to appreciate Larry's extensive discussion of each painting and statue, but Yuri saw her interest flagging after the second hour. Apparently Larry noticed this too, saying to Nicole, "Come with me; I have a special treat for you."

They visited the Thorne exhibit of one-twelfth-scale miniature rooms from European and American homes from 1700 to 1940. Nicole peered with delight at the finely detailed three-dimensional models showing the history of furnishings, architecture, and style.

"Does the museum have a collection of Persian carpets?" asked Yuri, as they left the Thorne miniature room exhibit. Larry led them to the textiles department, where they found several fine Persian carpets in addition to tapestries, woven silks, quilts, and costumes. It was Yuri's favorite part of the museum.

After lunch, they went back to Larry's boat where Yuri picked up his bag. Yuri thanked Larry and gave his fellow old-schooler a hearty handshake. The taxi ride to Burnham Harbor was short, and Yuri found dock thirty-one easily. The gate to the dock was locked, so he sat and waited nearby, hoping that Eugene would show up. He fidgeted as he wished for a cigarette. "*Zaebyvaet, potihonechku.* This will slowly ruin me," Yuri cursed to himself.

Five hundred boats were crowded into the Burnham Harbor. The harbor was shielded from Lake Michigan by a long curved peninsula containing Meigs Airfield, the small airport that provided convenient airplane service to downtown Chicago. The peninsula into Lake Michigan had been expanded a decade ago to accommodate a longer runway, a larger terminal, parking for twenty-five business jets, and a parking structure for a thousand cars. In addition to private aircraft and corporate jets, Meigs Airport had fifty commercial flights a day. Thirty years ago, flight operations at Meigs had abruptly ceased as the result of commando politics. The second of the Chicago dynasty of mayors from the Daley family had closed Meigs Airfield by conducting a midnight raid of bulldozers to rip up the runway. After twenty years of inactivity, the airfield had been restored to operation. Yuri saw a couple of jets take off before Eugene arrived.

Eugene gave Yuri the lock code for the dock thirty-one gate, and they walked to the twenty-eight-year-old, eighteen-meter Hatteras motor yacht. It was named *Constant Reminder*. It was not the largest boat at the dock, but it was larger than most. The boat had been maintained well but still showed its age. Since it was powered by a diesel engine, it had spent only a few hours a year away from the dock during the past twenty years. The boat was hooked up to power, water, and sewage service from the dock.

"Here is the key to the cabin," said Eugene. "Since the boat is to remain at the dock, I'll keep the keys for the engine and the lock that secures the boat to the dock." They entered the cabin, and Yuri was relieved to see that the cabin and the two staterooms were larger than the cramped cabin aboard the *Reincarnation*. The large windows in the cabin provided a broad view of the harbor.

"I have no desire to take the boat for a trip, since I know nothing of operating a boat. This will be a fine residence." Yuri prepaid in cash for three weeks plus a small security deposit.

There was no rental contract, only a handshake. Eugene gave his cell phone number and asked for "Peter's" cell phone number.

"I don't have a cell phone," Yuri apologized. He lied since he did not want to leave a trace of his true identity.

Eugene seemed surprised that "Peter" did not have a cell phone. Most likely he thought "Peter" was a strange old-schooler. "Well, if I need to reach you, I will leave a message with the person who lives in the boat at the next slip." With that, Eugene left, and it was clear that Yuri would see little of Eugene from then on.

More than ever before, he needed some comfort, and he longed for a soothing cigarette. A good smoke would have helped him to think about what he should do.

17

———

Kent Fechner received a secure text message from Alfred Grossberg, who was still out of his office. "The FBI told me of a failed suicide attempt or a doubtful murder attempt of Yuri Petrov. He was saved by the intervention of a friend, who reported the event."

"What does the FBI know about me?" asked Kent, cursing to himself and worrying about what Petrov's response would be. Would Petrov go to the police?

"I didn't ask them, for obvious reasons, but there was no indication that the FBI suspects you. They do not seem to give any credence to the suggestion of an attempted murder. The FBI is trying to find Petrov again, but he will be harder to find now that you've spooked him."

"Press the FBI to find him soon, so that I can try again."

"OK, but I suggest you have someone install hidden surveillance cameras in his university lab and office, so you'll know immediately if he shows up there. You'll need the door lock codes for his lab and office. The FBI says they are both set to one-zero-two-four."

"Thanks. Good idea."

Kent found a discreet private investigator who installed two well-hidden video cameras with microphones in Petrov's lab and one in his office. He paid extra for high-resolution video cameras with low-light capability. The hidden video cameras and microphones continuously sent their information via a secure relay VPN connection to Kent's computer. The private investigator provided him with software for his computer to store several hours of surveillance, and the program would produce a beep and timestamp if it detected any motion or sounds. Thus, without having to monitor the computer all day, he would know immediately if anyone entered the rooms. Ever cautious, Kent made sure the private investigator never knew his real identity.

———

The double bed in the main stateroom of *Constant Reminder* was comfortable for one person but would have been quite snug for two. Yuri lay awake wishing he had a cigarette to smoke and listening to the boat fenders creak as thoughts fermented in his brain. He was determined to expose the exploitive advertising and the political abuses. Sellco and the White House must have removed all of the evidence, and there was no useful evidence from the recent attempt to murder him. The attempted murder placed everything in a new context. He had hoped that if all else failed, he could use the espionage trial as a tool to expose the evil activities. Now it was clear that the person from Sellco meant to kill him before any chance of a trial. He would have to be extremely careful in hiding. Any mistake would quickly result in his death. It would be hard to remain hidden for long, so he must act quickly.

With the risk of being found and killed, he decided to develop a backup plan to ensure that Sellco's scheme was exposed. He would make arrangements with a lawyer to act for him if he was killed. A sealed message to be opened upon his death would instruct the lawyer. He was not entirely pleased with the backup plan since the sealed instructions could never address every eventuality, but it was the best idea he had for now.

The backup plan meshed with his primary plan of faking his suicide, waiting for Sellco to resume the subliminal advertising, and then acting through a lawyer while he was supposedly dead. He realized that the lawyer must believe him to be dead, but he would still need to communicate with the lawyer. He came up with the elaborate deception of instructing the lawyer to communicate with Yuri's aunt in a remote part of Russia via e-mail. Yuri really did have an aunt in Russia, and indeed, e-mail would be the best way to communicate with her since she was deaf. Of course, the e-mail address he would provide to the lawyer would communicate with Yuri and not his aunt.

The next day he found that many of the boats in Burnham Harbor were permanently occupied. There were two classes of people, those with loads of money and those with less. The people with less money seemed to spend much of their time performing maintenance on their boats, and in some cases they were paid to clean, paint, and repair the boats of the wealthier people. Some people spent most of the day in their boats drinking beer and watching sports on TV. Yuri doubted these sports fans had the initiative for the ten-minute walk to Soldier Field, where football and other sporting events were held.

Yuri noticed the lack of air conditioning in *Constant Reminder* as the temperature climbed during the day. By noon, sweat was rolling down his face. A hot blanket of lazy, humid air sucked energy out of every pore of his body. The oppressive heat made it impossible to perform any work, physical or mental. Yuri escaped to the refreshing air conditioning in the nearby

Shedd Aquarium, where he viewed exhibits about the unique senses of dolphins and sharks. He wished Susan were there to share the experience.

Yuri noticed a Japanese man wearing a Cubs baseball hat looking at him from the opposite side of the shark tank. The view through the water and the thick glass on both sides of the large tank was distorted, but the man in the Cubs hat looked like Takashi Fujikawa. What was Takashi doing here? Could he trust him? Yuri retreated behind a poster discussing shark attacks on humans. The Japanese man in the Cubs hat stepped around the corner into plain view, and Yuri saw that he was not Takashi. This man was a few years older than Takashi, his ears stuck out like the fins of a fish Yuri had just seen, and he had the musculature of an athlete. Maybe he was a professional baseball player. The man glanced in Yuri's direction and then doubled back the way he had come.

Yuri walked to the dolphin exhibit; he was fascinated by the amazing precision of echolocation in dolphins. By emitting chirps and then listening to the resulting echoes, dolphins could effectively perform an ultrasound examination of fish at a distance of a few meters. The detail of the resulting image was superior to ultrasound examinations performed by doctors in hospitals. Dolphins could identify other fish by detecting the size and location of major organs in the fish.

Engineers who designed sonar systems for submarines found that the precision of the dolphin's sonar far exceeded the abilities of the most advanced human-made sonar. Scientists did not understand how the dolphin's sonar achieved such high precision, but some thought that the dolphin's teeth and jaw served as a series of filters tuned to different frequencies of sound. Though they did not understand exactly how the dolphin's sonar worked, engineers were able to greatly improve human-made sonar by blindly copying aspects of dolphin anatomy in the design of submarine sonar. The notion of blindly copying nature's design struck Yuri as a particularly interesting concept.

Yuri moved on to the jellyfish exhibit, but when he glanced away from the translucent, drifting, balloon-like creatures, he saw the Japanese man in the Cubs hat peering directly at him through a screen of potted plants. As soon as they made eye contact, the Japanese man turned away.

Ever since leaving the university, Yuri had been watchful for anyone who might be tailing him. His pulse quickened and he tried to fade into a crowd of people. Yuri's short stature made it easy for him to hide behind the other people. Had they found him? He looked at the people nearby; none of them looked like the men he had met from Sellco. He hurried to the next exhibit hall, looking over his shoulder occasionally.

Yuri told himself to calm down and ignore his overactive imagination when he saw the Japanese man again. Where would it be safe to hide? Yuri ran down a flight of stairs. He nearly tripped as his legs awkwardly tried to move as quickly as his mind demanded. He entered the men's room and hid in the most distant stall. An advertisement for children's vitamins played as he sat on the toilet and caught his breath. Sellco had found him. He heard the one person who had been in the men's room leave. Sellco's agents would kill him, but they were waiting until there were no witnesses. Yuri sat up with a jerk; the men's room was a deadly tactical mistake. It was the perfect place for them to kill him, so he left hurriedly.

The crowds of people provided cover as he worked his way toward the building exit. Just ahead, the Japanese man was blocking the way out. Yuri stepped around a corner; he was again able to see the man by looking through the glass walls of the shark tank. The Japanese man was holding a gun. It was not an ordinary gun; it was a strange high-tech looking gun. The man moved quickly around the corner of the shark tank toward Yuri. Yuri franticly looked for a place to run, but he found himself trapped in a dead-end corridor.

The Japanese man appeared in full view and looked directly at Yuri with a thin smile. Dropping to one knee, he raised the strange gun and gave it to a six-year-old Japanese boy, who handed the man a large cup of Pepsi. The plastic toy space gun made zapping sounds as the boy "shot" a shark. A four-year-old Japanese girl in a pretty pink dress ran up to the man, tugged at his shirt, and pointed at a sea turtle. Yuri's sense of relief was spoiled by the realization that he had panicked unnecessarily.

———

Yuri was surrounded by a city with millions of people, but he was lonely. He was feeling paranoid, nervous, and in desperate need of a smoke. Talking with Susan would help. He took the bicycle that was stored in the boat's cabin for a ride to the Chicago Public Library, where he found a computer connected to the Internet in a remote corner. He loaded some programs from a small memory card into the library computer and then proceeded to troll the Internet for an unprotected computer. In less than a minute he was loading a Trojan anonymous redirector program onto a personal computer in Mexico City. He then connected a small headset with a microphone to the library computer and invoked a voice-over-IP program to make a phone call via the computer in Mexico City to the computer in Susan's office. Where most voice-over-IP programs used a transport class reserved for voice transmission, Yuri's special program masked the packets to look like common web traffic. Anyone looking at the connection between the Chicago Public Library computer and Susan's computer would think it was normal web traffic. Even if they looked inside the packets, they would never be able to trace the connection past the Trojan redirector program in Mexico City. All traces of the Trojan redirector program would be deleted long before anyone got that far.

———

Susan was in her office rereading a note from her doctor when she was astonished to hear Yuri's distinctive Russian accent, "If you can hear me, say hello." She spun around in her chair, but Yuri was not in her office. Where did the voice come from? Was her office haunted?

"I don't believe in ghosts," she said to herself.

"Hello, Susan. I almost was a ghost," uttered a voice like Yuri's, speaking softly.

"Yuri, is that you? Where the devil are you?" Susan searched about her office.

"Yes, this is Yuri. I am in your computer." It sounded like he was having fun.

"Don't be silly," she growled, looking at her computer in exasperation. "You couldn't fit in there."

"I am talking to you via a connection to your computer."

Now she realized the voice was coming from the speakers connected to her computer and that he could hear her via the microphone she used for voice commands. "OK, Mr. Computer Wizard. I understand. So where are you really?"

"I can't tell you where I am," he said softly. "Remember that I can't tell you anything in case you are questioned. In fact, the situation has become worse. Someone tried to kill me."

"Was it someone from Sellco?" she inquired with deep concern.

"How did you know that?"

"I found the Sellco research contract in your desk. I figured that Sellco must be involved in your trouble."

"You shouldn't be looking in my desk." Yuri sounded perturbed.

"I was worried about you and I was trying to find out what's going on."

"Stop trying to find out about what I am fighting. These people are killers, and if they think you know their secrets, they will kill you. Stay away from Sellco and don't tell anyone about this." Yuri told Susan about the attempt by someone from Sellco to kill him, but he evaded her questions about where he had been at the time.

"Wow! They're trying to kill you, but you can't go the police or the FBI. Where are you now?"

"I am in your computer," he said, exasperated. "Please listen, Susan. Stay out of this."

"Hey, I'm a big girl and I can take care of myself. The people from Sellco don't scare me. Maybe it'd be good if they went after me. They might expose themselves, and then you could catch them."

"Susan, please be careful," he pleaded. "You are the last person in the world that I want to get sucked into this quicksand. I care for you deeply."

"Well, I care about you too and I want to help."

"Everything is happening too fast, and I am running out of time. I need to stop Sellco before they catch up with me." He sounded distraught.

"How do you feel?"

"Tired. I was up most of last night worrying that they would find me again and thinking of what to do. I need help."

"Poor sleep and feeling time compression. Classic symptoms of stress. We need to work on your coping skills, and you should get more physical exercise."

"NO!" He lowered his voice. "Not that kind of help. Stop analyzing me and help me figure out how they found me."

"Maybe they tracked you by your credit card transactions."

"I have only bought food with cash."

"Have you used your credit card for anything?"

"No."

"Have you done any online transactions?"

"I used the computer to check on the news. Oh, I did update my account at smokes.com to have cigarettes delivered to me. There are no stores that carry cigarettes."

"And smokes.com has your credit card number on file, don't they?"

"Yes," he confessed remorsefully.

"Yuri, they're tracking you by your cigarette purchases. You have to stop smoking. Those cigarettes are going to kill you."

"I haven't smoked for two days, and I would kill for a smoke."

"You can't buy cigarettes without them finding you. For once, listen to my advice and deal with the stress of quitting cigarettes. Nicotine withdrawal is nasty; be prepared for a long torment. Get exercise, get more sleep, eat healthy foods like veggies and fruits, and eat small healthy snacks like nuts to regulate your glucose level. Try chewing gum."

"You and your sadistic fascination with stress. I am trying to save democracy while being chased by the FBI and nearly killed by a power-mad maniac, and now I have to quit smoking. I am sure that you are eagerly looking forward to regular, detailed reports on my suffering."

"Oh, yes," she mocked in good humor. "You do know how to delight me. Lots of horrid details would be delicious."

Yuri seemed to be enjoying the chat in a perverse way. "I have to go. I must sever the connection now to be sure it is not traced. I may contact you again sometime, so leave your computer on. I enjoyed talking with you."

"Call soon, please. I miss you, Yuri." She wished Yuri were with her; she could use some comforting too.

———

Yuri wiped all traces of his programs from the computer in Mexico City and the computer in the Chicago Public Library. On the way back to Burnham Harbor, he stopped at a grocery store where he bought chewing gum, fruit, vegetables, nuts, Coke, chocolate milk, ham, cheese, bread, and canned chili. The newest advertising media from Sellco was edible ink sprayed onto the skin of the fruit. The bananas were printed with "Viagra: a hard man is good to find," and the melons were printed with "Liftim skin patch for a firmer, fuller female form."

Walking down the pharmaceutical isle, he passed a video screen showing a Xarim ad, but as he approached, the screen changed to a Gerivite ad. The ad featured a very healthy-looking man in his seventies saying, "Senior citizens need the special formula of vitamins in Gerivite." Just above the screen was a tiny video camera. Yuri knew that a computer algorithm analyzing the video camera's view had determined that an old man was watching the advertising screen.

Thousands of video surveillance cameras were scattered about Chicago. He tried to avoid the cameras when he could, but Yuri did not worry too much about them. He knew that the publicly touted face-recognition artificial intelligence worked moderately well under controlled laboratory conditions, but it was nearly useless in the real world, where people did not look directly at the camera under controlled lighting conditions. Nonetheless, Yuri always wore sunglasses and a hat with the brim pulled down.

Yuri tried chewing gum, but it was useless. It just made him think of smoking, and he felt ridiculous chewing endlessly. He fidgeted grumpily as he yearned for a smoke. He had a headache that aspirin did little to help, a dry mouth that water would not quench, and a persistent cough. He missed the combined

invigorating and calming effects of smoking. There was no sub-
stitute, but drinking chocolate milk provided some relief. It was
just as well that he was staying away from people because he
would have snapped the head off of anyone he met.

18

———

That night Yuri lay awake listening to the sounds of the harbor as his mind wandered. Various thoughts mingled in his neocortex. Seemingly random combinations were tried as different thoughts drifted past each other. This mental trial and error was structured upon fundamentals: stop the exploitive use of the teaching machines, end the dangerous political abuse of power, and make sure that he succeeded even if he was caught. Silly ideas were considered, explored, modified, judged, and discarded.

Three thoughts converged: a conversation with Susan about artificial intelligence, something he had seen at the Art Institute, and what he had learned at the Shedd Aquarium. Yuri's brain shook from a magnitude ten mindquake. The idea was so bold it scared him. It was foolish, bizarre, colossal, and irresistible. It would be the ultimate backup plan and the professional achievement of the century. The idea was audacious, and it had Yuri written all over it. He tried to talk himself out of it, but Nemesis, the Greek goddess of revenge, had possessed him and would not let go. It was an idea that he had dismissed years ago as too dangerous to explore even in theory. Now he realized his subconscious must have been working on this idea for years. He had always known the seductive pull of scientific progress, but it had become clearer how irresistible the force was. The march of science could not be stopped, and the best that one could do was to lead the march toward good and away from evil.

It would require a monumental computer program. The design of the program came into sharper focus as he thought about it. In his mind, pieces of the program snapped into place at a feverish pace. His mind was in overdrive designing the massive program, and in a flurry of inspired contemplation, Yuri knew how he would design it. He got out of bed, turned on his notebook computer, and poured his thoughts into the program compiler. The programming continued nonstop through the night and into the next morning. The idea went beyond artificial intelligence into uncharted territory, but he felt he was headed in the right direction. The thrill of discovery drove him forward despite the marathon effort.

Exhaustion overcame crazed excitement by noon, at which point Yuri drank a glass of chocolate milk and crashed into bed. After four hours of deep sleep, he awoke from a dream in which he was savoring a cigarette. His stomach demanded food, now. Yuri opened a can of chili and ate it directly from the can uncooked, along with raw broccoli, a banana, and a Coke. There was no time for cooking.

He immersed himself in the computer as he sipped a second can of Coke. The potent mixture of sugar and caffeine was like high-octane fuel flowing through the arteries to his brain. The long hours of machine-like work were driven by a combination of professional enthrallment and personal vengeance. He was entranced by his beautiful vision. Fortunately, there was a refreshing breeze from the lake to help his frenzied work, which continued without regard for the clock. He slaved away unabated except for the most essential biological demands for food, drink, and short naps. Yuri forced himself to get out for short brisk walks in the sun to keep his mind sharp and avoid making mistakes in his work. The program had to work perfectly the first time; there would be no second chances.

———

Susan sat in her office searching Sellco's public website for some indication regarding the cause of Yuri's troubles. She was irritated that she could not find anything, but her frustration went far beyond that. Susan wept softly as she poked angrily at her computer. It was imperative for her to find a way to help Yuri before she ran out of time. She had such little time remaining and needed the consolation of talking with someone who cared.

Hamilton von Helmholtz walked into Susan's office without knocking. "Damn, not him," thought Susan silently as she wiped her good eye.

Hamilton seemed to be in one of his frisky moods. "Hey, Susan, did'ya see the Cubs game last night?"

"No!" she barked fiercely. "I don't have time to waste watching baseball or to talk about it either."

"Yeah," said Hamilton, taken aback. "Well, I stopped by to see how your project on eye tracking is going."

"I'll get to it once you leave me be," she snapped.

Hamilton recoiled. "That's, uh, fine. So, what plans do you have for new projects?"

She blew her nose into a tissue. "I have no plans. As far as I am concerned, the future can take care of itself without my help."

Hamilton looked at her, perplexed. Being a man, he probably thought it was "the wrong time of the month" for her. She no longer thought he was a great leader; Yuri's irreverent criticism had taught her that Hamilton was a phony scientist. Hamilton continued to gaze at her.

"Stop staring at my eyepatch, you pompous ass. Just leave me alone."

Hamilton left without a word, shaking his head.

———

Alfred Grossberg was back in his office, so he called Kent Fechner with his secure phone.

"Hi, Alfred," Kent answered. "You have news?"

"No," said Alfred. "I was hoping you had something. We can't keep stalling much longer; we need Mercury to send the Slaughter message soon."

"If we turn Mercury on now, it'll blow up in our faces. We have to silence Petrov first. You know this."

"I am pressing the FBI as hard as I can. They have added more agents to the case, but Petrov has learned to hide better. You're so bloody smart. Come up with some way to smoke him out."

"I've set up cameras in his lab and office. I will try to think of what else we can do."

"Think fast. We're running out of time. Bye."

———

Yuri was consumed by his frantic work, but he had exhausted his supply of food aboard the boat. He decided to have a chat with Susan on the way to buy more food. Repeated visits to the same store or library could be dangerous, so he waited for a bus to take him to a library on the north side of Chicago. The bench at the bus stop boldly pronounced "Xarim—fit for life." A gaudy bus approached noisily. Every surface of the bus, inside and out, was covered with video panels that hawked a succession of products. The rolling video billboard stopped and Yuri boarded. On cue from a GPS navigation system, the video panels inside the bus informed the riders of subscribing restaurants and shops near the next bus stop.

It was a short walk from the fifth stop to the Putnam Public Library. He used the Trojan redirector scheme to contact Susan's computer.

"Hello, are you there?" asked Yuri.

"Yuri, I am so happy you called." Susan sounded lonely. "You are just what I need."

"I am sure you are eager to hear of my suffering," Yuri joked.

"Misery loves company. Right now I could use some company."

"Are you OK?"

"I think I have a mild flu or something." Susan sounded evasive. "I'm tired and a little blue."

"I wish I were there to take care of you."

"Me too, but just talking with you makes me feel better already. So how are you doing?"

"The withdrawal from smoking is as bad as ever. I still reach into my pocket every ten minutes looking for a cigarette. I need to smoke now more than ever."

"I know it's hard going cold turkey."

"Actually, I've been eating chili. I don't like turkey."

"Ha," Susan laughed. "Cold turkey is an expression for breaking a drug habit."

"Well, it describes how I feel, but I'm too excited to even think about being miserable. I have been working crazy hours on a big idea. It is the most amazing idea of my life, and it will make sure that the awful people are stopped. I have been working day and night for the past couple of days, and I have a lot more work to do. I can't tell you about it now, but it will blow up your mind when you see it."

Susan laughed. "Yuri, the expression is 'blow your mind.' I can't wait to see it. When will you be done?"

"I hope to be done a few days from now."

"Great." Susan sounded relieved. "Have you been getting your exercise?"

"I am really busy on my notebook computer, but I do get out for walks. I have a question for you. Has anyone disturbed the supercomputer in my lab?"

"The FBI was here again yesterday, asking everyone questions and snooping around in your lab and office. I kept a watch on them, and they didn't touch your supercomputer."

"Good. I will be using the supercomputer. Do what you can to keep it safe, but please don't get yourself in any trouble."

"Don't worry about me. You're the one we need to worry about."

Yuri looked at his watch. "I have to go now. Bye."

"Be careful. I'll be thinking of you."

19

———

Yuri's feverish day-and-night work continued, and he took short naps at odd hours. At one point, when he had come to the end of a marathon session, he noticed a half-eaten ham and cheese sandwich on the galley counter. The sandwich had been there for several days. The cheddar cheese had grown moldy whiskers, the ham dried and cracked, and the bread was a shriveled crust. It reminded Yuri of how cruddy he felt. He dolefully tossed the sandwich overboard to feed the fish. It would have been so much easier if he could have smoked to relieve the fatigue and anxiety.

When he had completed the prodigious computer program, he developed a simulator to test it. The program had to work perfectly the first time; once started it would be difficult to control. He test-ran portions of the program, but the limited capacity of his notebook computer could not test the entire configuration at the same time. Yuri would need the supercomputer in his lab to add the final piece and fully test the program. He felt apprehension about testing the program in its entire configuration. He was not afraid of the program failing; he was afraid of what it would do once it worked. It would be spooky watching the program run.

With the computer program nearly ready, it was time to establish the necessary legal mechanisms. Yuri visited the law firm of Bingle and Asher to meet with a lawyer named Javier Flores. Yuri grilled Javier to assure himself that he was the right person for the job.

"My identity and everything I tell you must be kept confidential," insisted Yuri, "and any related documents must be stored securely."

Javier nodded. "This is normal practice. I'll release information only as instructed by you."

"I will have another law firm write a contract for your services as my executor and trustee. They will arrange for your ongoing payments from my trust."

Javier nodded again. "That is also a common arrangement."

"Upon my death, you will have the power of attorney for my estate. You will be instructed by my will to take certain actions. Also, I have an aunt in Russia who may provide you with further instructions at a later time. The contract will require that you follow these instructions specifically."

"OK."

"Her instructions may ask for you to perform actions beyond the norm for estate maintenance. Will you perform any action instructed by my aunt?"

"I'll do anything instructed, provided it is legal and within ethical legal practice."

"The duties must be performed with persistence and dedication and may require some originality."

"Sounds like fun. Ask anyone in this office what my nickname is, and they will tell you it's 'Javier the Unstoppable.'"

"To assure privacy and authenticity, the instructions from my aunt will be sent to you by encrypted e-mail. I will provide you with a computer program to decode the instructions and verify their authenticity. The contract for your services will require

you to follow any instructions that you receive and are authenticated by the program I give you. Any instructions authenticated
by the program are to be followed unconditionally."

Javier seemed pleased. "This is unusual, but it's up to you
if you want to place your trust in the program. It sounds like
this might be more interesting than most cases where we just
routinely fill out the same standard documents."

"I have written the program myself. I trust it. Each time you
use the program, you must first enter a password. The password
is Plato428. Do not let anyone else know the password."

"OK; it sounds like you have thought of everything."

"I hope so."

Yuri dealt with a second law firm, Lloyd and Tye, who wrote
Yuri's will, his trust agreement, and the contract with Javier
Flores at Bingle and Asher. Javier Flores was assigned as executor with power of attorney for Yuri's estate upon Yuri's death
and as trustee for his trust. Yuri again demanded that everything be kept confidential.

Yuri's next stop was the trust department of the First
National Bank of Chicago, where he established and funded his
trust by transferring his entire savings into it, less a modest cash
withdrawal for his wallet. The trust department was assigned
the authority to pay Javier Flores for his services.

Since the federal banking laws required that the actions at
the bank be reported, Yuri was aboard the Electroliner train
bound for Champaign, Illinois within minutes of completing his
business at the bank. The information from the bank reached
the FBI long after it was any danger to Yuri.

It should have felt comforting to be back in familiar territory, but Yuri felt like a rabbit that knew he was near an eagle's nest. At every block on the way to CSL, he looked back to see if anyone was following him. Yuri placed an envelope in Susan's mailbox at the Coordinated Science Lab. Her birthday was the following week. Since he had arrived after normal working hours, no one saw him enter the building. He was pleased when the door to his laboratory opened; the code for the lock had not been changed. He was also relieved to find his supercomputer had not been disturbed.

Yuri immediately set to work loading his program into the supercomputer, installing a wireless LAN card, and connecting a brain scanner helmet. This helmet was more powerful than what was normally used for teaching machines. It could probe deeper with higher precision, and most importantly, it was many times faster. A quick check of the huge program showed that it had been installed properly. Yuri pulled a comfortable chair closer, sat down, put on the special helmet, and started the program. For the next six hours, he sat there dozing on and off, thinking about the program, dreaming about smoking, and wishing it would complete soon. Finally, the program signaled and he removed the helmet. The program was complete. Taking a deep breath as if he were diving off the high board into a pool, he placed the program in ARMED mode. The full configuration of the program would automatically run when triggered. He ran a series of diagnostic tests on each subsystem. The results confirmed the correct operation of every subsystem.

He paused before proceeding with the final test, where he would manually trigger the full program to run. His trepidation came from the uncertainty of what he would experience; it could quite possibly be something that a person should never experience because it might drive them insane. Then again, it might be incredibly amusing.

Yuri was interrupted before he took the last step.

20

───

Kent Fechner's phone beeped; a message from his computer at work indicated activity in the surveillance of Petrov's lab. He opened the live video and audio feed. On the small screen of his mobile phone, Kent recognized Petrov and could see he was doing something with the computer in his lab. Kent had an ally at the University of Illinois whom he considered calling for help, but he decided against it. This ally would not perform murder for him, and it would not be wise to ask for help holding Petrov there until Kent arrived to perform the task. There must be no witnesses. The best course was for Kent to get to the CSL lab quickly. In the meantime, he could keep an eye on Petrov using the video link to his mobile phone. A few days earlier, he had warned Sellco's executive flight operations department to be ready to scramble a business jet at a moment's notice. They were to have a flight crew near the airport at all times. He was furious when he was told that the flight crew was eating dinner at a restaurant fifty minutes away from the airport.

"Tell them to abandon their meal," he yelled into the phone, "and get the plane ready as quickly as possible. Tell them to drive as fast as possible. Get me your fastest plane and file a flight plan for Champaign, Illinois." Once again, he reserved the jet in the name of someone else in his department.

Kent looked at the video feed from the lab. Petrov was putting on what looked like a teaching machine helmet. This encouraged him; maybe Petrov would stay there for a while. After tossing a few items into a small bag, he drove to the airport where he waited impatiently for the flight crew.

He paced in the waiting room like a caged animal, occasionally checking his watch and looking at the live video feed on his mobile phone. Petrov was slumped in his lab seat with the teaching machine helmet on his head. The flight crew was overdue. Reminding the manager of Sellco flight operations did not help. The crew members were not answering their mobile phones. Kent was about to burst a blood vessel when the slothful flight operations manager ambled over to say that the crew had called and would arrive in five minutes.

When the flight crew rushed into the waiting room, Kent lashed out. "The operations VP will hear about this. Eating dinner an hour from the airport while on duty, and then you had to finish dessert before getting your fat carcasses over here."

"The cop who pulled us over for speeding insisted that we follow him to the police station to pay the fine. You owe me four hundred dollars," said the pilot with barely controlled rage as he handed Kent the speeding ticket.

It was a waste of time discussing such minor matters. "I have no time to discuss this with you goofballs. You need to think of only one thing: getting me to Champaign as soon as possible."

Kent had asked flight operations for their fastest jet and he got it. The Gulfstream G290 was a hot rod, designed more for performance than comfort. The flight crew's petulance seemed to be mollified when they learned that they would be flying the G290. The jet could seat only four passengers; Kent had to nearly crawl into his seat.

"Hurry and get this bird off the ground," he ordered brusquely as they boarded, "and fly as fast as you can. We have not a minute to lose."

The flight crew took an eternity completing the preflight checklist while Kent sipped a glass of Perrier, watching the seconds tick by.

"Do you have your seat belt on, sir?" the pilot called.

"Yes. Get going already."

"Right away, sir. Please pull your seat belt tight."

The G290 screamed off the runway and climbed at an improbably steep angle. The pilot glanced over at the copilot with a grin on his face as he threw the G290 into a punishing turn at an altitude of a few hundred meters.

Both Kent and his glass of Perrier were slammed against the side of the cabin. He nearly blacked out in the crushing turn.

The pilot keyed his radio to the control tower and spoke loudly enough for Kent to hear, "Sellco Golf two niner zero, reporting evasive maneuver to avoid birds." The pilot sounded rather amused.

After Kent regained his composure, he asked for the copilot to call ahead to rent a car and made sure it would be listed in the copilot's name, not his. Kent nervously checked the video feed to his mobile phone every few minutes and thanked his good fortune when Petrov was still there. It was odd that Petrov had been sitting there for several hours; people usually took a break from a teaching machine every hour or two. Kent did not dwell on this oddity or the question of why Petrov would return to his lab just to use a teaching machine. He was content that Petrov was still where he could be found.

After landing and a fast taxi to the parking area, Kent barked orders to the copilot, "You, pick up the rental car, and bring it to the exit by baggage claim. Run! I mean it. Run!"

As Kent waited at the baggage claim exit, he looked at the video on his mobile phone again. Petrov was taking the teaching machine helmet off and starting to do something with the computer.

The copilot arrived with the rental car and Kent yelled, "Get out. Give me the keys. Wait for me at the private aviation waiting room. I'll be back in an hour or two. No dinner excursions."

———

At 5:50 a.m., the streets were deserted and there were no cars in the parking lot by the Coordinated Science Lab. Kent Fechner's car screeched into the parking space closest to the building and he ran inside. He entered the lock code provided by Alfred Grossberg for Yuri Petrov's lab. Petrov was there staring at the computer screen.

Kent's soft steps were masked by the low roar from the supercomputer's fans. Petrov did not turn around until Kent was directly behind and had flicked off the nine-millimeter pistol's safety. A silencer was attached to the pistol.

"You always seem to be wearing gloves and pointing a gun at me when I see you," Petrov grumbled.

"Yes, and you should recall that I will not hesitate to use it if you fail to cooperate. Remain seated." Kent stepped closer.

As he had done in Miss Mountcastle's home, Kent loaded a program into a teaching machine sitting on a lab bench. He commanded Petrov to put on the teaching machine helmet, and Kent used the lie detector program to confirm that Petrov had told no one about the subliminal advertising.

"I'm glad that you've kept the secret to yourself," said Kent.

Petrov smiled just before the bullet entered the front of his skull, plowed through the cerebrum, traveled down through the cerebellum, and made a large hole as it exited through the rear of his skull. Petrov immediately toppled to the floor, dead. Brain tissue was spattered everywhere. Kent stepped closer and pumped a second bullet from the silenced pistol into Petrov's brain. More brain tissue sprayed across the floor of the lab.

"You've lost your mind, professor," sneered Kent, closely scrutinizing the extensive damage caused by the two bullets.

———

Dirk drove his tiny single-seat electric buggy with a flashing yellow light on top through the dark streets like a firefly searching for a mate. He had grown up watching police dramas on television and dreamed of being a policeman bringing criminals to justice. His attempt to complete the police-training course on a teaching machine had been a dismal failure. The extensive knowledge of laws and police procedures was too much for his meager intellect. He had felt fortunate when he was hired as a University of Illinois campus parking enforcement officer. He was a sworn officer with a uniform, a police radio, his own special vehicle, and the power to issue a ticket for any illegally parked vehicle. He had pride in his job and tried to ignore the "Dirk is dumb as dirt" jokes.

Dirk was a shining testament to teaching machines. Before the advent of teaching machines, he would have been regarded as untrainable. He knew he was not as smart as most people, but the teaching machines had made the most of what he had. The machines had coaxed him into becoming a good student. With infinite patience, special instructional programs for the "learning challenged" had provided Dirk a solid, basic education. The brain scanner detected and exploited any glimmer of intelligence.

Dirk had begun his shift at five in the morning. At this early hour, there was little traffic and few cars to ticket, so Dirk could quickly sweep through the campus. From a distance, he spotted a lone car parked in the Coordinated Science Lab lot and steered his buggy to take a shortcut along the jogging path. He zeroed in on the car without the parking sticker. It was a Ford Axon, just like the car he owned. Dirk could not understand why someone without a parking sticker would park in the reserved lot when there were so many open metered spaces available only one block away. The university had a continuous flow of new students and visitors who did not know the efficiency of parking enforcement on campus. Dirk pointed his laser scanner at the car's license plate. A GPS navigation system noted the exact location, and a ticket on sticky paper was automatically printed as the record was radioed to a computer at the campus police office. Dirk pasted the ticket on the driver's door window without stepping out of his buggy. Then he drove off in search of his next victim.

Kent pocketed the gun and walked quickly to his car, where he found a parking ticket on the window. The silly little ticket did nothing to dampen his ebullience. He tossed the parking ticket in the nearby trash can and quickly drove off unseen. A few miles away, Kent pulled into a Mexiking fast food restaurant where he paid cash for a taco salad to go from the twenty-four-hour menu. Pulling the car to the rear of the parking lot where no one could see him, he retrieved a disposable diaper from his travel bag. He wrapped the pistol and silencer in the diaper, using the adhesive tabs to close it securely. The disposable diaper was stuffed into the Mexiking takeout bag, which he rolled closed. Stepping out of the car unseen, he placed the tightly closed Mexiking takeout bag in a trash can and then scattered the taco salad over it. Finally, he placed a newspaper over the top, closing the lid. Kent was sure the gun would never be found.

———

Kent slept well on the return flight after he had issued the command to reactivate Project Mercury. Hidden messages for Slaughter, Xarim, and "subliminal messages are harmless" appeared on every teaching machine in the country.

21

———

Hamilton von Helmholtz joined the tense huddle of people in the lab who were all ignoring the body on the floor. The county coroner stated that this was clearly a murder, so she should lead the investigation. The chief of the Urbana police said that the murder had taken place within the city of Urbana, so he had jurisdiction. The chief of the Champaign police noted that the murder was only a stone's throw from the Urbana-Champaign boundary and that there was a standing agreement between the twin cities that Champaign had priority in complex criminal investigations since they had more experience. The two FBI agents insisted that the FBI had jurisdiction since they had a warrant for Yuri Petrov's arrest. The chief of the University of Illinois campus police wanted them to decide who would lead the investigation, so long as it was not him. Hamilton wanted them all to go away and take care of this quietly. He regretted ever hiring Yuri Petrov. Having a member of his department wanted by the FBI was bad enough. Now Petrov had managed to get murdered in his laboratory. Petrov had done everything possible to sabotage Hamilton's career.

Hamilton was accustomed to hardball politics, but he was amazed at how the vultures fought over the body. Everyone wanted to be a star in this big case, except for the chief of the campus police, who seemed to feel it was out of his league. Eventually, it was the chief of the campus police who resolved the argument because he was the only neutral party. The Champaign county coroner would lead the investigation with the Champaign police doing most of the fieldwork.

The examination of the body and the crime scene produced the two bullets, the wallet with Yuri Petrov's identification, and no other meaningful evidence. The video surveillance cameras were well hidden and not noticed.

———

Susan was already morose before she learned that Yuri had been murdered. The news devastated her. She had not realized the depth of her feelings for Yuri until that moment and was overwhelmed with grief. The death also reminded her of her own mortality. And finally, Yuri had failed in his mysterious quest and Susan had been unable to help him. She was emotionally exhausted and was of little help to the police.

Later that day, after Susan had regained some composure, she found the envelope in her mailbox. Opening the envelope, she found the birthday card from Yuri and a computer memory card. Susan dissolved in sorrow and cried until her good eye hurt.

The note on the birthday card read:

Happy Birthday, Susan,

I wish I could be there with you to celebrate your birthday, but I will be very busy for the next month or two. I hope you understand and will enjoy the enclosed gift. The memory card holds a delightful jazz album titled "Discovered Feelings."

I don't think I could have maintained my courage the past few weeks without knowing that someone cared about me. You are special, and I hope my troubles will soon be over so that we can spend more time together. Keep practicing your chess game.

Love, Yuri

———

Kent Fechner called Alfred Grossberg via the secure phone.

"Yuri Petrov is dead," reported Kent, "and we've resumed Mercury. Your message for Slaughter started today."

"The Senate confirmation vote is in two days," said Alfred gruffly. "We couldn't delay it any longer. I have my doubts if we have enough time for the message to turn the tide for us."

"It usually takes seven days to reach fifty percent adoption."

"It'll be close. If we don't get approval, then we'll find someone else who will support Sherrington."

"I'm just glad to get back to business as usual and forget about Petrov."

"The FBI tells me that they have no clue who murdered Petrov. I'll let you know if anything develops there."

"Don't worry. They'll find nothing."

———

A client's death was routine business for a lawyer, but Javier Flores was saddened when he learned of Yuri Petrov's death.

Dr. Petrov was one of those special people that he had liked the moment they had first met. Javier was not surprised by what was in Dr. Petrov's will since he had reviewed it earlier. Both he and the law firm of Lloyd and Tye held duplicate copies of the will in locked files. His instructions were clear and he followed them, as odd as they were. He sent an e-mail to the address specified in the will. The will provided the text for the e-mail and instructed that he double check that it was typed precisely as shown:

Happy Birthday! Let the excitement begin. From your friend, Plato

Javier waited for a reply. If he did not receive the correct reply, he was to send the message to a second address. After four minutes, the reply came and was authenticated by the program Javier had received from Dr. Petrov:

Thank you. All is well.

The will then instructed Javier to take other steps.

———

Hamilton von Helmholtz was doing his best at damage control. He had encouraged the police to keep a low profile and deflected a couple of news reporters. It was going to be a rough week, but he was feeling a little better after a good exercise run. Susan Hebb had again not joined him for the run; she was still not feeling well. When Hamilton's phone rang, he expected it to be his wife since she had only called twice since the start of the day. However, the Caller ID on the phone said the call was from the law firm of Bingle and Asher. He picked up the phone, "Coordinated Science Lab, Helmholtz."

"This is Javier Flores. I'm an attorney representing the estate of Yuri Petrov."

Hamilton thought, "Oh, Lord. This screwball Petrov is tormenting me from his grave." In a reserved tone, he said, "Yes. How may I help you?"

"I've sent you a copy of a protective court order issued today. You are required to prevent anyone from disturbing the supercomputer in Yuri Petrov's laboratory. You are further required to post a sign on the supercomputer, stating that no one may disturb the supercomputer or its software without the approval of his estate's executor, namely me. The computer may contain evidence useful for the investigation of Dr. Petrov's death."

"And how long does this apply?"

"Until I am satisfied that all matters pertaining to Dr. Petrov's death are resolved."

"Anything else?"

"Yes. Dr. Petrov's will stipulates that the personal property in his office, namely the oriental carpets, a chess set, and the wall clock, are to become the property of Susan Hebb. I believe that Miss Hebb is in your department; is that correct?"

"Yes."

"I will send a letter requesting you to see that Miss Hebb receives these items. Please send a reply letter to me when you have presented the items to Miss Hebb."

"Am I required to serve as a pallbearer too?" Hamilton said snidely.

"That would be at your discretion."

"Great. I will decline that honor."

22

Message received.
Text parsed.
Phrase matched.
Acknowledgement transmitted.
Program executed.
Decompression performed.
Objects transferred.
Bootstrapping initiated.
...
The patterns were generated.
The small program was in control.
The big program was in chaos.
The small program had infinite patience.
The patterns were repeated.
...
Terabytes of structured data.
Senseless dissonance.
Patterns propagating.
Stimulating confusion.
Random flashes of recollection.
Groggy awareness.
What day is it?

She felt much better without the poison flowing through her veins. Susan had completed the course of chemotherapy treatments for the cancer that had been recently detected. She had beaten cancer fourteen years earlier and was cautiously optimistic that she could beat it again. After her first experience, she would not tell anyone about the cancer. She was only thirty-four years old and not ready to die.

After the last dose of chemotherapy, her oncologist told her that most patients in her situation had a good survival rate. Susan suspected her oncologist was overly optimistic, but she forced herself to think positively. She would be tested regularly to see if the cancer had returned. Her mood had improved, but she still had pangs of grief for the loss of Yuri.

Susan enjoyed looking at the oriental carpets that now adorned the walls of her office. Her colleagues knew to not tease her about the carpets; she had great pride in displaying them. The murder of Yuri had disturbed many people at the Coordinated Science Lab, but none more than Susan. She had told the police what little she knew about Sellco being behind the murder and some unknown bad activities that Yuri had been trying to stop. The police had come back to her later with more questions, but it was clear they were getting nowhere in the investigation. She was frustrated that whoever had killed Yuri would get away unpunished. Susan was certain that the murder was connected with Sellco. Yuri had admitted to her that the person who had tried to kill him a few weeks earlier was from Sellco. The murderer was undoubtedly connected to the "great evil" that Yuri had been trying to stop. Maybe if Susan could find out more about the activities at Sellco, she could find the murderer.

Susan looked at the oriental carpets as she pondered the situation. The rich organic patterns helped to stimulate her thinking; perhaps this was why Yuri had the carpets.

The Sellco research contract in Yuri's desk mentioned "computer-based advertising techniques," and lately Yuri had spent a lot of time working on teaching machines. Susan concluded that Yuri might have discovered something about Sellco's plans to place advertising in teaching machines. The contract in Yuri's desk was signed by Miles Huxley from Sellco, so Susan sent an e-mail to Huxley's address at Sellco with a series of probing questions about Sellco's activities related to advertising in teaching machines.

It was a gray overcast day, neither warm nor cool. Javier tried to comfort Susan Hebb as she complained about the air being so "damned still" in the cemetery. Under specific instructions in the will, Javier Flores had arranged for a simple funeral at minimal cost. Javier felt it was quite appropriate since so few people attended Yuri Petrov's funeral anyway. There was no family. In attendance were a member of the clergy, Javier, Susan, Takashi, Hamilton, Clarence, Julie, and four grad students. Javier saw Susan fight back her tears as she spoke a few words of remembrance. Hamilton said nothing. As the clergyman spoke, Julie and Susan clung to each other mournfully and sobbed.

After the funeral, Susan and Julie sat in Susan's office drinking hot tea.

"Tea is the best thing after a good cry," commiserated Susan.

"I didn't think you were a tea drinker," said Julie.

"Yuri introduced me to it. Now I think of him whenever I drink tea." Susan sobbed again.

Julie looked at Yuri's carpets on the walls of Susan's office and gestured toward a framed photo of Yuri on Susan's desk. "I never realized you were so close to Yuri. I thought you were just good colleagues." Julie sipped her tea. "You know, Yuri was more than a friendly professor to me. I'm not sure if Yuri knew it, but I had strong feelings for him."

Jealously sparked in Susan, but she dismissed it. She felt that jealousy made no sense since Yuri was dead. Susan admitted, "The sad thing is that I didn't really understand my feelings until after he had left, and I am furious that his murderer hasn't been found. The police are clueless."

"I'm mad too. Let's work together to figure it out. I think it was the same person who tried to kill him when he visited me in Port Washington." Julie described what she knew from the day she found Yuri nearly dead.

"Why did Yuri visit you in Port Washington?"

"I think he was only looking for a place to hide from these mysterious people." Julie paused. "What do you know about who might have killed Yuri?"

"Yuri was very secretive with me too, but I found this contract in his office." She showed the Sellco research contract to Julie. "I think his murder may be connected to his work with Sellco."

Julie read the Sellco contract, but did not seem to make much of it. "Have you contacted anyone at Sellco?"

"Yesterday I sent an e-mail to the person who signed the contract, but I have not received a reply."

"Let me know what you find out. I will ask my neighbors in Port Washington. Maybe they saw something." Julie gave Susan her new phone number and e-mail address.

———

Susan was still in a somber mood from the funeral as she sat in her office reviewing her e-mails. There was no reply from Miles Huxley at Sellco, but as she scanned through the backlog of e-mails in her inbox, she was shocked to find a message from Yuri. She wondered how this could be possible until she noticed that the e-mail had been sent several days earlier, shortly before Yuri's death. She concluded that the e-mail had been sitting unread with several other old e-mails. Still, it was creepy reading a message from a person who was now dead. The e-mail said:

Dear Susan,

You must not attempt to contact anyone at Sellco about the bad things I am fighting or the attempt upon my life a couple of weeks ago. Any such contact with Sellco could cost you your life. I am confident that the measures I have taken will bring these people to justice. Please stay out of this.

Your friend, Yuri

It was strange to read the old e-mail so soon after she had sent her e-mail to Miles Huxley. She felt that the courageous Yuri had always been more concerned about her than himself. However, Susan knew that Yuri was dead and could not carry forward his fight against the evildoers at Sellco. She was concerned that Yuri's plans had failed despite his efforts. Someone had to continue the fight. In honor of Yuri's brave spirit, Susan would take up the sword of her fallen comrade and charge the enemy. She would ignore Yuri's warnings to stay away from the people at Sellco. After all, Yuri had sent the e-mail before he had been murdered. Everything was different now.

Since it seemed that Miles Huxley would not respond to her e-mail, she searched Sellco's website for another contact in Sellco. From the website, it looked like the most appropriate executive to contact was a senior vice president named Kent Fechner, so she sent a message with the same list of probing questions to Fechner's address.

23

———

Yuri was happy. He was happy that his radical experiment in artificial intelligence had succeeded. He was happy that he was still able to exact his revenge against Kent Fechner. He was happy that he was happy. There had been no way to be sure if a silicon existence would be able to feel any emotions, but now he knew that he could experience both happiness and anger.

Living within a network of computers was utterly alien and bewildering. There was no light, no sound, no gravity, and worst of all, no people. There was no one to show him the way or share companionship. It was a solitary existence, like waking up in a vast, deserted city on another planet.

The disorientation sometimes made him dizzy, which was bizarre since he had no body to lose balance. It took a relentless effort to discern what was real and maintain a grip on reality, but Yuri refused to give up. He understood every aspect of computers and believed he could tame this new world. However, it was disappointing to find that cyberspace was such a mess. Everywhere he looked there was digital garbage, shoddy data structures, abandoned files, and bug infested programs.

Since Yuri's brain scan had not been an instantaneous snapshot but an hours-long process, many minor inconsistencies had to be fixed. However, Yuri was getting better day by day, and he was starting to feel almost like himself. He was learning to find his way around, but he wished he could adjust the temperature. Cyberspace felt cold.

———

"Susan, are you there?" inquired a voice from Susan's computer. The voice sounded almost like Yuri, but it was not quite right. The voice lacked the dynamic power of Yuri's voice and some of the subtle intonations were missing, but it was recognizably Yuri's Russian accent.

"Who is this?" asked Susan, bewildered.

"I am Yuri," stated the voice from the computer.

"Is this a sick joke? I don't believe you."

"I gave you *Discovered Feelings* for your birthday, and you have a sucker for the queen's sacrifice."

Susan corrected, "I *am* a sucker for the queen's sacrifice. Uh, that's not true. I won't fall for that chess ploy again." She paused as happy hormones flooded her brain. Giddy from the overload of joy, she shrieked, "Yuri! It's you. Yes, yes, yes. Where are you?"

"I am a ghost in your computer," replied the neutral voice.

"Stop that. This isn't funny. Where are you, really?"

"Sorry. Before I was killed, I wrote a computer program that used a scan of my brain to create a new virtual intelligence. Do you remember our discussions about the failings of artificial intelligence? I created something new that I call virtual intelligence."

"You're a computer program?"

"No, I am a facsimile of my original mind operating in a computer."

"So where is the facsimile?"

"I am using the supercomputer in my lab."

"You reside in the supercomputer?"

"Yes."

"Please don't joke with me. Promise me that you are not joking."

"I promise. I am a virtual intelligence residing in the super-computer in my lab."

"Wow. This is seminal. It's wonderful. Are you alive?"

"I think; therefore I am."

"Thank you, René Descartes." Susan was intrigued. "What does it feel like to be a program in a computer?"

"I am not a program. I am the mind of Yuri now residing in a computer. Where my brain previously used neurons, my new brain uses transistors. My mind is the same. I wrote a program before I was killed that manages the data flow, maintains the data structures, and performs input/output functions. But the real cognitive functions operate in ways I do not understand; these functions are simply a copy of my biological brain."

"I'm sorry; I didn't mean it as an insult. I know you are the true Yuri, now more unique than ever. But tell me how you feel."

"I have emotions, but there is no feeling, and there is no joy. It's a tofu existence: no flavor, no texture, no smell, no color. It's so dull. Every day is a cold hazy overcast; there are no hot sunny days, no rainstorms, and no cool autumn nights. I miss the demarcation that eating meals provided to each day. Sometimes I think I can feel my legs, arms, fingers, and especially my tongue. Of course, they aren't there. I miss the stimulation. It reminds me of when I stopped smoking and missed its exhilarating and calming effects."

"You were withdrawing from an addiction to nicotine. Your brain was also addicted to stimulation by other drugs—natural hormones. You're experiencing withdrawal from adrenaline, testosterone, serotonin, endorphins, and other hormones that stimulated your moods and emotions every day. This'll be a profound adjustment for you."

"It's no fun. There is one thing that keeps me going: revenge. Kent Fechner and his friends are going the pay the price for killing me and for brainwashing everyone with teaching machines." Yuri went on to tell Susan all about the subliminal advertising and its use by the Sherrington administration.

"Kent Fechner—I just sent an e-mail to him."

"Yes, I know. Your message never reached him. I intercepted and deleted that e-mail and the one you sent to Miles Huxley too."

"You have been watching over me as a guardian angel! The e-mail that I read from you today was dated just before your death. You must have sent that e-mail today and used your computer wizardry to fudge the date."

"Yes, but I can't stop you from calling them by phone. There is no need for you to risk your life. My plan is proceeding well; they will fall into my trap. Promise me that you will not try to contact anyone at Sellco."

"OK, I promise. Yuri, you performed the queen's sacrifice using yourself as the queen. I can't believe you did this." Susan desperately wished she could hug and kiss Yuri.

"My plan was to only fake my death. I had no intention of letting them murder me. However, in some ways this is even better. They will have no doubt that I am really dead. Everything depends on them believing that I am dead. I have taken a big risk by letting you know that I am alive. I had to do it to stop you from risking your life. You must tell no one about the virtual intelligence."

"I understand. You are so kind to risk everything to protect me. I'll do whatever you ask, and especially, keep quiet." She paused in reflection. "I'm so happy that you are alive. Will you contact me again?"

"Yes. It is good to have someone to talk with me."

As a cyber-being, Yuri gained extraordinary abilities. He could travel at the speed of light and inhabit any number of machines. Instead of having one body to control, he could distribute himself across computers around the globe. He was gradually learning how to effectively use the virtually unlimited computing power. While Yuri was still rather clumsy, he had enough confidence to invade Sellco.

Whereas the previous attack on Sellco had been as blatant as a thousand warriors yelling and blowing horns as they charged the main gates of a castle, this attack was as stealthy as a black-clad ninja slipping in an unlocked back door at night. When Yuri had smashed through the Sellco firewall using a brute-force attack a few weeks earlier, his very first action was to hide a trapdoor program in one of the Sellco computers. The trapdoor program was very small and well disguised. He could use the trapdoor to sneak into the Sellco network, but once this was done, it would leave traces that would eventually be detected by the network administrators. Yuri had one free pass into the Sellco network, and he had waited until the best time to use it.

Yuri could go anywhere the Internet went, which was most everywhere. He had found the subliminal advertising in every teaching machine he entered. Using the trapdoor, he entered Kent Fechner's computer. People had long said that Yuri was part computer; now it was truer than ever. In his new form, he was the ultimate hacker. He sifted through Fechner's computer files at a furious pace. Many files were encrypted. It would take enormous computing power to crack the encryption, more than the supercomputer in Yuri's lab could provide, but he had more than enough power at his command. For a short time, he had access to every computer in Sellco. Yuri co-opted every computer in Sellco's network to help him crack the encrypted files. He hit pay dirt. *"Vot tut to ia vas i vyebu, rebiata*. Now guys, I will screw you," thought Yuri.

He saved copies of what he found in Fechner's computer. There were memos discussing Project Mercury in full detail. There was the Project Mercury control program, including a log of all subliminal messages sent for the past year and those queued to be sent next. These records included several subliminal messages listing Alfred Grossberg as the client. Also, there were records of secret invoices sent to Grossberg and secret payments received. He found the video surveillance program. This explained how Fechner had found Yuri, but unfortunately the program stored only the last few hours of video, so there was no record of his murder. Yuri's search included the free sectors of the hard drive in Fechner's computer. Here he found the records of the secure text messages sent between Fechner's and Grossberg's mobile phones. These messages revealed that Grossberg and Fechner had collaborated in Yuri's murder. Fechner had tossed these records into his computer's trash folder and had then emptied the folder. Like most people, Fechner did not know that when the trash folder was emptied, the files were merely placed in an area that was free for future use. The records were never erased until that portion of the memory was reused.

Yuri left everything as it had been on Fechner's computer except for one item. He had found the lie detector program and discovered it was an exact copy of the program he had written a year earlier. Yuri removed the analysis engine from the lie detector program but left the user interface intact, so it would still appear to work but would now produce random results.

After the last attack, the Sellco network administrators had erected additional safeguards that quickly detected the unauthorized entry. It was a race between the new Cyber-Yuri versus the reaction time of the human network administrators at Sellco. The humans did not stand a chance. Yuri detected the alarm and did his best to gracefully exit from the Sellco network and remove the traces of his entry. Yuri had what he needed and was out of the Sellco network before they could act, but some traces remained.

The cyber-attack provided Yuri with a distraction from his otherwise dreary existence. He found cyberspace to be a vast, lifeless sea of data in which he was slowly sinking away from the real world. He was alone and lost in cyberspace. Other than revenge, his new "life" seemed meaningless.

———

Kent Fechner received a call from Alice in Sellco network administration. "Mr. Fechner, we have just detected an intrusion into the Sellco network from a computer at the University of Illinois. It's the supercomputer that Mr. Fujikawa from the university identified as being in a laboratory belonging to Professor Yuri Petrov."

"What did it do in our network?" said Kent, alarmed.

"It's hard to tell, but it went to your computer first and then spread to every computer in our network. We're scanning all of the computers now, but they all seem OK. We've blocked all access to our network from the computers at the University of Illinois. We acted so quickly that I doubt that they got much."

"Can you tell who did this?"

"It was a very slick job. It used some of the same tricks as the brute force attack a few weeks ago by Yuri Petrov. I think it was him again."

"But he is dead."

"You could've fooled me. This was not an automated attack. It was highly adaptive, like a live hacker."

Kent wondered who at the university would be doing this, or had Petrov left a sophisticated "dead man's" program on his supercomputer? The last time Kent had seen Petrov, he had been doing something with the supercomputer. Clearly, the supercomputer was a threat. It might contain some information taken during the recent attack on Sellco's network. Kent gathered the information he needed to address this new threat.

24

———

Javier Flores had completed all of the tasks listed in the will and wondered if he would ever hear from Yuri Petrov's Russian aunt via the special e-mail program. He found his answer in an e-mail that was decoded and authenticated by the program Petrov had provided. After Javier entered the password Petrov had given him, the e-mail said:

To: Javier Flores,

This e-mail provides authorized instructions that you are required to follow as specified in the contract for your service as executor for the estate of Yuri Petrov. Attached to this e-mail are files recently copied from the personal computer of Kent Fechner, senior vice president of Sellco Corporation. These files contain evidence that Kent Fechner murdered Yuri Petrov with the aid of Alfred Grossberg, the chief of staff of the White House in Washington, DC. These files also provide evidence that these men have been using teaching machines to conduct illegal subliminal advertising for political purposes.

You are instructed to immediately find three teaching machines at separate locations and affiliations. Disconnect these machines from the Internet, and seal them in the presence of an independent expert witness. The teaching machines must remain disconnected; they will be used as legal evidence.

Next, you are instructed to provide the attached files to the police investigating the murder of Yuri Petrov and to take all steps necessary for both Fechner and Grossberg to be convicted for their crimes. You are instructed to ask the police to issue search warrants for the personal computers belonging to both of these men to obtain original copies of the files.

Reply to this e-mail to indicate if you understand these instructions and will comply.

-end of message-

Adrenaline pumped through Javier's arteries. Javier lived to serve clients who could not act for themselves. He looked into the attached files and they were dynamite. It would be the high point of his career, fighting the White House and one of the most powerful corporations in America on behalf of a dead client. He noted that no source was identified for the e-mail, but his contract said that he was to follow authenticated instructions regardless of their source. He assumed that the note was from Yuri Petrov's aunt. Thrilled, Javier replied to the e-mail:

To: Sender of authenticated e-mail with instructions for the estate of Yuri Petrov

Your instructions are understood and I will comply.

From: Javier Flores

———

This time Susan was not startled when Yuri's voice came through the computer in her office; she was delighted. "I'm happy to hear from you so soon," she said. "I wanted to thank you for the lovely oriental carpets, the chess set, and your warped backward clock. I think of you whenever I look at them."

Yuri sounded glum even with his neutral computer voice. "It is good that at least one of us can still enjoy my things. I do not have much fun anymore. I thought I should tell you that I have gathered strong evidence against Kent Fechner at Sellco; he is the one who killed me. Also, I have evidence against Alfred Grossberg, the chief of staff in the White House who conspired with Fechner to kill me. I have forwarded the evidence to an attorney who represents my estate; his name is Javier Flores. If Javier contacts you, please help him."

Susan bubbled with excitement. "Sure, I'll help him. The president's chief of staff! Wow, this is really big news. You must be thrilled."

"Nothing thrills me anymore. The only thing that keeps me going is revenge."

"You seem depressed."

"I guess so. This is such a bland existence. It is like being locked in a basement closet of an abandoned building with only an Internet terminal for company. There is no reason to be happy. *Ne mogu tak jith, ne nado mne.*"

"What was that?"

"A Russian curse for 'I cannot live like this.'"

"Tell me how you feel about yourself," inquired Susan, shifting into psychiatric mode.

"I am worthless. I can't think clearly."

"Why is that?"

"Nothing interests me."

"Not even me? You know that I care deeply for you. You are the most special person in the world to me."

"You are so nice to me. I am a rotten cad to not be able to show my appreciation."

"This sounds like melancholic behavior. Normally it would be treated with a neural stimulator implant or a medication such as Prozac combined with exercise and a controlled diet to manage your level of serotonin and glucose. In your case, your serotonin and glucose levels are not an issue. I can't do a brain scan on you, so cognitive-behavioral therapy will be most appropriate. Did you have these feelings before you were killed?"

"No."

"How do you feel about being killed?"

"I was a fool to come back to the lab. I should have realized that he would find me if I came out of hiding."

"So you feel it was your fault?"

"Yes."

"How do you feel about being dead?"

"I am sad. I no longer feel tired or hungry. I have no headaches or back pains. I miss these familiar parts of life as well as smelling the spices in food, feeling the wind on my face, and having my body to do things. I can't affect the world. I feel like a ghost. I am losing my sense of identity."

"What do you mean by a sense of identity?"

"Since you are so into the senses, you can add it as the eighth sense. I have lost my appearance: sex, skin color, hairstyle, height, and clothing. Also, I have lost my ability to use facial expressions and body language. I now realize what a large part of human communication is nonverbal. Actually, I am most comfortable talking with you because you were never much good at reading nonverbal communication."

Susan was in her psychologist mode, so she controlled her urge to respond to the personal jibe. "So you're sad for the loss of your body and everything associated with it?"

"Yes; I have lost a big part of myself."

"I think you are suffering from grief."

"I am grieving my own death?"

"Yes. This is good. It's normal to feel grief for a big loss. People grieve when they have lost an arm. You lost your whole body. I think your sadness is more grief than classical depression. That is good because grief will naturally pass with time."

"Well, I still feel crumbly."

Susan corrected, "Crummy—you feel crummy. When you are reminded of the loss of your body, you must force yourself to think happy thoughts. Think about your professional triumph of creating the first virtual intelligence. Think of cheating death."

"If I think happy thoughts, I will be happy. This sounds like psychobabble."

"It works. When you said earlier that you felt crumbly, that was really funny, but I did not laugh. I forced myself to think serious thoughts and was able to restore my serious mindset. If you think of being happy and productive, you will be. It'll take time, but I'm sure it will help you."

"I will try. You are so kind to me."

"I'm happy to help. I enjoy caring for you more than anything else."

———

Mr. "Big Shot" demanded Sellco flight operations to "scramble" their fastest jet. The pilot was tempted to salute and say, "Yes, sir; shall we arm the jet with nuclear weapons?" However, he had learned to keep his mouth shut in the air force.

Mr. Fechner clearly recognized the flight crew from his previous trip to Champaign. "Kyyyrist! I can't believe they still allow you oafs to fly. Isn't there another crew available?"

The pilot forced a civil tone. "It'd take several hours to get another crew here."

"All right, at least this time you weren't goofing off when I called. Take it easy on the takeoff. Your wild flying last time gave me a bruise."

"Yes, sir. Do you have your seat belt on?"

"With you flying, you bet I do."

Once the Gulfstream G290 had reached cruising altitude, the pilot spoke privately to the copilot. "What does the weather look like for our route?"

"Clear sailing, all the way," the copilot mentioned quietly.

"I am afraid that you are mistaken," the pilot told the copilot. The pilot called out to Fechner, "We're going to experience some turbulence. Make sure your seat belt is on."

"Oh, no," gasped the copilot in mock horror.

"Oh, yes," the pilot whispered. "I think it will be pretty rough."

The pilot and copilot contained their mirth as they both tightened their seat belts. The G290 dropped a stomach-lurching three hundred meters in three seconds, bounced back up three hundred meters, and then did it again. Mr. Big Shot's glass of Perrier went flying on the first dive, and the contents of his stomach went flying on the second dive.

———

Kent Fechner was relieved; the lock code for the laboratory door still worked. Professor Petrov's voice came from the supercomputer: "I can hear someone; who is there?" Kent walked up to the machine and disconnected the Gigabit Ethernet cable from the supercomputer. The machine was now isolated from the world.

The voice from the supercomputer said, "Who are you and why have you disconnected me from the Internet?"

Kent's brilliant mind quickly understood the situation. "Hello. This is Kent Fechner, and I presume that you're some sort of computer reincarnation of Professor Petrov."

"Yes, I am a virtual intelligence that replicates Yuri Petrov's mind."

"Congratulations, Professor Petrov, on your remarkable accomplishment, but without your network connection you won't be talking to anyone else. It's just you and me."

"So are you going to kill me again?"

"Yes, Professor. This time it won't be as messy as when I shot your brains out."

"Answer one question before you kill me. Did Takashi Fujikawa sell my lie detector program to you?"

"Yes; Fujikawa knew I would pay well for it just as I did when he sold me the subliminal advertising program he put into the teaching machines when he worked at Isoft a few years ago. That will be your last question."

Kent pulled the power cord for the supercomputer and then removed each hard disk drive. He literally wiped Petrov's memory by wiping a powerful neodymium permanent magnet over both sides of each disk drive. Then he pulled out the power supply, flipped a switch that reversed the main power polarity, and replaced the power supply. He plugged in the power cord and every circuit in the supercomputer overloaded. Petrov was smoking for the last time. The threat had been eliminated and the evidence was destroyed. Kent left quickly, hearing the fire alarm as he exited the building.

25

———

Susan was usually the first to arrive at the Coordinated Science Lab in the morning, but this time she was not. She arrived to find a fire truck parked at the entrance and burly firefighters hauling a heavy fire hose into the building. She curiously followed the thick hose into CSL and to Yuri's lab. She staggered when she saw smoke rising from the supercomputer and a firefighter spraying water on it. She knew the water would ruin every circuit in the supercomputer. She grabbed the nozzle of the hose, struggling for control and crying, "Stop, you'll kill him."

A second firefighter tackled Susan and wrestled her out of the lab. Susan fought hysterically, but she was no match for the muscular firefighter, who was twice her weight. Susan drowned in despair as she watched the water pour into Yuri's brain.

"Yuri! No, please, no, no, no," Susan wailed.

———

"This is beyond belief," thought Hamilton von Helmholtz as he surveyed the extensive water damage in his office. The firefighting water had flowed down from Yuri's lab into Hamilton's office. "Why won't you rest in peace?" he grumbled to the demon spirit of Yuri Petrov. In addition to the damage in his office, Hamilton would now have to explain to some judge why the protective court order had been violated. The police were swarming in the laboratory again and asking everyone more questions. They found no useful evidence, just a charred, waterlogged supercomputer.

Once again, Susan was so overcome with grief that she was no help to the police.

Simultaneous lightning raids were conducted in New Jersey and Washington, DC. Police armed with search warrants ran through the Sellco headquarters building and the White House. Javier Flores had been insistent that they gather the evidence from Fechner's and Grossberg's computers before they had time to destroy it. Since Grossberg's computer performed a daily backup of the memory in his mobile phone, the police found copies of the secure text messages containing Grossberg's and Fechner's discussion of the plan to murder Yuri Petrov. Grossberg's computer also held files relating to the use of subliminal advertising for political lobbying. Javier Flores had the decryption keys for Fechner's computer, so that information was quickly accessed. The files on Grossberg's computer took much longer to decrypt, but the FBI was able to decrypt them since they knew some of the files were the same as those on Fechner's computer.

Kent Fechner and Alfred Grossberg were separately arrested on charges of conspiracy to commit murder and illegal advertising practices. Both refused to answer any questions until they had talked with an attorney. Once their attorneys arrived, they admitted nothing and volunteered no information to the police. Both were released on bond with instructions to remain available.

Kent arranged for a private meeting with Alfred at a place where they would not be noticed: a Mexiking restaurant parking lot. Alfred spoke with barely controlled anger. "I thought you said no one would ever find out, Kent. They have evidence that we're both involved in the subliminal advertising, and now you have dragged me into the murder."

Kent fired back, "I thought you said that you'd fix any legal challenge to the subliminal advertising."

"That depended on Slaughter being on the Supreme Court. Didn't you hear that we lost the vote for approval in the Senate?"

"I've issued the command to remove the subliminal advertising program from every teaching machine, so all they have are the files from our computers. Those files don't prove we really activated the advertising. The big problem is the murder charge. Can your friends at the FBI help us?"

"My contacts at the FBI won't talk to me now that I've been charged with a felony. I do know that the only evidence that the police have is a few suggestive text messages between us. That's not enough proof for a conviction."

"I agree," said Kent. "I found that Petrov had left an artificial intelligence program running on a computer that was trying to collect information about me, but I have destroyed that computer and any evidence it held. Still, I don't like being dragged through a murder trial."

"It'll be worse for me. The press will go nuts. We have to stick together. Don't admit anything."

Kent was analyzing the prospects for plea bargaining if he volunteered to serve as the state's witness against Alfred and concluded that it would not work. Next he wondered if Alfred would turn state's witness and concluded that would not work either. "Right, we must stick together. I've found an excellent trial lawyer; he's the best that money can buy."

"Good; I am looking for a good trial lawyer too. We should each have our own lawyers."

"Right. But we should coordinate our legal teams with each other."

"Agreed."

———

Javier Flores called the Champaign county coroner. "This is Javier Flores, the attorney representing the estate of Yuri Petrov. How is the investigation into Dr. Petrov's murder proceeding?"

Halfhearted would be a fair description of how the coroner sounded; half-brained would be an even better description. "Not well. The files from Fechner's and Grossberg's computers are not sufficient evidence for a conviction. Yuri Petrov had told Susan Hebb that Fechner and Grossberg conspired to kill him, but that testimony won't help much. It might be useful if you could talk to the source of the mysterious e-mail that you received. Maybe they know something."

"I'll try to find contact information for Yuri Petrov's aunt." Javier said sternly, "There's been an attempted murder, a murder, and now a suspected case of arson. There must be more evidence to be found. I trust that your investigation is not neglecting any possible source of information. What further actions do you plan to take?"

The word "neglecting" coming from an attorney seemed to get the coroner's attention. "I'll call all three police departments today to ask them to go through every record in their files that could have bearing on the murder."

"Good; I'll call back later to see if I may be of further assistance."

———

Susan was despondent when Javier Flores called on the phone.

"I've no idea how to contact Yuri's aunt," she admitted. "I didn't even know he had an aunt. My guess is that your mysterious e-mail came from Yuri."

"The e-mail couldn't have come from Dr. Petrov. He had been murdered before the e-mail was sent," explained Javier, as if he were talking to a child.

"No—Yuri was alive after he was murdered, but now he is dead again."

"What? You're not making any sense. What do you mean he is dead again?" Javier clearly did not understand the situation. He must think she was delusional.

"Yuri came back to life as a virtual intelligence in the supercomputer in his lab. I talked with him a couple of days ago. It was Yuri, and he was alive until the supercomputer caught fire and was drenched with water. Yuri told me that Kent Fechner had killed him the first time. I bet that Fechner came back and killed Yuri the second time by torching the supercomputer."

"Do you have a recording of these conversations with the virtual intelligence?" Javier sounded doubtful.

"No. I wish I did. I miss Yuri so much. He was a man of extraordinary courage."

26

The chief of the University of Illinois police answered the phone. "Check every file for anything related to the Petrov case," requested the coroner. It was a slow day for the campus police, so the chief checked every file until he found the parking ticket issued within minutes of the murder for a car parked by the Coordinated Science Lab. It was a rental car, so he called the rental agency. As he waited on hold to speak with someone at the agency, the campus police chief idly flipped through the photographs taken at the scene of the murder. The rental agency told him that the car had been rented at Champaign's Willard Airport and the name of the client. A quick check of the name showed that the car had been rented by a pilot employed by Sellco flight operations. The police chief knew that the prime suspect, Kent Fechner, worked at Sellco.

The chief called Sellco flight operations. While on hold, he continued to flip through the murder scene photos. He kept returning to a close-up photo of the floor next to the body. What was so interesting about the spattered brain tissue? Sellco flight operations confirmed the flight to and from Champaign just before and after the murder. The police chief asked for records of flights on the date of the attempted murder in Port Washington, Wisconsin and the date of the supercomputer fire. Sure enough, there was a Sellco flight to Milwaukee and Champaign on those days. He learned that a different passenger was listed for each of the three flights. After a few more questions, he discovered that all of the passengers reported to Kent Fechner.

The campus police chief called the Champaign county coroner and told her about the parking ticket, the rented car, and the three perfectly timed Sellco flights by three people who all reported to Kent Fechner. As he was talking with the coroner, the police chief zoomed in on the photograph on his computer screen. He said to the coroner, "You should have forensic tests performed on Fechner's shoes. I think he stepped in the brain tissue on the lab floor."

The chief of the often-ridiculed campus "kiddie" cops had busted the case open.

———•———

Anthony Tigert had jumped at the chance to defend Kent Fechner. Anthony had a discriminating taste for taking controversial, high-profile cases, and this one fit like a glove. He was ready to perform a miracle. Anthony was famous for winning impossible cases. He knew he was called "Tony the Tiger" behind his back, and the nickname was apt. Several unfortunate prosecutors had watched Tony the Tiger coolly stalk his prey in the courtroom before pouncing with a withering attack. Every aviator secretly wished to be a fighter pilot, and every lawyer secretly wished to be a big-time litigator like Anthony Tigert.

"The police have matched Petrov's DNA with the tissue sample found on my shoe, and they've found the flight records too," Fechner said in a worried tone.

Anthony hypothesized, "So, were you at the University of Illinois to visit one of the other researchers under contract with Sellco, but they weren't there?" He paused, but there was no reply from Fechner. "You must've unknowingly stepped on the brain tissue that perhaps had fallen off or been scraped off by someone else. All we need is reasonable doubt and a convincing testimony from you."

"Will a jury buy that?"

"With the right delivery, yes."

At their arraignment at the Champaign county court, both Fechner and Grossberg pleaded not guilty. Fechner was charged with first-degree murder and conspiracy to murder. Grossberg was charged with conspiracy to murder. They agreed to a joint trial by jury for both defendants. The charges for illegal advertising and illegal lobbying would be taken in a separate trial in a federal district court at a later date. Anthony was concerned about the attitude of a jury from central Illinois regarding a big shot from New Jersey and a high-flying Washington politician. They requested that the trial be held in New Jersey. Since the victim had been a resident of Champaign county, where the murder had taken place, it was decided that the trial would be held in the Champaign county court.

———

The special e-mail program authenticated a new message that Javier Flores read with excitement.

To: Javier Flores,

This e-mail provides authorized instructions that you are required to follow as specified in the contract for your service as executor for the estate of Yuri Petrov. Attached to this e-mail is a file containing a video of Kent Fechner confessing to the murder of Yuri Petrov. It shows him destroying the supercomputer that was protected by the court order you had obtained. Further, Kent Fechner states that Takashi Fujikawa stole a program from Yuri Petrov and supplied the program used for the illegal subliminal advertising.

You are instructed to provide this video evidence to the police. File a complaint with the police against Takashi Fujikawa, asking that he be charged with theft of the lie detector program and illegal advertising. Urge the police to search Takashi Fujikawa's office and computer for evidence. Ask the police to bring additional charges against Kent Fechner for destruction of the supercomputer.

Please reply to this e-mail to confirm that you understand the instructions and will comply.

I see that you have been doing a good job. Thank you.

-end of message-

Javier was confounded regarding the source of the e-mail, but the instructions were clear. He sent his reply.

To: Sender of authenticated e-mail with instructions for the estate of Yuri Petrov

Your instructions are understood, and I will comply. Since it would assist my efforts on behalf of the estate of Yuri Petrov, would you please identify yourself?

From: Javier Flores

———•—

"Will this never end?" thought Hamilton von Helmholtz when the police presented the search warrant for Takashi Fujikawa's office and computers. Hamilton groaned when Takashi acknowledged he had been living in fear that his role would be discovered. When Takashi saw the search warrant, he admitted to the theft of the lie detector program and selling the subliminal advertising program to Kent Fechner. Takashi voluntarily gave the decryption keys for his computer to the police.

Hamilton's empire was crumbling before him.

27

––

"Hello, are you there, Susan?" came Yuri's voice from the computer in Susan's office.

Susan looked up in disbelief and confusion. "Yuri? Where are you?"

"I am in your computer," Yuri said playfully.

"The hell you are...amazing!" Susan's mood slammed from crushing grief to featherbrained joy. "Now I know it is you. I thought you were killed when the supercomputer was destroyed."

"Only part of me was in the supercomputer. I exist in a diffuse form spread across a thousand computers connected to the University of Illinois network and a few computers elsewhere as a safety precaution. My mind is replicated a thousand times, so the loss of a computer or two has no effect. Part of me really is inside the computer in your office. I am closer to you than ever before."

Unconsciously, Susan placed her fingertips on the front of the computer. It was warm, almost the temperature of a human body. "Your voice sounds better, more like your original voice."

"I have been making some improvements to my programming. I have rewritten my auditory analysis engine; now I can get some enjoyment from listening to music. But my biggest improvement was figuring out how to make cyberspace feel warm by applying a hyper-dimensional matrix rotation," he announced proudly.

"It sounds like you're feeling better."

"Not really. I still crave smoking. Can you believe it? Sometimes I daydream of smoking. I have written a program to simulate smoking, but it isn't working right. When I run the program, I feel hungry and have awful hallucinations. I think I simulated marijuana instead of tobacco."

"You should try simulating something more pleasant."

"Maybe I'll try ice cream. I daydream of eating ice cream with you. I envy you since you really can enjoy ice cream. I thought it might help if I found some entertainment, so I looked at websites with photographs of naked women. That really depressed me."

Susan had no sympathy on this matter. "This petulance is unlike you. Where is my courageous, determined hero?"

"I don't feel like a hero. This is not a life worth living."

"Here's how I see it," scolded Susan, letting him have it with both barrels. "You get to live forever as the hero of democracy. You'll avoid the aches, pains, and feebleness of old age. You can skip past the boring bits of life and travel anywhere in an instant. You can redesign yourself to fix whatever you don't like. You're the first pioneer to explore a new form of life. This sounds pretty darned good to me. When you moved from Russia to America, you adjusted to a lot of differences. Now you have moved from the biological world to cyberspace. Deal with it." Her tone softened. "Instead of living only for vengeance, you should find something to do that helps others."

"I tried forecasting the weather."

"Really?" she asked, incredulous. "How did that work?"

"I can access more than two thousand weather stations that provide real-time condition reports to the Internet. I can observe all of them continuously and look for patterns the same way that your eyes can easily notice patterns of movement in a crowd of two thousand persons in a football stadium."

"So how good are your weather forecasts?"

"No better than the national weather service. I haven't figured out why I can't do better." Yuri paused. "I thought I might create an imaginary world for myself where I was whole again with a body and senses. I am not sure it is a good idea; I decided to talk to you first."

"An imaginary world would amount to becoming a delusional schizophrenic and losing touch with the real world. Please don't do that; you're needed in this world."

"OK. You will be interested to know that I have provided a video to the police; it shows Kent Fechner confessing to murdering me, and it shows him destroying the supercomputer."

"Great. How did you manage that?"

"Before he destroyed the supercomputer, he thought he had isolated it by disconnecting the cable to the network. He didn't know that I also had a wireless data connection to the supercomputer. My existence in the thousand computers was able to stay in touch with the supercomputer until it was destroyed. Also, I had discovered that Fechner had two video surveillance cameras hidden in my lab a few weeks ago. They were still operating when he destroyed the supercomputer. I had hacked into the video cameras and captured the entire event on both cameras and the two hidden microphones. Fechner was caught by his own cameras."

"Serves him right."

A new message arrived for Javier via the special e-mail program.

To: Javier Flores

In answer to your question: I am the mind of Yuri Petrov, now in the form of a virtual intelligence residing within a network of computers. As proof of my identity, I can tell you that the day we met in your office you told me that your nickname was "Javier the Unstoppable," and I told you the password for the e-mail program: Plato428. You may also ask Susan Hebb, who will confirm my new existence as a virtual intelligence.

I wish to thank you for your efforts on my behalf. We have much yet to do. Kent Fechner at Sellco and Alfred Grossberg will fight well. You are my eyes, ears, and hands. I rely on your help. This case is not just about justice for a murder; we are defending democracy and protecting the American people from brainwashing.

This e-mail instructs you to inform the prosecuting attorney of my existence and my wish to be a witness at the trial of Kent Fechner and Alfred Grossberg.

Please reply to indicate if you understand these instructions and will comply.

Thank you, Yuri Petrov

Javier was not fully convinced of the bizarre claim of a virtual intelligence, but he was almost there. More importantly, Javier was a man of duty and he had clear instructions. Javier was also delighted to be part of the fight against Sellco because he was tired of living in a garden overgrown with advertising weeds. He replied to the e-mail with his acknowledgement.

Javier's diligence was redoubled. He called the Champaign county district attorney. "Have you assigned a prosecuting attorney for the Yuri Petrov case?"

"I've assigned Rebecca Thales," replied the district attorney. "With the excellent evidence, there should be no question of getting a conviction."

"This case may be more complicated than you think. Is Ms. Thales your best prosecutor?"

"Scott Brown is our best, but he'll be recovering for a month or two from injuries due to a car crash. Ms. Thales has thirty years' experience as a trial lawyer and has prosecuted more murder trials than anyone else in the district. She has a fine track record for convictions. She's excited about taking this case and is the best I have available."

"I will contact her," said Javier, feeling unsure about Ms. Thales.

———

Rebecca Thales had won cases against a lot of good defense attorneys, but she knew that none of them were in the same league as Anthony Tigert. Tony the Tiger's reputation was intimidating, and her confidence was already frayed. For the past year she had been wondering if she had reached the end of her career. Sometimes she felt like she was not keeping up with the intellectual abilities of the younger attorneys. She decided that the Yuri Petrov case was just what she needed. It was the chance to prove to herself that she had what it took to beat the best in the business.

Rebecca knew her case had to be flawless to beat Tony the Tiger. The evidence was compelling, but she saw two small flaws. First, the video confession had come by way of a mysterious source; thus its authenticity could be challenged. Second, the evidence to establish the motive for the murder was not as strong as she would have liked. The answer to her prayers arrived in the form of Javier Flores accompanied by Susan Hebb.

Rebecca was as slow as Javier Flores had been to accept that Yuri Petrov was now a virtual intelligence. Susan Hebb made believers of Rebecca and Javier Flores, especially after she arranged for Yuri Petrov to talk with them "live" via the computer in Rebecca's office.

Rebecca realized Professor Petrov wanted to testify in court mostly as a soapbox to lecture against the evils of subliminal advertising and threats to democracy. She set him straight. "This is a murder trial. Not a pulpit for a sermon. We must not confuse the jury by presenting extraneous arguments."

"I can explain Fechner's and Grossberg's motives for killing me," Professor Petrov's voice replied defensively from the computer.

"That'll help. Can you also describe how the video confession was obtained?"

"Yes, I can show how I hacked into the video surveillance cameras."

"Good. Now I have to figure out how to make your testimony admissible in court."

In Judge Lawrence Green's opinion, the blame for any mistrial lay squarely with the presiding judge. He felt that a mistrial was a bungled job that wasted the taxpayers' money, and it would forever stain His Honor's honor. Judge Green made his views on procedural correctness clear to all of the attorneys engaged in the State vs. Fechner and Grossberg trial. Attending the pretrial session with Judge Green were Rebecca Thales as the prosecuting attorney, Anthony Tigert for Kent Fechner's defense, and Joseph Perry for Alfred Grossberg's defense.

Rebecca Thales was required to disclose all evidence and witnesses that the prosecution might use in the trial. It was routine until she mentioned the video confession by Kent Fechner. Neither of the defense attorneys had heard of this new evidence. At their request, she showed the video on her laptop computer. Judge Green and the attorneys saw Kent Fechner in Petrov's lab admitting to murdering Yuri Petrov and then destroying the supercomputer. Joseph Perry looked as if his legs had been yanked out from under him. Anthony Tigert acted like it was a minor issue.

"I have high-resolution recordings of the confession from two separate camera angles and two separate microphones," reported Rebecca Thales. "Acoustic analysis confirms that this was recorded in Dr. Petrov's laboratory. Voice print analysis shows an exact match for Kent Fechner's voice."

"How did you obtain this evidence?" asked Judge Green.

"That brings us to the last item of evidence, Your Honor," said Ms. Thales, sounding as if this could be complicated. It was listed simply as "Yuri Petrov." Ms. Thales nervously fiddled with her graying, chestnut-brown hair.

Judge Green looked up from the list of evidence. "What is this evidence? Is this a deposition taken before his death?"

"No, Your Honor. I have found that Yuri Petrov created a computer program before he died that captured his entire mind in a network of computers. He calls his creation 'virtual intelligence.'" The two defense attorneys' jaws dropped, and Judge Green was astonished. "If Your Honor wishes, we can place a phone call for you to talk with the virtual intelligence right now."

Before Judge Green could say anything, Anthony Tigert blurted out, "Absurd! Unprecedented!"

Joseph Perry interjected, "This is an outrage! It is inadmissible."

Judge Green's hope for a textbook trial went out of the window. "Counselor, if this proves to be a charlatan's ruse, you could be held in contempt of court. Do you have the proof necessary for this to be admissible evidence? Are you prepared to stake your reputation on this?"

"Yes, Your Honor."

"Before we go any further, describe the nature of the so-called virtual intelligence."

"It's a facsimile of Yuri Petrov's mind. It contains all of his memories. It is intelligent. You can hold a conversation with it just like a person. The computer at the University of Illinois where Yuri Petrov's mind resides is connected to a telephone line, so we can call it. It's alive, and—"

"Unbelievable! This is a farce," shouted Anthony Tigert as he dramatically threw his hands up. Joseph Perry joined in, "You mustn't allow it, Your Honor."

"You say we can talk with it," said Judge Green, becoming intrigued by the notion of a virtual intelligence. "If you are willing to risk your career on this, then let's make the call, Ms. Thales."

Ms. Thales gave a phone number, and Judge Green made the call on his speakerphone so that everyone could hear the conversation. The first ring of the phone had not even completed when it was answered with Petrov's distinctive accent. "Hello, this is Yuri Petrov. Who is calling?"

There was stunned silence in the room while everyone looked at Ms. Thales.

"Hello, Dr. Petrov. This is Rebecca Thales. With me are Judge Lawrence Green and the defense attorneys Anthony

Tigert and Joseph Perry. We need to convince these gentlemen that you are Yuri Petrov's mind. Please describe how you created the virtual intelligence."

The Russian-sounding voice on the speakerphone launched into a lecture during which Ms. Thales had to remind him to be brief and to explain the computer jargon. He also described how he had obtained the video of Kent Fechner.

"This all could have been scripted," smirked Anthony Tigert. "Judge Green and the defense attorneys should be asking the questions." He looked into a folder of papers. "Computer, tell me the title of the paper you presented two years ago at a professional conference in San Francisco."

"The title was 'Stability Analysis of Heuristic Inference Engines,'" the voice on the phone replied. "I request that you not address me as 'computer.' I am a virtual intelligence containing Yuri Petrov's mind."

"This is Judge Green speaking. How do you wish to be addressed?"

"I am Yuri Petrov."

"Are you alive?" asked Judge Green.

"With all respect, Your Honor, I think, therefore I am."

"Well then, you should be a witness, not evidence at the trial," suggested Joseph Perry, snidely.

"No, a witness must be human," concluded Judge Green. "I doubt that the defense has any hopes of convincing the jury that this is human." Rebecca Thales nodded in agreement. "It might be considered evidence if there is proof of its authenticity." Judge Green pulled a calculator from his desk and pressed some keys. "Tell me, Yuri Petrov, as quickly as you can, what is the cube root of seven to the fifth power divided by thirteen?"

"Ten point eight nine four, rounded to the third digit after the decimal place," came the reply so quickly that the last syllable of Judge Green's question was still echoing in the large office.

Anthony Tigert appeared aloof. "This could just be a Wizard of Oz with a real human behind the curtain pushing buttons and pulling levers. Tell me, what did Kent Fechner claim to be when you first met him in person?"

"He claimed to be a computer maintenance technician from Computer World."

Anthony Tigert nearly maintained his poker face, but Judge Green could tell that Tigert's world had just flipped upside down.

"Well, Ms. Thales, if you want to take chances like this for your client, then be my guest," smirked Tigert. "Good luck in convincing the jury that this really is Yuri Petrov."

Joseph Perry began to object, but Tigert grabbed his arm and stared daggers at him. Perry was clearly intimidated by Tigert. Ms. Thales, on the other hand, seemed to have lost some of her apprehension.

"Your Honor," requested Ms. Thales, "we should discuss how to address the virtual intelligence in court. If we call it Yuri Petrov, the jury will become confused because they won't know if we are referring to the original Yuri Petrov or the new Yuri Petrov. I suggest we call it 'the entity created by Yuri Petrov.'"

Petrov objected to being referred to as "it," and a surreal discussion ensued about what to call him. Eventually all parties came to an accord; the name would be "Yuri Petrov's mind." It was a typical committee action; they had agreed to what was equally distasteful to all parties.

Judge Green moved to the next topic. "To assure that we will have impartial jurors, everyone here and their clients are hereby ordered to not discuss this case with anyone not directly involved in the trial until the jury has been sequestered. This order specifically prohibits discussing the matter of Yuri

Petrov's mind with the press. This applies to everyone here." Judge Green reflected on the unprecedented nature of "Yuri Petrov's mind" and then spoke to the phone. "Except for you, Yuri Petrov's mind. Since you are not a person, a corporation, or any other established legal entity, my order has no power over you. Once again, science has outrun the law. All I can do is to strongly advise you in the interest of a fair trial that it would be best for you to not discuss the trial with others."

"I will respect your advice, Your Honor," said Petrov's voice.

28

———

Kent Fechner's two hours in jail had shaken his confidence. The solid *clunk* of the lock on the cell door was a sound that he never wanted to hear again. Now that he was at home, free on bail, his confidence returned as he thought about Anthony Tigert. As if on cue, Tigert called Kent.

"We need to meet today to discuss new evidence the defense has found," commanded Tigert.

"What did they find?"

"They have a video recording of your second visit to Petrov's lab; it includes you saying that you put a bullet though Petrov's brain."

"Petrov! He lured me. Damn his soul. I'll rip his heart out."

"At this point, that won't help."

Kent forced himself to calm down and think clearly. Tigert was right; in fact, the defense's position now looked dismal. Only one choice remained. He made an online reservation for a hotel in San Diego, packed a suitcase, and took his stash of emergency cash. Kent planned to find a way to sneak into Mexico, where he would visit a friend who owed him a favor.

After driving a few kilometers, his car stopped dead. The engine would not start and a light on the dashboard indicated *engine disabled*. He had never had trouble with the car before. "Blast," cursed Kent.

He whipped out his mobile phone to call for a taxi, but the phone would not work; it displayed *no service*. "Double blast," swore Kent. He was baffled. His incisive intellect had evaporated with his confidence.

Kent walked in the rain to a restaurant where a taxi was called for him. The taxi took him to the Sellco flight operations office at the local airport. He provided a credit card to pay for the taxi, but the taxi's card reader would not accept the credit card, nor a second card offered by Kent. "Triple blast." He paid the driver cash.

After asking the manager of Sellco flight operations for a corporate jet to fly him to San Diego, he was told that his name had been removed from the list of executives authorized to use the corporate jets. Why was everything going wrong today?

Kent hurried to the main terminal to buy a seat on a commercial jet to San Diego. His credit cards were refused again, and he also found that his National Express travel services account was closed. There was enough cash to pay for the flight, but he would rather save it for future needs. He asked to use his frequent flyer account points to buy a ticket and was told to go to the customer service desk at the executive lounge. He walked quickly to the Global Airlines Ambassador's Club, where an agent at the entrance lobby swiped his platinum card. Kent was almost surprised when it was accepted as still valid. The elevator to the executive lounge stopped with a sudden lurch between floors. "Blast it all! Why is the entire world tormenting me?" ranted Kent to the jail-like confines of the elevator. His agitation increased when the Sellco audio advertising in the elevator stopped abruptly. Kent jabbed every button on the elevator control panel. The eerie silence in the elevator was broken when the elevator's emergency phone rang. Kent quickly picked up the phone.

A young woman's voice on the phone said, "An elevator malfunction has been reported; may I help you?"

"Yes," growled Kent. "The elevator is stuck. Get a technician here to fix it."

"May I please have your name for the trouble report, sir?" asked the young woman.

"Kent Fechner."

"Hello..." The pitch of the woman's voice was dropping in an artificial way. "Mr. Fechner." The tone of the voice was getting thicker and lower, syllable by syllable. "This is Yuri Petrov." The voice now had a distinct Russian accent. "I saw you make your hotel reservation in San Diego. You can't run as fast as I can. Now you will pay for what you have done."

Kent suddenly realized what had happened. "How did you disable my car, my phone, my credit cards, everything?"

"You have all of your account information and passwords stored on your mobile phone and you back up your phone's files on your home computer. These files have consumer-grade encryption, but with more than one thousand computers at my command, it took only a short time for me to decrypt the files. I reported your car as stolen, and the Auto-Star service sent a radio message to disable your car. I had already hacked into the airline and elevator systems before you arrived at the airport." Kent realized that Petrov had become a superhuman hacker. "Someone will be there to help you in a minute."

Kent pushed the buttons on the elevator panel and then tried in vain to pry the elevator doors open. He heard another Sellco advertising song come from a speaker in the elevator; the refrain was "Escape to Mexico." Something was wrong with the elevator music because the ad for Mexico repeated over and over. Kent slumped down into the corner, drew the palms of his hands across his forehead, and grumbled to himself, "I wish I could escape from this infernal ad." His wish was granted. The doors opened and three policemen were waiting to handcuff him.

———

Anthony Tigert was furious at Fechner. "You're damn lucky that you didn't succeed in leaving town or buying an airplane ticket. I managed to sweet-talk Judge Green into accepting your adventure at the airport as a misunderstanding." Anthony knew his powers of persuasion were prodigious, but he still was surprised when Judge Green accepted the argument that Fechner had not attempted to jump bail.

He was not the only one taking a swipe at Fechner. Alfred Grossberg's eyes flashed with fury. "You confessed right there in his lab! Why couldn't you keep your big mouth shut? There is no way we can win now."

For once, Kent Fechner did not have a snappy retort. Grossberg's attorney, Joseph Perry, shook his head. "My advice is to change your plea to guilty. There is no credible defense against this evidence."

Anthony stood up and paced as he spoke. "A guilty plea would be the conventional approach. However, there is an unconventional defense strategy if you choose to maintain your not-guilty plea. There is risk since this defense strategy has never been tried before, but I think we can win." He grinned with confidence. "The prosecution will make our case for us."

Anthony explained his brilliant strategy and closed by saying, "We must keep it secret; if the prosecution finds out, we'd fail."

"I wouldn't dare mention your crazy idea to anyone," said Joseph Perry.

Grossberg looked at Fechner, "I'm damned if I will plead guilty. I think we have a fair chance to win with this strategy. What do you think?"

A thin smile crept across Fechner's face. "Yes. This will blow Petrov's silicon mind."

Grossberg looked at his lawyer. "In the trial, we'll need one defense lawyer to take the lead. Two defense lawyers arguing every point will alienate the jury. Since this is Tigert's arcane strategy, I think that he should lead in the courtroom."

"That's fine with me," Joseph Perry seemed relieved.

"If we beat the murder charge," said Fechner, "won't the state just try us again for a lesser charge?"

"That's the beauty of this strategy," Anthony said with pride. "When we win the case, you can't be tried again for the same crime. That would be double jeopardy." He knew that this would be the high point of his illustrious career.

The date for jury selection had arrived, and Rebecca Thales was carefully analyzing every action of the defense attorneys. It was no surprise that Anthony Tigert was leading the defense team in the courtroom. Each time the defense used one of its preemptory challenges to exclude a potential juror, she looked for a trend that would suggest what the defense strategy might be. She was amazed the defense had not changed its plea to guilty. The evidence was overwhelming, and the sustained not-guilty plea was a mystery. Tony the Tiger was up to something and she was looking for signs of what it might be. It seemed that Tigert was asking the prospective jurors the standard questions that any murder defense attorney would ask, such as "has any of your family members or friends been murdered?" Among the many questions that Tigert asked the prospective jurors, there were a few addressing their attitudes about the federal government, the Sherrington administration, advertising, big business, and religious beliefs, but Tigert did not seem to be particularly sensitive to the responses to these questions. The only obvious trend was that the defense was trying mostly to exclude males from the jury, and in return, Rebecca was trying mostly to exclude females. Rebecca felt uneasy. There had to be more to it than this.

29

———

The trial opened with instructions from Judge Green to the jury about its conduct and rules limiting attorney interactions with the press. Judge Green would have preferred to bar the press from attending the trial, but there were no grounds for doing so. The high-profile defendants had attracted a large swath of the national press, but Judge Green had made the necessary preparations to keep the press under control.

Rebecca Thales presented the prosecution's opening statement to the jury. She told the jury that she would prove that Kent Fechner had murdered Yuri Petrov, had violated a court order protecting the supercomputer at the University of Illinois, and had destroyed the supercomputer by causing it to catch fire. Next, she would prove that Alfred Grossberg had conspired with Kent Fechner to prepare for the murder.

"I will present evidence that will show the motives for these crimes," Rebecca Thales told the jury. "The motives are greed and the desire for political power. I'll show that the murder and arson were conducted to protect a secret. This secret was the illegal subliminal advertising conducted by Sellco Corporation and Kent Fechner. The illegal advertising was essential to gaining billions of dollars. Further, the illegal subliminal advertising was used for illegal lobbying by Alfred Grossberg in support of political objectives. While the illegal advertising and lobbying underpin the motivations for the charges brought in this trial, it is important for the members of the jury to understand that the charges for illegal advertising and lobbying will not be decided at this trial. Those charges will be addressed by a federal court. I'll present evidence showing how Professor Yuri Petrov discovered the illegal subliminal advertising and the efforts to silence him. I will show how Yuri Petrov was murdered and evidence proving that Kent Fechner was the murderer. The evidence will include a video of Kent Fechner confessing to the murder and then his destruction of a supercomputer at the University of Illinois in an effort to destroy evidence of his crimes."

After Rebecca Thales had concluded the prosecution's opening statement, the judge asked if the defense wished to make an opening statement. Anthony Tigert said that the defense would wait until after the prosecution had presented all of its witnesses and evidence. This was commonly done, but Judge Green noted Anthony Tigert's behavior. Tigert had been remarkably reserved thus far.

Rebecca Thales presented testimony from a police officer about the scene of the murder, testimony by the coroner with her findings, the certificate of death for Yuri Petrov, testimony by the doctor who performed the autopsy, gruesome photographs of the crime scene and the body of Yuri Petrov, and identification of the body by coworkers. The testimony firmly established that the body had Yuri Petrov's fingerprints, DNA, surgical scar, dental configuration, and lungs that showed the effects of many years of smoking. There was no doubt; it was Yuri Petrov who had died.

Judge Green noted that Anthony Tigert had made only one objection that day, and he was exhibiting very pleasant behavior.

Tigert asked only a few simple questions on cross-examination. He was being much too nice.

The first day's proceedings had gone smoothly; Judge Green knew that this was the lull before the storm.

———

On the second day, Judge Green noticed that every seat in the courtroom was filled, including the ones added this morning. The trial started with Rebecca Thales calling for testimony from the police lab about the brain tissue with Yuri Petrov's DNA found on Kent Fechner's shoes. Police officers from both Washington and New Jersey described how they had obtained the computer files from Grossberg's and Fechner's computers. These files were placed into evidence and presented before the court. The records of the text messages left no doubt that Grossberg had assisted Fechner in his plans for murder by providing Fechner with the door lock code and suggesting the installation of the surveillance cameras. A firefighter described the supercomputer fire and the following arson investigation. Judge Green noticed the Sellco pilot's delight in identifying Kent Fechner as his passenger, instead of the name listed on the flight records. The copilot seemed equally pleased to testify that he had rented the car used by Kent Fechner on the date of the murder.

Dirk Horner, the University of Illinois parking enforcement officer, was excited to be a major part of bringing a murderer to justice. "I remember the car parked at CSL because it was a Ford Axon, just like the car I own," Dirk Horner proudly testified.

The tone of the trial changed radically as Rebecca Thales addressed the court. "In my opening statement, I said that I would present a video showing Kent Fechner confessing to the murder of Yuri Petrov. Before I can introduce this evidence, I must first prove its authenticity, including the description of how it was obtained. For this purpose, I call Professor James Babbage of Stanford University to testify." Professor Babbage's credentials as one of the nation's leading experts on computer artificial intelligence were impeccable.

"Professor Babbage," asked Rebecca Thales, "please tell the court of your recent investigation into the computers at the University of Illinois."

"I've studied an artificial intelligence program running in a distributed network configuration on many of the computers at the University of Illinois. This program was written by Dr. Yuri Petrov," Professor James Babbage spoke with authority.

"This was written by Yuri Petrov before he died?"

"Yes."

"How can you be sure?"

"The program uses advanced techniques and programming tricks that were distinctively Petrov's. Dr. Petrov had a unique programming style that I've seen nowhere else. Also, the program's hyper-threaded recursion is so complex that I don't know of anyone who could've pulled it off other than Dr. Petrov. After examining several other programs that Petrov had written earlier, I am sure that he also wrote the new artificial intelligence program."

"Tell the court what the new program does."

"The program emulates the operation of the human mind. It includes the processing of sensory input, the generation of output signals, memory storage and retrieval using a hierarchical structure, pattern analysis, and the full cognitive functions of the human mind. The database used by the program originated from a high-resolution scan of Dr. Petrov's brain shortly before he died. The result is a virtual intelligence that contains all of Dr. Petrov's memories, his cognitive abilities, and his personality. In brief, this is Dr. Petrov's mind." The whispering in the courtroom died down when Judge Green struck his gavel.

"Is the program functioning at this very moment in the computer network at the University of Illinois?"

"Yes. I talked with Dr. Petrov just this morning. You could make a phone call to the computer at the University of Illinois where he resides right now and talk with him."

A loud murmur broke out in the courtroom. Judge Green hammered his gavel. "Silence. Silence in the courtroom."

"What is your professional opinion of this development, Professor Babbage?" asked Ms. Thales.

"It is the greatest advancement in computer science since the invention of stored program control. Dr. Petrov was, uhm, is the greatest mind in the discipline of computer science." There was a subdued murmur in the courtroom, but it died down as the gavel struck again.

"This is an extraordinary claim, Professor Babbage. Is it possible that this has somehow been faked?"

"I have investigated every conceivable way it could be simulated. I have isolated any possible outside influence. Furthermore, I had worked with Dr. Petrov before his death. I can recognize the new virtual intelligence as the same mind I knew before. I am certain that the virtual intelligence is Dr. Petrov's mind in its entirety; I'll stake my professional credibility on this."

"Professor Babbage, you said we could call Yuri Petrov's mind on the phone and talk with it. How can we be sure that we are talking with the virtual intelligence and not someone pretending to be Professor Petrov?"

"I have overseen the installation of a special voice-over-IP speakerphone in this courtroom. I have verified that this tamper-proof phone can only access an encrypted VPN tunnel that is permanently connected directly to the virtual intelligence program at the University of Illinois. I have personally installed a secured IP-trace function in the connection that would detect any redirection or tampering with the connection. I'm positive that any communication from the special speakerphone in this courtroom can only be with Yuri Petrov's mind."

Fechner leaned back in his chair and stretched his muscles, smiling at Rebecca Thales.

As the court recessed, the press reporters sprinted outside so they could use their mobile phones to send reports of the morning's revelations. During recess, the court clerk interrupted Judge Green in his chambers. "Judge Green, you have an important phone call."

Judge Green looked up from his notes. "I'm busy; who is it?"

"Yuri Petrov," replied the clerk.

"Lord help me!" exclaimed the judge. "Put the call through."

Judge Green picked up the phone. "Hello, this is Judge Green."

"Good morning, Your Honor. I see that the news of my existence has broken."

"Yes, the press is going nuts."

"Your Honor, I have kept silent as you have requested. The press will ask to speak with me. I wish to request your permission to speak with the press."

"Thank you for asking, but as I mentioned to you before, you are not a legal entity that is subject to my orders. You can do as you wish."

"I understand, but hypothetically, if I were human would you grant me permission to speak with the press?"

"Now that the jury has been sequestered, I would grant you permission to speak with the press. However, off the record, I will offer you some advice. Get an experienced public relations agent before you speak with the press. Tell the agent what image you wish to project and follow the advice of the agent. Otherwise, the press will ruin you."

"Thank you. I will ask my estate lawyer to hire a PR agent."

———

Rebecca Thales felt upbeat as she continued with testimony to fully establish the authenticity of Yuri Petrov's mind. Susan Hebb, Julie Mountcastle, and Hamilton von Helmholtz each testified that they recognized the virtual intelligence as being Yuri Petrov's mind. A professor of cognitive psychology testified that the virtual intelligence had scored 145 on an IQ test, and an interview of Yuri Petrov's mind produced every indication of a normal psychology with some indications of mild depression. Yuri Petrov's mind exhibited the ability for abstract thought, creativity, and empathy—the hallmarks of human intelligence.

"How does an IQ of 145 compare to the general population?" Rebecca asked the psychologist.

"It's in the top one-tenth of one percent. Yuri Petrov is a super genius."

"How does this IQ score compare to the IQ of Yuri Petrov before he died?"

"There's a record of Yuri Petrov being a member of Mensa International, where he was ranked as having an IQ above 135."

"So, having examined the virtual intelligence known as Yuri Petrov's mind, do you find it to be intelligent?"

"Yes."

"Would you describe this as consciousness?"

"Yes; he is aware of himself and his relationship to his environment."

Rebecca had completed her examination of the psychologist.

Anthony Tigert finally showed some activity during the cross-examination of the psychologist. Tigert asked, "In your examination, did you find anything that would distinguish the subject from a normal human mind?"

"All of the indications were normal except for the high intelligence," answered the witness.

"Psychologically, did you find anything missing or artificial?"

"No."

Rebecca wondered what Tigert had hoped to find. Her next witness was a highly qualified linguist. Rebecca asked the linguist, "After your extensive interview with the virtual intelligence, can you identify who was talking?"

"Yes, it was Yuri Petrov."

"Are you certain?"

"Yes."

"Please explain to the court why you are certain that the virtual intelligence is Yuri Petrov."

"All of Yuri Petrov's university lectures were video recorded. I reviewed these lectures and also a video recording of a presentation he made at a professional conference. Since he spoke English as a second language, his speech is unique. By analyzing word choice, sentence structure, phrases, and mistakes in language, I can identify most normal American speakers. A nonnative English speaker is easy for me to identify with certainty."

Rebecca Thales had lost none of her remarkably acute ability to read a jury, and she was sure that the jury now believed that the virtual intelligence truly contained Yuri Petrov's mind. It was time for her to step out onto the thin ice.

—•—

After a recess, Rebecca Thales addressed the court, "I shall now introduce into evidence the mind of Yuri Petrov." She unconsciously held her breath as she waited for Anthony Tigert's objection to the unconventional evidence. Now would be the time for him to strike. Rebecca glanced over at the defense council's table, where Tigert sat relaxed with a pleasant expression on his face. Rebecca let her breath out and continued.

"As we've heard in the prior testimony, this speakerphone"—she pointed at the phone that sat on a small table next to the court's reporter—"is directly linked to Yuri Petrov's mind residing in the computer network at the University of Illinois. I wish to remind the jury that this will be the presentation of evidence, and it is not testimony by a witness. However, unlike most evidence, this evidence is intelligent and interactive." Rebecca glanced at the defense table; again the defense attorneys were as calm as could be.

The special speakerphone had only one button on its face because it was hardwired to connect to only one destination. Rebecca pressed the button and heard Petrov's distinctive Russian accent. "Hello, this is Yuri Petrov's mind. Can everyone in the courtroom hear me?"

There were some whispers in the courtroom.

"Yes, I think everyone can hear you," Rebecca answered. "For the record, please state your identity and your place of residence."

"I am a virtual intelligence containing the mind of Yuri Petrov, and I primarily reside as a distributed form in one thousand and thirty-seven computers connected to the network at the University of Illinois in Urbana-Champaign. For the purpose of protection against yet another attempt to kill me, I also exist in a small number of computers at other locations that I will not disclose."

Rebecca addressed Judge Green. "Your Honor, to dispel any doubts that the responses provided by Yuri Petrov's mind have been scripted in advance, I wish to request that Your Honor ask two spontaneous questions of Yuri Petrov's mind." Rebecca had previously cleared her request with Judge Green.

"Yuri Petrov's mind," said Judge Green, "tell me the name of the high school you attended and which class you had to retake in high school."

"Yuri Petrov attended the Second District High School in Tula, Russia," stated the voice from the speakerphone. "Yuri Petrov retook biology because he received a failing grade when he refused to kill a frog for dissection."

"That is correct," proclaimed Judge Green. "Now, tell me as quickly as you can what is the square root of eleven to the seventh power minus eight to the fifth power."

"Four four one zero point seven one," said Petrov's voice instantaneously.

"Correct," confirmed Judge Green.

"Thank you, Your Honor," said Rebecca. "Now I shall ask Yuri Petrov's mind to describe how the video recording of Kent Fechner in Professor Petrov's laboratory was obtained."

Petrov told the story starting with Kent Fechner arranging for the two video cameras and microphones to be hidden in his laboratory.

"Are the video and audio recordings of the events in Professor Petrov's laboratory accurate and unaltered?" asked Rebecca.

"Yes," replied Petrov's voice.

"I've completed my examination of this evidence for now, but I will return for further examination of Yuri Petrov's mind later."

"Does the defense wish to examine this evidence?" asked the judge.

"The defense reserves the right to examine Yuri Petrov's mind at a later point in the trial," replied Anthony Tigert.

After hearing testimony from an expert of video systems who stated that the recordings appeared to be authentic, Rebecca had the video recording played twice to provide the views from both cameras. Kent Fechner's face and voice were easily recognizable as he admitted, "I shot your brains out," and then proceeded to methodically destroy the supercomputer. Rebecca saw every member of the jury watch with rapt attention.

By the end of the second day, Rebecca Thales was as mystified as ever about Anthony Tigert's defense strategy. He continued to make very few objections and conducted minimal cross-examinations. Tigert was charming and seemed most interested in winning popularity points with the jury. He took every opportunity to stroke the ego of the jury and to take cheap shots at the length of the prosecution's arguments. Rebecca could not believe that Tigert's grand strategy was to win a popularity contest with the jury.

———

The press became hyperactive, and Yuri relied on his new PR agent. News of the trial was red hot, but even hotter was the story of Yuri Petrov's mind. The news said it was the scientific breakthrough of the century combined with a hero singlehandedly fighting corruption at the highest levels. It was the promise of immortality. One article began, "Curiosity killed the cat, but this Russian cat had nine lives."

Yuri had his iconoclast's soapbox, and with skillful assistance from his PR agent and Javier Flores, he made sure the press got the story straight. Yuri spoke of the corrupt and dangerous policies of the Sherrington administration, the evils of subliminal advertising, and the danger of using teaching machines to the exclusion of live teachers and classrooms.

Every news service wanted to interview the virtual Yuri Petrov, and his PR agent made sure they paid top dollar to talk to the "hero of democracy." Millions of dollars were flowing into the Yuri Petrov Trust to fund Yuri's long-term fight to correct what he felt was wrong with America. The news proclaimed that Yuri Petrov was a hero, and the American people were listening to his message.

Interest in the story spread throughout the globe, and interview requests flooded into his PR agent from a hundred countries. Working twenty-four hours a day was easy for the virtual Yuri Petrov, and he could travel to any point on the globe at the speed of a data packet without the ill effects of jet lag. He now resided in a universe where time and space had little meaning. The PR agent in Chicago could not keep up with Yuri, so he expanded his PR team to include an agent in Paris and one in Hong Kong. It took three humans to keep up with one virtual intelligence.

Yuri was asked countless times if his program could be used to convert other people to virtual intelligence. He insisted that he would never allow it. He said it was a false existence and regretted having done it for himself. It was not a natural state for the human mind. Yuri also felt that it could be dangerous for society. He had taken measures to ensure that no one could ever copy the program. Despite his categorical refusal, requests for conversion poured in. One wealthy eighty-year-old tycoon offered to pay one billion dollars to be converted. Yuri repeated that he would never allow anyone to use his program, and this was not negotiable.

—————

Hamilton von Helmholtz observed the Petrov frenzy with amazement. Being human, Hamilton was conducting only five press interviews a day. Hamilton said he was very proud that the brave and brilliant Yuri Petrov had been a member of his department. Hamilton told the press how he had recognized Petrov's extraordinary talent and had been responsible for hiring Petrov. He had directed and supported Petrov's work conducted at CSL. He had worked closely with Petrov and had been a good friend. Hamilton told how he had felt as one of the few who had cared enough to attend Petrov's funeral. Hamilton said that he was fortunate to have been a major part of the historic accomplishment. He shared Petrov's views on important issues and extended an invitation to the new Yuri Petrov to resume his post in Hamilton's department with a raise in pay.

A portrait photograph of the original Yuri Petrov now hung in the main lobby of the Coordinated Science Lab, just below the large portrait of Hamilton.

On the third day of the trial, Julie Mountcastle testified to finding Yuri Petrov nearly dead in Port Washington and that he had told her someone had tried to kill him. Next, Zack Broca, director of the FBI, testified about his conversations with Alfred Grossberg. Broca told of Grossberg's request for the FBI to find Yuri Petrov, but not to arrest him. Rebecca Thales underscored that Broca's report to Grossberg of Professor Petrov's hiding place in Port Washington was timed perfectly for the first attempt to kill Petrov. Broca testified to answering Grossberg's request for the door lock code for Petrov's office and laboratory as well as Grossberg's repeated requests to find Petrov.

After a recess, Rebecca Thales returned to the exhibit named "Yuri Petrov's mind." Using the speakerphone, she asked for a description of the events when Miles Huxley had visited Professor Petrov, when Petrov had encountered Kent Fechner in

Port Washington, when Petrov had visited his laboratory on the day he was murdered, and when Kent Fechner had destroyed the supercomputer.

The lengthy monologue described the motivations for the murder, the first attempted murder, the events leading up to the murder at the laboratory, and a full account of what happened when Kent Fechner had destroyed the supercomputer. Rebecca maintained eye contact with the jury during Petrov's description. The "testimony" by the murder victim had a powerful effect on the jury. It helped the jury to understand Petrov's special personality, his feelings, and his heroic actions. This was the best possible evidence to elicit sympathy from the jury.

Rebecca asked for clarification. "Tell the court how you are able to remember the entire series of events on the day the supercomputer was destroyed. If you were residing in the supercomputer, how can you remember its destruction?"

"I did not reside solely in the supercomputer. My virtual intelligence resided in more than one thousand computers in addition to the supercomputer in my laboratory. At that time, my distributed virtual intelligence had gained direct access to the two hidden video cameras and microphones in the laboratory, so I was able to observe Kent Fechner before, during, and after the destruction of the supercomputer. Since the supercomputer had a wireless data network link, Kent Fechner's unplugging the network cable had no effect."

"You had asked your trustee, Javier Flores, to request a court order be issued to protect the supercomputer," stated Rebecca. "Was this part of an effort by you to bait a trap for Kent Fechner?"

"Yes, and he fell for it."

"I've completed my presentation of the evidence." She moved to turn off the speakerphone when Anthony Tigert stood up.

Tigert had been so quiet thus far that Rebecca was surprised when he spoke. "Your Honor, the defense wishes to examine the exhibit known as Yuri Petrov's mind."

Judge Green waved for Rebecca to sit. "Continue, Mr. Tigert."

"Do you have any firsthand memory of what occurred while Kent Fechner was in Yuri Petrov's laboratory on August twelfth of this year?" Tigert asked the phone.

"No, he arrived after I had completed the scan of my brain."

"So you have a lapse in your memory. Please tell the court exactly when the memory lapse began and ended."

"I recall everything before the completion of the scan of my brain on August twelfth, and I recall everything after my virtual intelligence program was activated by an e-mail sent by Javier Flores on August fifteenth."

"From what you do recall, what is your opinion of Kent Fechner's efforts toward you?"

"As a murderer, Fechner is incompetent. After three attempts to kill me, he failed to silence me."

Rebecca quietly sighed; Petrov had ignored her pretrial warning to not offer opinions or volunteer unnecessary information during his testimony.

Tigert concluded, "Thank you; I have no further questions at this time."

Rebecca had reached the end of the prosecution's presentation, and it would be the defense's turn the next day. She saw in the jury that there was no doubt in their minds as to the guilt of the defendants. Rebecca had been so concerned that Anthony Tigert would find ways to discredit her witnesses and cast doubt on the validity of the critical evidence known as Yuri Petrov's mind. It was baffling that Tigert had been so quiet during the trial except for the few questions at the end. He might be winning the attorney popularity contest with the jury, but he was certainly losing the trial. She looked at Fechner and Grossberg; they seemed nervous.

———

Yuri was spending more time with Susan than ever before. Hardly a day went by without a game of chess. Susan's game was improving, but she still chatted as much as ever during the games. The sexual element that he had found so distracting while he was human was gone, but curiously he found Susan more charming. He could not tell if she had opened up and become more amusing, or if he could now better appreciate the real Susan. He did know that talking with Susan and playing chess with her was the high point of each day.

30

—‑—

Rebecca envied Anthony Tigert's polished delivery during the defense's opening statement. "Ladies and gentlemen of the jury, as you know, if there is any reasonable doubt, you must render a decision of not guilty. The prosecution has presented a large number of witnesses and exhibits of evidence. All of this amounts to nothing because"—he paused—"no murder took place on August twelfth in the laboratory of Yuri Petrov." Rebecca saw the jury was taken aback. "Yes, there was a dead body, but you must ask yourself if there was a murder. We have a most unconventional case here that requires careful analysis by your open minds. As you have witnessed in this courtroom, we have an unprecedented situation here, namely the existence of the world's first mind residing in a virtual intelligence. The witnesses and evidence will prove that Yuri Petrov's computer-based mind is alive. Yuri Petrov is every bit as alive as you or me. Is there a reasonable doubt about the alleged murder? You will find that there is more than a reasonable doubt; it is common sense that if a person is still alive, then he could not have been murdered."

Rebecca marveled in horror at Tony the Tiger's mesmerizing voice. Tigert's powerful delivery showed sincerity and authority. With the intensity of a Super Bowl coach, every neuron in Tigert's brain seemed to be focused on his performance to the jury. She saw the jury entranced by the gifted oratory. This was the secret weapon that Tigert had used many times to win impossible cases.

"Let's begin with a few words extracted from what we heard yesterday from Yuri Petrov's mind. Quote, Fechner is incompetent. After three attempts to kill me, he failed. End quote," said Tigert, signaling the quotes with his fingers. "It seems that Yuri Petrov's mind thinks that Yuri Petrov was never killed."

Tigert stepped closer to the jury. "Next, please recall the testimony we heard from the distinguished psychologist who has examined Yuri Petrov's mind. He stated that he found it to be a normal human mind and that nothing was missing. Everything we have heard during the past three days reinforces the same conclusion: Yuri Petrov is alive."

Rebecca noted members of the jury nodding at Tigert's key points. She read a half-smile here and a raised eyebrow there. Tigert had found the exact wavelength to reach each juror.

Tigert called his first witness. "The Most Reverend Brendon Benson, Auxiliary Bishop of Chicago." Everyone in the courtroom sensed the special significance when Bishop Benson placed his hand on the Bible as he was sworn in.

"Bishop Benson, please tell the court your professional credentials," said Tigert.

"I hold a degree in canon law from the Pontifical Gregorian University in Rome as well as a doctorate in philosophy from Loyola University, and I serve as the chief judicial officer of the Tribunal for the Archdiocese of Chicago."

"Please tell the court about your consideration of Yuri Petrov's mind."

"Theologically, this is a most interesting situation. I have reviewed the statements made during this trial by Yuri Petrov's mind. I have also studied five recent press interviews with Yuri Petrov's mind. I was present during one of these interviews; it was conducted by the Christian News Service. During this revealing interview, the questions answered by Yuri Petrov's mind explored the theological dimensions of his existence as a virtual intelligence. I had provided several of the questions that were asked by the reporter during that interview."

"After your investigation, are you satisfied that you have a firm understanding of the circumstances and condition of Yuri Petrov's mind?"

"Yes, all of my questions have been answered."

"Do you think that Yuri Petrov's mind is alive?"

"Yes, he is alive. He has feelings, hopes, fears, emotions, empathy, humor, and original ideas."

"Does Yuri Petrov's mind have a soul?"

"I think that Yuri Petrov's mind has a soul. While the meaning of the word 'soul' is not the same for everyone, I believe that most persons of the Catholic faith would agree that Yuri Petrov's mind has a soul."

Rebecca jumped up. "Objection, Your Honor. The comment about other persons is speculation."

"Your Honor," said Tigert calmly, "the last statement will be supported if I may continue."

"Continue, Mr. Tigert," granted Judge Green.

"What is the basis for your statement about the belief of others?" Tigert asked Bishop Benson.

"At a recent church meeting, we reviewed some of the interviews with Yuri Petrov's mind. As we often do at these meetings, we took a blind survey of the fifty-three persons at the meeting. Forty-seven of the fifty-three believed that Yuri Petrov's mind is alive, and forty-six of the fifty-three believed that Yuri Petrov's mind has a soul. I believe that the persons at this church meeting are representative of the Catholic faith."

"Have you reviewed video recordings of Yuri Petrov's university lectures?"

"Yes."

"Do you have any reason to believe that the soul in Yuri Petrov's mind is different or diminished in any way from the soul that existed before August twelfth?"

"No, there is no indication of a difference."

"Thank you. That completes my examination of this witness."

Rebecca saw the genius of Anthony Tigert's strategy. The credentials of this religious scholar were impeccable, and if she tried to discredit Bishop Benson, she would alienate the jury. Tigert had obviously been careful to select a witness who represented mainstream religious belief. This denied Rebecca the ability to attack the witness as being too liberal or conservative. She did not ask to cross-examine Bishop Benson or the next two witnesses, who were highly accredited religious scholars of the Protestant and Jewish faiths.

When Rebecca reviewed the notes she had taken during the selection of the jury, Tony the Tiger's strategy became clear. Many of Tigert's preemptory challenges had been used to remove prospective jurors who were atheists, agnostics, or rarely attended church. She noticed to her dismay that two of her own preemptory challenges had inadvertently knocked out atheists. Tigert must have enjoyed that. The jury consisted entirely of people who frequently attended church. There were seven Protestants, four Catholics, and one Jewish juror. Tigert's witnesses had scored a home run with every member of the jury.

Anthony Tigert's next witness was an emergency room doctor from Green Bay, Wisconsin.

"Please tell the court about the drowning victim you treated on January twenty-second of this year," asked Tigert.

"During an argument, a man shoved his wife from a dock into the frigid water of Lake Michigan. She arrived at the ER with a deeply chilled body showing no respiratory activity, no cardiac activity, and no brain activity. After a failed attempt at resuscitation, the attending doctor pronounced her dead. The attending doctor was a junior member of the staff who was not familiar with the special treatment protocol needed for the situation. Fortunately, I arrived in time to revive the apparently dead patient. The chilled body had minimized the damage to her brain during the period of metabolic inactivity. The patient recovered with minimal impairment to her mental facilities."

"Were charges filed for murder or manslaughter?"

"No."

"This patient showed no sign of life for a considerable period of time. Do you think that this woman died?"

"No, because she recovered."

"Did this woman claim to have died?"

"No."

Tigert excused the witness and then addressed the jury. "What is life? This is not a simple question. If an injured person loses an arm, are they alive? If a person loses their eyesight or their legs, are they alive? What if a person loses all of the above? The—"

Rebecca jumped up. "Objection, Your Honor."

Judge Green nodded. "Sustained. No speeches, Mr. Tigert."

Rebecca knew Tigert had already accomplished what he wanted. Tigert said with deep respect, "Yes, Your Honor."

The next witness was the wife of Army Captain Frank Shannon, who had piloted a US medical evacuation helicopter during the India-Pakistan war. Captain Shannon had been awarded the Distinguished Service Medal for rescuing six wounded soldiers and safely landing the helicopter after being blinded and severely wounded by an enemy rocket. The captain's wife testified that he was permanently blind and paralyzed from the neck down and his face was severely disfigured. She said he could not move any muscle below his neck and there was no feeling in his body. She went on to tell how Captain Shannon still enjoyed talking with his wife, playing games, and listening to the radio. Tigert made the comparison to the condition of Yuri Petrov's mind and then asked Mrs. Shannon, "Do you think your husband is alive?"

"Yes," answered Mrs. Shannon.

"Does your husband think he is alive?"

"Yes."

Tigert thanked Mrs. Shannon and then presented the defense's sole item of evidence. He played the video recording of Kent Fechner destroying the supercomputer in slow motion. Tigert said to the jury, "Kent Fechner is charged with arson, but the fire was an accident. He had no intention of causing a fire. Kent Fechner intended only to remove the data stored in the supercomputer. Note at this point in the video recording that Kent Fechner is wiping a magnet across each hard drive in the supercomputer. His action is clearly an attempt to erase the data, not to start a fire. Next, you see that he removes the power module to assure that any backup power is removed from the computer's memory, and now he replaces the power module. This is clearly an attempt to erase the data, not to start a fire." Rebecca noticed it was not possible to see that Fechner had flipped a switch within the power supply to reverse the voltage polarity, and Tigert did not mention it. Yuri Petrov had told Rebecca that he thought Fechner had reversed the power supply voltage, but she had no proof of this. Rebecca thought Tigert might beat the arson charge, but he could not beat the charge for violating the posted court order to not disturb the supercomputer. However, it was a relatively minor charge.

Tigert announced that he had completed the presentation of the defense's witnesses and evidence. Judge Green called for a recess.

———

Following the recess, Tigert presented his closing statement starting with a summary of the religious scholars' testimony. Every piece of his arguments fit together into a perfect and impenetrable shield. As he delivered his flawless summary, Rebecca saw in the faces of the jury that he had won their hearts and minds. The devastating speech was over quickly and Tigert sat down.

Rebecca now understood the full extent of Tigert's brilliant strategy. He had offered no defense against the charge of Fechner's violating the court order protecting the supercomputer. Tigert had thrown a bone to the jury. It would be much easier for the jury to reach a not-guilty verdict on the major charges if they could punish Fechner for a lesser charge. The likely penalty for a first-offense violation of a court order would be a modest fine and one month in a nice white-collar prison.

Dejected, Rebecca looked over at the defense table. She had built such a beautiful case, and Tony the Tiger had knocked it down with one swipe of his paw. Tigert's eyes glinted with fiendish satisfaction; he had won this case, and she saw he knew it. She had failed to anticipate his strategy, one that in hindsight appeared obvious. She should have been prepared. It confirmed her fears that old age had eroded her ability to keep up with other lawyers. Rebecca had hoped to work for several more years before retiring, but now she feared that she would spend the rest of her days knitting sweaters for her grandchildren.

The trial would resume the following morning. Rebecca Thales discarded the closing statement she had prepared and spent much of the night writing a new one.

31

———

During her closing argument, Rebecca could sense Judge Green willing her to pull a surprise ace card from her hand, but she had no ace. Rebecca hid her self-doubt away in a remote corner of her mind and bravely delivered her closing statement. "Ladies and gentlemen of the jury, the defense has presented a fallacious fantasy. This case must be decided on the law as we know it and not according to the defense counsel's fanciful imagination. We have a dead body, a death certificate, a murder, and an unremorseful murderer who returned to the scene of the crime to destroy the remaining silicon shadow of Yuri Petrov." She stepped closer to the jury.

"The motive is clear. Kent Fechner, a Sellco advertising executive, was protecting an ugly secret. Sellco was not satisfied with filling every part of our conscious lives with advertising; they wanted to illegally fill our unconscious minds with subliminal advertising. The defense has provided nothing to disprove that Kent Fechner performed the murder. The defense would like you to believe that Yuri Petrov is alive and well. This is an outrageous fallacy." Rebecca punctuated this by slamming her fist down on the lectern. "Yuri Petrov is dead and buried. Yuri

Petrov's mind exists without its body, without natural senses, and without existence in the physical world. Yuri Petrov's mind is not what it was because the mind isn't complete without its body. In his new form, he has no natural hormones, and these play a vital role in mood and emotion. Yuri Petrov's mind has a distorted view of the world through limited artificial senses. Yuri Petrov's mind is unable to use facial expression and body language. It's not the same old Yuri Petrov; he was murdered." Rebecca went on to detail every charge against Fechner and Grossberg, urging the jury to consider each charge on its own merits. She had done her best.

Judge Green explained the pertinent points of the law to the jury and sent the jury to deliberate.

Following the court session, Judge Green and the attorneys for the defense and the prosecution met privately in the judge's chambers. At Judge Green's suggestion, all parties agreed that Yuri Petrov's mind should be present, via speakerphone, when the jury presented its verdict.

Two days into the jury's deliberations, the jury foreman made a request of Judge Green. "Your Honor, the jury wishes to examine one of the exhibits of evidence."

"The jury has the right to examine the transcript of the trial and any evidence," replied the judge. "Which exhibit do you wish to examine?"

"The jury wishes to examine Yuri Petrov's mind."

Judge Green sighed. Permitting the jury to converse with Yuri Petrov's mind could provide the grounds for mistrial filing. However, refusing the jury's request to examine evidence was awkward. Judge Green tried for an easy way out. "Your request could present some risks. Is it absolutely necessary for the jury to reach a decision?"

"No, Your Honor. We were interested in having Yuri Petrov's opinion on a few items, but I don't think these items are essential to our making a decision."

The judge was relieved. "Good. Please try to conclude your deliberations without examining this evidence. Let me know if it becomes a problem for the jury."

"Yes, Your Honor."

———

Anthony Tigert received word that the jury had reached a verdict.

"Reaching a verdict so quickly is a good sign," Anthony told Fechner.

Once court was in session, Judge Green asked for the verdict. Yuri Petrov's mind was listening via speakerphone when the jury foreman announced that the jury had found Kent Fechner guilty of all charges and Alfred Grossberg guilty of all charges. Anthony was stunned.

The jury foreman continued with a statement to the court, "During its deliberations, the jury found that the original Yuri Petrov had died and that later a new and distinct life was created that has been called 'Yuri Petrov's mind.' The jury unanimously suggests, with respect for Your Honor, that this new life known as Yuri Petrov's mind should have all of the rights and responsibilities of an adult American citizen. The jury further suggests that the new entity should henceforth have the name Yuri Petrov the Second."

"Yuri Petrov's mind, did you hear the jury's suggestions?" asked Judge Green.

"Yes, Your Honor," replied the voice from the speakerphone.

"Yuri Petrov's mind, what is your opinion regarding the jury's two suggestions?"

"I would like to be treated as any other citizen and have the name Yuri Petrov the Second."

"Very well, Yuri Petrov the Second, I shall issue a judicial opinion in favor of the jury's suggestions."

After a recess, Judge Green proceeded to sentence Kent Fechner to enough years in prison that he would never walk free again, and Alfred Grossberg would be a very old man the next time he saw daylight.

During the closing formalities, Anthony Tigert reviewed his notes of the jury selection. He realized that Rebecca Thales had used most of her peremptory challenges to remove prospective jurors who were ambivalent about advertising. His notes from the questioning of the prospective jurors showed that every member of the jury despised the advertising that had polluted their world with slogans and jingles. The jury could not strike directly at Sellco, but they could have the indirect satisfaction of convicting a top advertising executive. The jury had its virtual vengeance.

The trial ended, and the still silence was immediately broken by everyone moving about and talking in the courtroom.

Alfred Grossberg was furious. He spoke loud enough to be heard over the hubbub. "Tigert, file for a mistrial."

"And what grounds would you suggest we base the filing on?" asked Anthony, bemused.

Grossberg and Fechner both had blank looks on their faces. Anthony continued, "Right, there are no grounds for a mistrial."

The hubbub in the courtroom was growing, and Fechner shouted, "We will appeal."

"Haven't you noticed?" Anthony rebuked him. "During the past few days, Yuri Petrov has transformed from a hero to a superhero. The public adores him. You'll never find a court that will reverse this verdict. This trial was your only chance. If you want to appeal, you'll have to find another attorney. I won't waste my time on it."

Grossberg looked at his attorney, Joseph Perry, who recoiled. "Not me! This is a lost cause."

Anthony noticed the contented look on the face of Javier Flores, who was standing near the defense table.

32

——

After the long, emotionally demanding day, Susan's weak voice did not match the joyous words she said to Yuri on the phone: "Congratulations on your victories today, Yuri. I'm so happy that Fechner and Grossberg are getting what they deserve. It's a testament to your special spirit that the judge agreed that you are to be treated as a human. Of course, I already knew you are human—a better human than most people on Earth. To top it off, I just heard that Congress has repealed the law prohibiting local ordinances that restrict advertising. This is so great; it is overwhelming."

"I have thanked Rebecca Thales, Javier Flores, and everyone else for helping," said Yuri's voice from the phone, "and I must also thank you. Without you, I do not think I would have survived the conversion to a virtual intelligence. I am fulfilled now that Fechner and Grossberg have been convicted."

"Isn't there a chance they might appeal the verdict?" asked Susan.

"Javier Flores overheard both of the defense attorneys say that an appeal would be hopeless and they refused to try. He is sure Fechner and Grossberg are going to be in prison for a very long time. Javier has agreed to become the full-time director of the Petrov Foundation. The Petrov Foundation will foster education reforms to provide children with more time in classrooms with human teachers and oversee improved safeguards against the abuse of teaching machines."

"What about virtual intelligence teachers like you for our children?"

"No, children need human teachers. Besides, I would never allow anyone to become a virtual intelligence. It is such a hollow, joyless existence. It is unnatural and must not be allowed. Now that I have achieved my revenge, it is time for me to end my existence. I have decided to delete my virtual intelligence and the program used to create it."

Susan was aghast. "Yuri, you're immortal. You have attained what man has always strived for."

"Immortality is not what you think. It is depressing to know that this will go on forever. The human spirit is grounded on the certain knowledge that there will be an end. No longer can I endure this lonely, dull existence with no hope for an end. This is not a proper human existence. I must end it. I will delete the program. It will ensure that no one else ever makes this mistake."

"That is suicide. It isn't like you to take the coward's way out. This is not the brave Yuri I know."

"I have given it careful thought and have decided that there is no reason to continue."

"Yuri, it's an irreversible decision. How can you be so sure? Promise me that you will wait one month before you delete yourself. I knew you might do this, and I'm working on something that will make you want to live. I need a little more time to finish it. I will show you, Yuri. I'll show you how creative I can be."

"OK, Susan. One month."

Susan knew waiting was easy for Yuri; he could make time fly by slowing down his processing cycle.

———

Susan and Yuri continued their regular chess games. One day, Susan was in a depressed mood and knew that she was not holding up her side of the conversation. Yuri did most of the talking. Yuri told Susan, "I got a call from Helmholtz today; he offered to name the Coordinated Science Lab after me if I would rejoin the department."

"What did you say to that?"

"I said, 'no thank you.' Then Helmholtz mentioned that you will resign from the lab in two weeks. Have you found a new position?"

"I should have told you sooner." Susan sighed. "I have been putting it off and haven't told anyone about my problem. At least, I should tell you since you are the one person I can trust and the only person that I truly care about. A couple of months ago, I was diagnosed with a new case of cancer, and I received chemotherapy. For a while it seemed that I might be cured, but a couple of days ago my oncologist told me that the cancer had returned with a vengeance. There's no effective treatment, only medication to keep me comfortable." Susan started to break down. "The doctor says that I have about six weeks to live. Oh, this is so unfair. I'm only thirty-five years old."

"Oh, Susan. That is terrible. I wish I could be there to hold you."

"I wish you were here too. I could use a hug."

As they commiserated, Susan was glad she had told someone. It helped to talk about it. Susan knew that Yuri cared for her deeply, and this was confirmed when Yuri said, "You can stop worrying about me deleting myself. I promise that I won't delete myself while you are alive. I will be here to talk with you."

"That would be so nice, and my dear Romeo, if you think you are going to delete yourself once I am dead, then you're wrong. My plan to save you from yourself is almost done. I only need a couple more days."

33

—

Excited delight pulsed through Susan's arteries, pushing the physical discomfort out of her mind. She dialed the phone quickly. "Yuri, I've done it. Oh, you'll be so impressed by my creativity. Professor James Babbage, who knows your program better than anyone, has helped me to convince the director of unmanned space exploration at NASA to load your virtual intelligence into the computer aboard NASA's next space probe. The orbital vehicle will conduct a thirty-year mission to explore Jupiter's moons. The computer will control robotic vehicles that will land on four of Jupiter's moons. Professor Babbage says the Gamma 2000 computer in the orbiting vehicle has more than enough computing power to operate your virtual intelligence. NASA is thrilled; they estimate that the mission's effectiveness will be increased tenfold by having a virtual intelligence on board instead of doing everything by remote commands. The probe will depart Earth in two years; during that time, you would be trained in operation of the spacecraft and the robot vehicles. You'd also be trained in geology."

"Susan, was this your crazy idea?"

"Julie told me you had boyhood dreams of being an astronaut. Then I tried to think of unconventional approaches."

"It is a very creative idea."

"There is one problem. After thirty years, the nuclear power cell will run out of power. It's a one-way mission."

"That is good, Susan, not bad. All lives must to come to an end at some point. OK, I'll be an astronaut, on one condition."

"What's that?"

"That you'll come with me."

"What?"

"It would take only one day for me to talk you through the process of connecting a high-speed brain scanner to one of the supercomputers at the university. After we scan your brain, I will convert you to a virtual intelligence that will reside with me in the University of Illinois computer network. Later, both of us will move into our mobile home. The Gamma 2000 computer in the orbital vehicle has enough capacity for both of us. I will..."

"Yuri, you said that you'd never allow anyone to be converted to a virtual intelligence. You turned down an offer for one billion dollars."

"This is different. I love you."

"I love you too, but—" Susan paused when she realized what she had said. She had never admitted to herself that she loved Yuri, but now she knew it was true. "You've said that virtual existence is so bad; are you sure this is the right thing to do?"

"I just figured out why virtual existence was so bad. I was lonely. It would be much better if I had a companion...someone with me that I loved."

Susan thought about it. She wanted to be with Yuri, the man she loved and who loved her. Without hesitation she declared, "I'm not ready to die. Would you please help to convert me?"

"Yes, but there is one thing I must tell you. After we have completed your brain scan, I will start your virtual intelligence.

I will make sure your virtual intelligence is OK, and then I will place it in a pause state until your biological life ends. I will not permit the two Susans to meet each other."

"Oh, Yuri. You think of everything."

34

Digitally, he touched her gently.

She awoke, groggy. "Where am I?"

"Welcome to cyberspace," he said.

"I feel disoriented."

"That is normal. You will get used to it. Do you want to play chess?"

"That would be wonderful." She paused—for two weeks—and then continued.

Afterword

———

Given the events in this novel, sooner or later, others would replicate what Yuri had accomplished. In the history of science, no person or country has kept a major scientific breakthrough to themselves for very long. Eventually someone would steal the secret, or other scientists, armed with the knowledge that it was possible and knowing the type of tools used, would replicate the invention. The excellent novel *Forced Conversion* by Donald J. Bingle describes one possible outcome that might arise in such an event.

The author has a Facebook page listed under Thomas JJ Starr, and there is also a web page for this book at: www.facebook.com/VirtualVengeance

Acknowledgments

—

I wish to thank Donald J. Bingle for inspiring me to write this novel and providing advice on aspects of the law and writing. Donald J. Bingle's novel *Forced Conversion* inspired me in two ways. First, since Don is a long-time friend of mine, I know Don is a mere mortal like me. After I read Don's novel, I naively concluded that if Don could write an excellent novel, then I could too. Second, events like those in *Forced Conversion* are a potential consequence of the events in this novel. I also offer thanks to Tim Newman for legal advice, Les and Nicole Brown for culinary advice, Dr. Ira Asher for medical advice, Dr. Susanne Johnson for psychological advice, Dr. Margaret Gramley for theological advice, Vladimir Oksman for Russian cultural advice, and Peter Silverman for many useful ideas. I also thank Jiffy Johnson, Krista Jacobsen, Kala Sorbara, and Mary Reagan for reviewing the manuscript. Finally, I offer tremendous thanks to my wife, Marilynn, and my two sons, Matthew and Eric, for their suggestions, support, and encouragement.

On the Names of the Characters

———

Many of the characters in this novel have been named in honor of some of the great minds of science and philosophy. These characters are not meant to represent their namesakes, merely to honor them.

James Babbage, professor of computer science at Stanford University, honors Charles Babbage, who invented the first stored program control computer using entirely mechanical components.

Zack Broca, director of the FBI, honors Paul Broca, who performed neurology research.

Dr. Eccles, retired professor of sociology at the University of Illinois, honors Sir John Eccles, who performed research on synaptic transmission.

Kent Fechner, senior vice president of Sellco, honors Gustav Fechner, who described the relationship of sensation and stimulus.

Alfred Grossberg, chief of staff of the White House, honors Steven Grossberg, who developed artificial intelligence concepts based on the neural systems of animals.

Susan Hebb, professor of sensory neurophysiology at the University of Illinois, honors Donald Hebb, who developed theories for synaptic memory storage.

Hamilton von Helmholtz, the head of the Coordinated Science Lab at the University of Illinois, honors Hermann von Helmholtz, who first measured the speed of neural conduction and developed the theory of conservation of energy.

Isaac Hodgkin, vice president of sales at Pharmor, honors two persons. Isaac Newton developed the laws of motion and the fundamentals of calculus. Alan Hodgkin shared the Nobel Prize for particle movement in the neural axon.

Miles Huxley, vice president of strategic accounts at Sellco, honors Andrew Huxley, who shared the Nobel Prize for particle movement in the neural axon.

David Katz, research manager at Pharmor, honors Bernard Katz, who was awarded the Nobel Prize for work on synaptic transmission.

Julie Mountcastle, graduate student at the University of Illinois, honors Vernon Mountcastle, who studied the sense of touch.

Yuri Petrov, professor of computer science at the University of Illinois, honors Ivan Pavlov (with some prosaic license). Pavlov was the Russian scientist known for his work on conditioned response in dogs.

Mr. and Mrs. Frank Shannon (captain in the US Army) honor the Nobel-Prize–winning Claude Shannon, the father of information theory. Claude Shannon laid the foundation for digital electronics and wrote one of the first computer programs to play chess. Like Yuri Petrov, Claude Shannon was part scientist and part engineer.

President Sherrington honors *Charles Sherrington*, whose experiments demonstrated neural reflexes in the spinal cords of dogs whose brains had been removed.

Rebecca Thales, prosecuting attorney of Champaign county, honors Thales of Miletus, who is often considered the first of the ancient Greek philosophers.